Mountaintop

GEOFF DRESSER

DEDICATION

For Pearl

TABLE OF CONTENTS

EVICTION

Dr. Reginald Franks, grandfatherly dean and CEO of Redeemer Christian College, would never kick David Singer out. At least David hoped not. Not after David graduated with highest marks. Not after David and his grandmother had given the college all their money. Not after his grandmother died and David took out student loans to continue his studies. And certainly not after all that talk of Redeemer College being a family. David had done everything they'd asked of him, and he'd believed every promise they made to him: that he was being prepared for a fruitful career in ministry. Yet, despite all that, he'd applied to over a hundred churches over the last six months and no one had offered him a job. At least not a paying job. Some churches had offered to take him on without pay, with a vague promise that the role would eventually become a paid position. But working for free was a luxury well beyond David's means. Although he was certainly a gifted musician, no church was willing to take a chance on hiring him, not when they had people of their own who could do an adequate job, and do it for free.

And so, after his graduation, when his classmates moved on, David simply stayed at Redeemer College. A few of his fellow graduates found jobs in ministry, but most had either moved back home or moved on to further their studies and their debt load. At first, David thought he would stay for a few days, until he came up with a plan or until one of those churches offered him a job. But days turned into weeks. He almost left when the college turned off his internet access, but he still had nowhere to go. So he stayed, reading, playing his guitar, singing, praying and hoping he wouldn't be kicked out. But it was now August. New students would be arriving soon, and the dorms would be filled with actual students. Paying students.

David's phone buzzed with an incoming text message.

"This is your final notice."

It was from his cellular service. He'd stopped paying the bill in May, when the student loan money was gone. David was wondering where he'd find the money for his phone when he heard the knock on his door.

"David?" said Mitch, through the door, "Dr. Franks wants to see you."

Mitch was the campus caretaker and handyman. David had been helping him out over the summer. He was a patient and soft-spoken man, perpetually clad in his olive-green work pants and shirt.

David opened the door.

"Mitch, I know. I tried to stop by his office yesterday, but he wasn't there. Thanks for letting me know. I'll go see him today."

"David, I'm sorry. Actually, I'm supposed to take you to see him right now."

"Why?"

"Dr. Franks told me I'm to come get you and bring you back with me to his office. We have to go, both of us, to his office. Right now."

"What's so urgent?"

Mitch shrugged and looked away.

"OK. Well, let's go."

Neither spoke as they walked down the stairs, through the doors, and across the quad to the admin building. They both knew what this was about. David had been avoiding this meeting for two weeks.

They reached the door to Dr. Franks' office. Mitch stopped, reached up to knock, hesitated, and then turned to David.

"David, thank you for all your help this summer. It was nice having someone to work with. And, I'm sorry."

"Don't be sorry, Mitch. Nothing you could do about it," said David.

Mitch knocked on the door and opened it a crack. "Here he is."

"Thank you, Mitch. Come in, David. Mitch, you'll be carrying on, will you?" Dr. Franks looked over David's shoulder at Mitch.

"Yes, sir." Mitch looked nervously between David and Dr. Franks.

"Thanks, Mitch. David, please sit down."

David sat in a worn leather chair opposite Dr. Franks. Between them was a shabby antique oak desk, bare except for two envelopes. Dr. Franks folded his hands and placed them on the edge of the desk and exhaled. Then he looked David in the eye.

"David, it's time."

"Time?"

"You know exactly what I'm talking about. It is time for you to move on. You need to leave campus."

David shifted his feet. "Well, I was wondering if I could enroll in some extra courses for the fall semester."

"David, you've already graduated top of the class from our music ministry program. There's nothing more we can teach you."

"I was thinking some of the churches I applied to wanted someone who could do music *and* youth, so I should probably take some youth ministry classes. Dr. Franks, you know all I've ever wanted to do is serve in a church. I think some youth courses could help me realize my dream. I mean, God's calling on my life."

"David, you'd be better off volunteering in a church youth ministry. It wouldn't cost anything and you'd probably learn just as much. Besides, how would you propose paying for another semester?"

"Is there any unclaimed scholarship money?"

"No. Well, I mean yes there is, but not for you. It is time for you to move on." The dean let out a sigh. "David, you must understand this is really for the best. I hope you know I want the best for you. I care about you, you're part of the Redeemer College family. I hope you won't be angry with us."

"Dr. Franks, how could I ever be angry with you? You've been like a father to me. Especially after my grandmother died."

Dr. Franks' shoulders sagged. David saw his opening and pressed his advantage.

"I mean, you know my situation. And when Nan died... I had nowhere to turn. Redeemer was my family. You know, the rest of the class, well, they all either found jobs or went back home to their families. Redeemer College is the closest thing I have to a home and a family." David looked out the window behind Dr. Frank's desk, then up the ceiling and threw up his hands. "I mean, if I had somewhere else to go, I would. But, well, what option do I have? And it's not like I haven't tried to earn my keep. Mitch has really appreciated my help. He's told me so, many times. It all makes me think that maybe God wants me to stay here."

Dr. Franks shook his head slowly, unfolded his hands and slowly drummed his fingers on the desktop. "David, I appreciate the help you've given Mitch over the summer. I really do, and yes, so does Mitch. However, I am informed by our board of directors that we have likely broken several labour code regulations by allowing you to do that. I shudder to think about the situation we'd be in if you'd fallen off a ladder or some such thing and injured yourself." He folded his hands again. "When you didn't leave after graduation, I thought it would be OK for me to look the other way. I don't regret that, but it has been three months and you're still here. Regardless, the board has also instructed me in no uncertain terms to resolve this situation, no later than today. David, my hands are tied."

"So you're kicking me out?"

"David, don't make this any harder than it has to be, please. Look at it from my point of view."

"From the point of view of someone who has a job and a place to live?"

Dr. Franks' hands slowly closed into fists. He took a breath, relaxed his hands and looked back at David.

"I happen to have a job and a place to live because forty years ago when I graduated from college I took responsibility for my life, started working and haven't stopped since. It's time you did the same. But lest you think I am completely heartless, I have some good news. I am giving you a choice in how this plays out."

"A choice?"

"As I was agonizing about this yesterday, I received a phone call from a former student, Rick Avery. He pastors a small church in Lachance, about three hours north of here. They need a worship pastor, and Rick is highly motivated to hire one as soon as possible. It's an entry level position, full time. I told him about you. I told him you are the most gifted music student we've had here at Redeemer College in a long time. They're very interested in you. If you're interested, they'll send someone to pick you up. Today. Are you interested?"

"Well, yeah. Of course I'm interested."

Dr. Franks slid one of the envelopes across the desk toward David. "Here's the job posting and some information about the church that my assistant printed off their web site. Have a look at it."

David took the envelope and began to open it.

Dr Franks continued, "The deal is, David, that if you say yes, once they pick you up and take you away, you can't come back here. Regardless of whether or not you get the job. Understand?"

"Oh, I see. It's a way to get rid of me. Dr. Franks, I appreciate you setting this up, but I've applied to about a hundred churches all across the country and not one of them wanted to hire me. What makes you think this will be any different?"

"David, I know Rick. Their situation is unique. I think you stand a very good chance. And I sense the Lord's hand in this."

David had sensed the Lord's hand before, but the Lord's hand always turned out to be wishful thinking.

"So, I could end up stranded there if they don't hire me? In a strange city where I don't know anyone? I don't really like my chances. What's the other choice?"

"The other choice is that Mitch drives you into town and drops you off at the homeless shelter with this envelope which contains fifty dollars cash."

"What? I can't believe that! You wouldn't do that to me, Dr. Franks. You just couldn't! Just give me another week. I'll go out to this church, but chances are they'll turn me down like every other church has."

"David, you head to Lachance or to the homeless shelter. Which is it?"

"You would seriously throw out an orphan?"

"David, you're twenty-one years old. You're a grown man, orphan or not."

"Can I have some time to think about it?"

"No. I need an answer now."

"What if I refuse? Are you going to drag me away?"

"The board informs me that if you refuse, then you are trespassing and it becomes a legal matter."

"A legal matter? What does that mean?"

"It means we call the police, they arrest you for trespassing, you probably pay a fine and end up at the homeless shelter. Without the fifty dollars."

David sighed and looked across at Dr. Franks. "I'm sorry I've been difficult. Thanks for letting me stay here over the summer. I guess I'll take my chances with the job."

"Very good, David. I think you've made a wise choice. Pastor Rick is a good man and he'll teach you a lot."

"If I get the job."

"Yes, but it sounds to me like you'd be a perfect fit. I'm hopeful. I'll call them and let them know. You can go start packing up your room, but before you go, I'd like to pray for you."

"Sure. I need it." David felt the tension in his neck and shoulders as he bowed his head and closed his eyes.

"Dear Lord, I thank you for David and that you have a perfect plan for his life. I thank you that you care for him and will be with him. Lord, if it is your will, I pray that he would find favor with the folks at Lachance Community Church, that this would be the beginning of a long and fruitful ministry. Amen."

"Amen. Thanks Dr. Franks." David got up and shook the dean's hand across the table. "Dr. Franks, can I ask you one more thing?"

"Of course, what is it, David?"

"Can I still have that fifty bucks?"

DRIVEN

When David got back to his room he found Mitch, standing next to a stack of three plastic bins filled with all of David's belongings. At the beginning of the summer Mitch had begun giving half his sandwich to David at lunch. After a few days, Mitch began bringing two sandwiches. Some days, that was all David ate. A couple times a week, Mitch would invite David to dinner where his wife Sarah would dote on him, their own children having grown up and moved away.

"I'm sorry, David. Dr. Franks told me I had to. I mean, the board is really making us do this. I don't mind having you stay here. I'd even let you stay with us, but the seniors' residence doesn't allow overnight guests."

"Mitch, thanks for everything. Thanks for all you've done for me. Tell Sarah thanks, too. I'm really going to miss both of you."

"It was our pleasure. Really, it was. It was nice having someone to help me out. So, are you going to go for that job interview?"

"Yes. I have nothing to lose, really."

"Yeah. You're a real good singer. I think you'll be a great music leader. And you can keep these bins. The bottom one has your books, so be careful. It's real heavy."

"Thanks, Mitch."

David's phone rang before Mitch could respond.

"I better take this. It might be my new boss."

Mitch smiled, waved and left. David stared at his phone. He had heard that your voice sounds better on the phone if you're smiling, so he forced a smile onto his face and answered the call.

"Hello, David Singer."

"David! This is Rick Avery. Dr. Franks told me all about you.

I'm so glad you're willing to come up and see us this weekend."

The voice on the other end of the phone was confident and smooth. Rick Avery was probably smiling.

"Yes, so am I. I am also glad about that I am coming." David winced at his awkward response, then remembered to keep smiling.

"Um, great. Well, here at Lachance Community Church, or LCC as we call it, we are on the cusp of some great things. And we need the right kind of leader for our music ministry. From what I hear, you are just the type of man we are looking for."

"I hope so, Pastor," said David.

"Well, my right-hand man, Wayne, will be at the campus in about three hours to pick you up, OK? We've got a meeting here tonight with some of our key leaders in the church, and then we'd love for you to share a song in our service tomorrow morning. How's that sound? I hear you play a mean guitar. You'll bring your guitar?"

"You bet! I'll bring all my stuff." David stared at the plastic bins.

"We'll see you later tonight. God Bless, David."

"Thanks, Pastor. And thanks for this—"

Pastor Rick had already hung up.

David was sitting on a bench outside the dorm building, holding his wallet open and staring at the fifty dollars. It had been quite a while since he'd held that much money. He looked up as he heard a truck making its way down the lane where it stopped in front of him. The driver rolled down the window. "You David?"

"You must be Wayne?"

"That's right."

Wayne got out of the truck. He was tall, thin, wiry and looked about 40 years old. He was wearing work boots, jeans, and a navy work shirt that said "Dawkins Construction" on the sleeve. He looked at David and then at the three plastic bins, duffle bag, and guitar case on the bench beside him.

"Is that your stuff? You need all that?"

"Well, I sort of do, yeah. Is that OK?"

"Yeah, sure. I'll just have to make some room."

Wayne went to the back of the truck, opened the tailgate, lifted the box cover and started rearranging the contents to make room for David's things. David wondered if he should offer to help, but the tools and other materials he could see looked heavy. How embarrassing would it be if he wasn't able to lift them?

"OK, that should be good for the bins. We can stuff your guitar and the duffle bag in the cab. Let's go."

David handed Wayne the bins, one by one. They found room behind the seats in the cab for the rest of his things, and then David sat in the passenger seat. Wayne got in, started the truck, and pulled away. As the truck wheeled around to head back out the lane, David saw Mitch coming out of the dorm building, waving goodbye. David waved back and wondered if he'd ever see Mitch again.

"OK, three hours and we're there. Sit tight," said Wayne.

Three hours. That's a lot of small talk. David hated small talk, but he wanted to impress Wayne. He tried to initiate some light conversation.

"That's a lot of tools you have back there."

"Oh yeah. Being in construction, this is my rolling office and workshop. You gotta be ready for any situation. That means having the right tools with you at all times. Like, for instance, say lightning hit that light standard there and knocked it down in front of us. We'd be stuck here, right? Well, no sir. I have an angle grinder that would cut through that steel like butter. There'd be sparks flying everywhere, but we'd cut it up, clear it from the lane, and be on our way."

David wondered what an angle grinder looked like.

"Is that why you brought all that stuff?" asked Wayne. "To be prepared?"

"Yes." Technically, David was telling the truth. He needed to be ready to move into the nearest homeless shelter should he fail to get the job.

"Well I admire that. You never know what might happen. Best to be ready."

A surge of satisfaction came over David. He had impressed Wayne. He relaxed and settled back into his seat. "So tell me about the church."

"Oh, yeah, I guess you'd like to know all about the church. Well it's roughly thirteen thousand square feet, brick exterior, wood frame construction. Overall, it is pretty well-built. Roof was replaced fifteen years go, probably good for another ten. H-VAC is underpowered if you ask me, but nobody asks me. Of course, it was built before the sewer lines made it to our end of the street so we're still on septic. The city won't pay to connect us to the sewer. I figure it's because we're a church. If we were an abortion clinic I bet they'd hook us up, no questions asked. Bunch of baby-killin' commies at city hall. Anyways, in the meantime, we're still on septic. Can you believe that?"

"Believe what?"

"That we're still on septic." Wayne took his eyes off the road to look at David.

"Um, I don't really know what septic is." David instantly regretted revealing his ignorance.

"Really? Man, I don't know how, in this advanced country, we let a grown man graduate from college without basic knowledge, like what a septic system is. Well, it's basically a localized sewage treatment system for a building that isn't serviced by a municipal sewer. First, the waste goes into the septic tank…"

Wayne spent the next forty-five minutes or so explaining how septic systems work. He talked about various tanks, the drain field, sludge, the scum layer, the importance of regularly scheduled maintenance, and how to tell when the tank needed to be pumped. At times, he held the steering wheel still with his knee so he could use both hands to indicate the relative size and locations of the various components of a typical septic system. David did his best to feign both interest and comprehension.

They stopped for dinner at a rest stop off the highway. David was relieved when Wayne paid for both their meals, since he didn't know how long he'd need to stretch the fifty dollars from Dr. Franks. Over their hamburgers, Wayne went on to describe the H-VAC system along with something about BTUs without ever explaining what a BTU was.

As they got back into the truck, Wayne lamented that the church's electrical service was barely adequate and how even an expensive upgrade of the main panel would not prevent the women's ministry from plugging four fifteen-amp coffee makers into a single twenty-amp circuit.

"Well, we got about an hour left. And I haven't even told you about the sanctuary renovation we did last year. All new carpet, seating, sound system, lighting, newly renovated foyer. It looks as good as any new mega church you'll ever visit in there."

"Really? What kind of sound system does it have?" David

perked up. This was good news. As the prospective worship pastor, he would be responsible for all the music at the church. The idea of a state-of-the-art sound system was enticing.

"Well that's the funny thing. The building committee brought in this sound consultant who wanted ten grand just to design the system. That's without even buying a single speaker! So I told them to forget that. I've been to lots of churches and it's pretty easy to see that all you do is hang some speakers and point 'em where the people sit. So that's what I did. And you know why I did that?"

"Why?"

"Because I care about quality."

David shook his head, bewildered. "How does ignoring an expert help with quality?"

"Because with the money we saved on the sound system we were able to do the main bathroom floors in tile instead of linoleum." Wayne looked pleased with himself.

"So, how does the sound system actually sound?"

"Oh, man. I guess it sounds OK. I'm half deaf from working with power tools my whole life. But with the way our band plays, maybe you don't want to hear them anyway! And most people can't tell the difference, but everyone knows the difference between linoleum and tile."

David kept his opinion on linoleum versus an acoustic engineer to himself. "Well, can you tell me about the people in the church?"

"Oh yeah. They're great!"

David waited to hear more, but Wayne was not forthcoming.

"They're great? Like, what do you mean? In what way?"

"Oh, they're great. I mean, most of them are. There's some people that cause problems for Pastor Rick, but for the most part, they're great. You know, they're church people."

They crossed a long bridge over a river. On the other side was a large faded wooden sign reading "Welcome to Lachance! The luckiest place on earth!" Behind the sign was a lumber yard piled high with logs.

"Here we are." Wayne waved a hand. "This is the old lumber yard. Still going, even though they've been threatening to close it for years, but it still keeps going. It used to be the main employer in town."

David silently watched as the piles of dead trees drifted by his window. The scenery changed as they entered an industrial area with nondescript warehouses, then a business district.

"Here's Main Street," said Wayne, "There's the city hall, the war memorial, and Lachance Park. Lots of stuff happens there in the summer."

They passed through the business section into an old residential neighbourhood and then turned left on Cedar Road.

"There she is, down at the end of the street."

David looked down the road at the thirteen thousand square foot building and wondered who was waiting for him inside. He prayed silently as they approached it. *Dear God, help me make these people like me.*

INTERVIEW

They pulled into the parking lot of Lachance Community Church, past an illuminated sign, the lettering advertising the upcoming "FALL KICKOFF 2010! SUNDAY SEPT 13." Wayne and David got out of the truck. David counted six cars in the parking lot.

"Bring your guitar. They're probably gonna want to hear what you can do. I'll get your duffle bag. You think you'll need any of the boxes?"

"No, just the duffle bag. Thanks for the ride, Wayne."

As they came to the glass double doors of the church, David read the handwritten sign taped to the left door — "PLEASE!! USE OTHER DOOR." The 'PLEASE' was underlined three times. Wayne dutifully opened the correct door and David walked through with his guitar into the foyer. He was surprised at how well appointed the foyer was. It had new carpet, and reminded him of a modern hotel lobby.

"Well, hello there, you must be David! Welcome, welcome, welcome!"

David turned around to see who had welcomed him. A man approached him, mid-forties, black dress pants and a shiny grey dress shirt, tucked in and stretched tight around the stomach.

"I'm Pastor Rick. We are all really looking forward to getting to know you. Glad you could make it on such short notice! "

"Hi, I'm David Singer. Thanks for inviting me. Pleasure to meet you." David tried to produce a smile that projected 'confident and comfortable religious professional.' Inside, he was terrified.

"I hope the ride was OK and that Wayne didn't talk your ear off. Anyways, we've got a group interview with some of our music team tonight. Then tomorrow morning we'll have you participate in the service. After that, there's potluck lunch and I'll meet with the council to decide what direction we're going with all this. Sound good? Well the gang is in the boardroom, let's go meet everybody. Wayne! Thanks for picking him up."

"You know it, Pastor, anything you need, as always," said Wayne.

David, Pastor Rick, and Wayne walked into the boardroom where three people were already seated. It was obvious that the recent renovations had not made their way into this room. It contained two square wooden stacking tables, pushed together, surrounded by cushioned stacking chairs. Some of the chairs had tape covering frayed sections of the fabric. In the corner was a chair with a handwritten sign taped on the back "Broken. Do not sit." A flowery wallpaper border along the wall near the ceiling was peeling off at the seams.

"I'm Carissa! Welcome!" said a woman who appeared to be in her late thirties. Everything about her looked expensive. Her hair was shimmering blond, salon styled. Emerald earrings matched her green sleeveless blouse, which revealed tanned muscular arms. A gold watch on one wrist, designer charm bracelet on the other. She wore a wedding ring with an enormous diamond. She reached out a hand with manicured nails to David. He wondered if the combined value of her jewelry, clothing, manicure and haircut would be the equivalent of his entire student debt.

"The Lord bless you, David!" She looked sweetly into his eyes, head tilted to the side.

"Thank you, you too." David wanted to say her name, but he'd already forgotten it. He was nervous and wasn't off to a very good start.

The woman smiled, blinked furiously and sat down.

Next, a middle-aged man approached, receding grey hair pulled back in a ponytail, black button-down shirt unbuttoned over a concert jersey. There was a fedora on the table where he was sitting. "Inq Lang. Salutations."

Inq shook David's hand, turned, and sat down.

"Ink?" said David.

"That's correct. I-N-Q. It is unusual, I know. Its origin is actually somewhat interesting"

"But we don't have time for that story tonight," interrupted

Pastor Rick, to the apparent relief of the rest of the room, as though they knew the story well.

"And this is Trisha," said Pastor Rick.

"Hello." Trisha stood to shake David's hand. She appeared in her early twenties, with short brown hair, delicate features, beautiful but not glamorous. She was dressed in jeans and a long sleeved T-shirt. She had an intelligent, serious look in her eyes, perhaps even a little sad. But she smiled as she shook David's hand. He realized he was beginning to stare and shook himself out of it.

"Very nice to meet you, Trisha." David truly meant it. He began speculating whether he had a chance with her. As he shook her right hand, he looked at her left hand. Good. No wedding ring.

"David, we'll start by telling you a bit about us. I'm Pastor Rick, the lead Pastor here at Lachance Community Church. I'm married to Elizabeth and have two grown daughters, Sarah and Rachel. I've been here at Lachance for seventeen years."

"Well, I'm Carissa."

Ah, that was her name, thought David, repeating it to himself so as not to forget again.

"I spend most of my time looking after the twins, Skylar and Brodie."

And getting your hair and nails done. And shopping and working out, thought David.

"Bob is my husband and he's really busy with the business. I sing on the worship team, I'm passionate about ushering God's people into His glorious presence in worship! I've been coming here to Lachance for eight years."

The man with the strange name spoke next. "Well, I'm Inq Lang. I'm a software consultant and I've been attending here for about ten years. I play bass in the worship team as well as in my Jethro Tull tribute band called "The Aqualung Experience." In my opinion, the energy, sophistication and aesthetic moral imperatives of progressive rock reached their zenith in the artistry of Jethro Tull, and we, in the Aqualung Experience, endeavor — "

"That's fine, Inq. We all appreciate Jethro Tull, I'm sure," interrupted Pastor Rick again.

"Well," huffed Inq. "I'm simply sharing for the benefit of Mr. Singer." He gestured deferentially toward David.

David nodded, then turned to Trisha when she began to speak.

"I'm Trisha Bain. I've been attending this church my whole life

15

and I play piano in the worship team. I teach primary school."

David wondered if she had a boyfriend and then scolded himself. *First get the job, then get the girl.*

"Well, David, that's us. We know a little about you from your resumé, but why don't you tell us your story. Start with growing up."

David knew this was coming. He didn't like talking about growing up, but he took a deep breath and began. "I was raised by my grandmother. My mom wasn't really a part of my life growing up. I only remember being with her a couple of times when I was very young. I've never met my Father." David paused to clear his throat. "But my grandmother took care of me. She was a strong Christian and I grew up going to church regularly. I answered an altar call at Vacation Bible School one summer and gave my life to Jesus. I also began singing in church. I remember that every time I sang, the pastor would make the same joke about my last name being 'Singer' so I really had no choice."

They all chuckled at this. David started to relax. Of course, they'd chuckled in all the other interviews at the other churches as well, but he wasn't offered any of those jobs. It would take more than chuckles this time.

"My grandfather died before I was born, so all we had was his pension to live on, but Grandma sacrificed so I could have voice lessons. When I was fifteen, she surprised me with a guitar on my birthday. I think she sold half her jewelry to afford it." He inadvertently looked at Carissa as he said this, then shyly looked away.

"Anyway, I began singing regularly in church and that's when I knew that was what God made me to do. It was everything to me. It still is. When I graduated from high school, I enrolled at Redeemer College."

"My alma mater!" Pastor Rick interjected.

"Yes. Grandma sacrificed a lot to put me through college. She passed away two years ago."

"Oh, I'm so sorry," said Carissa.

The rest of the room nodded in sympathy.

"Well, thank you. But I really had to learn to trust God through all of that. It was sudden. She didn't suffer. I'm just sorry she never got to see me graduate and become a pastor. That was her dream for me."

Carissa was wiping tears from her eyes. It made David wonder if his story struck the right balance between pathetic, a poor orphan, and a comfortable and confident religious professional.

"At college, I joined the worship team right away and it really was my passion. It's my dream to become a worship pastor and share that passion with a church like yours."

Now Carissa was nodding and looking around at the rest of the people in the room. It looked like he had at least one vote in his favor.

"That's really great, David. I've asked the committee here to prepare some questions for you. Why don't you start us off, Carissa," said Pastor Rick.

Carissa smiled and picked up her designer purse on the table, digging out a small journal with a floral pattern on the cover. She opened it and found her page, reading a question written in purple ink.

"David, we've all heard a lot about the need for the church to be *missional*." She slowed down and emphasized this last word, a satisfied look on her face as she nodded toward each one in the room. "What would you do to ensure that our worship is *missional?*"

"Oh, well, I guess we should start with defining *missional*. It can mean a lot of different things to different people. What does *missional* mean to you?"

"Oh!" replied Carissa, looking confused now. "I guess, well, it's sort of a way of saying that... well, I guess that's something I thought you would know!"

Trisha rolled her eyes and smiled at Carissa, who smiled back and shrugged. Inq looked sideways at her, annoyed.

"OK... well, let's not worry about Bible College buzzwords," said Pastor Rick. "Inq, what's your question?"

"Tell me, David. Are you familiar with the work of the great medieval philosopher Boethius?" asked Inq.

Now Carissa looked annoyed. Trisha stifled a giggle. Pastor Rick rubbed his forehead.

"I told you we shouldn't have invited him," said Wayne.

"Inq, nobody's ever heard of him," said Pastor Rick. "David, Inq has an unhealthy fascination with this Boethius person. Usually we humor him, but you don't have to answer that."

"Well, actually, I wrote a paper on Boethius," said David.

17

Carissa, Trisha and Pastor Rick all stared at him with stunned expressions.

"You don't know what a septic tank is, but you heard of Boethius?" said Wayne.

Inq looked around triumphantly.

"Really? I half thought Inq had made him up," said Pastor Rick.

"No, he was real," said David. "He wrote that 'All fortune is good fortune, for it either rewards, disciplines, amends, or punishes — ' "

"And so is either useful or just!" said Inq, finishing the quote with David.

The room was silent for a moment until Inq, beaming, stood, picked up his fedora from the table and smartly put it on. "Pastor, I've heard enough. It is my recommendation that you hire this man immediately." Inq stepped back from the table, walked out of the room. They all looked silently out the door until they heard a car start and pull out of the parking lot.

"You are the first person I've ever met, other than Inq, who's heard of Boethius," said Pastor Rick. "But don't worry. We won't hold it against you."

"Well, actually I slept in one day and was late to my church history class. We were picking project topics and Boethius was the only one left. But please don't tell Inq," said David.

They all laughed.

"Trisha. You're up."

"David, you've spent a little bit of time with us now. What are your first impressions of us?" Trisha looked earnest and David couldn't read her at all. Was she fishing for a compliment? Or was she testing him to see if he was observant?

"Well, I'm pretty impressed with how quickly this has all come together. You didn't even know who I was until yesterday afternoon, but you arranged to pick me up, set up this entire candidating weekend for me. You all cancelled your Saturday night plans to meet with me, arranged the church lunch for tomorrow. I think that means you're all very committed and decisive. You must think this role of Worship Pastor is important if you can work so quickly to arrange all of this. It really is quite humbling that you've done all that for me."

David was happy with his answer. He hoped it made the committee members and Pastor Rick feel good about themselves.

However, after he spoke there was only awkward silence in the room. Carissa and Trisha both looked at Pastor Rick and then down at the table. Wayne looked at the ceiling, shaking his head.

"Well," Pastor Rick said. "David, we truly believe that God chose you to be here with us this weekend. That's the truth. And, it is also the truth that we arranged this candidating weekend two months ago for another young man. On Friday morning we found out that he accepted a call to another church and neglected to inform us. Now, due to a peculiarity with our budgeting approval process, we need to fill this position before the end of the month or the funding will be reviewed and possibly revoked. So that's when we called you! Now the Lord rarely plans things out with straight lines, and this is just one of those times. We are very glad that *you* are here."

It took David a few seconds to comprehend what Pastor Rick said. But as he understood it, he felt a sting of humiliation. All this was meant for someone else. David was not their first choice. He didn't know quite what to say. Most of all, he felt foolish for thinking all this was arranged just for him. He hoped he wasn't blushing.

"Well, I'm glad to be here, too." He tried to sound positive, wondering why they hadn't told him this until now.

"Would you like to sing something for us?" asked Carissa.

"That's a great idea, Carissa," said Pastor Rick. "Let's go into the auditorium. You can see it and then we can hear you sing something."

As Pastor Rick led them out of the conference room, a matronly middle-aged woman was waiting in the foyer. She wore a brightly patterned blouse with shiny gold buttons and shoulder pads. Her arms were folded over her stomach with a large black handbag dangling from her elbow. Crimson lipstick outlined the scowl on her face.

"Oh Elizabeth! What perfect timing!" said Pastor Rick. "David, this is my wife, Elizabeth. Elizabeth, this is David, our candidate for worship pastor."

Elizabeth's scowl quickly transformed into a benevolent smile as she thrust out her hand towards David. "Aah! So nice to meet you, David. We are glad you're here. We're looking for someone who can bring some real spiritual depth to our music ministry."

David noticed that she glanced at Carissa while saying this.

"Well, I'm happy to be here and hope that I have a chance to help out."

"Very nice. Good to meet you, David. And Carissa, how are you? And how are things with Bob?"

"Oh, Bob's doing great," said Carissa.

"It would be so nice to see him at church some time. I do keep him in my prayers. I can't imagine what you go through, being spiritually single like that."

"I certainly appreciate your prayers," said Carissa as she turned away and walked into the auditorium with Trisha following close behind.

Elizabeth turned back to Pastor Rick. "Rick, how long will you be?" She stretched out her arm to look at her watch.

"I can get a ride home with Wayne. You go on ahead, Sweetheart," said Pastor Rick.

Elizabeth said nothing, but turned to leave, digging car keys out of her handbag on the way out the door.

David followed Pastor Rick and Wayne across the foyer, through a set of double doors into the auditorium. It was beautiful, newly renovated with theatre-style seating. David thought he could smell a trace of new carpet. He figured it would sit five hundred people.

Two large projector screens flanked the stage. A set of drums, an electronic keyboard, some monitor speakers, and guitar amps were arranged on the platform. A microphone stood at centre stage.

"Why don't you use that mic there, David. I asked our sound man to leave it set up and there should be a cord for your guitar too if you need it," said Pastor Rick.

David went up on stage with his guitar, took it out of the case and plugged it in. The PA system popped as he did so. He walked up to the mic, strapped on his guitar, prayed silently to himself asking God to calm his nerves and give him strength. He began to play the introduction to his favorite song, Tom Lindsay's hit worship song, *Mountaintop*.

His voice echoed through the auditorium, beginning softly with the verse and then growing more passionate as he reached the chorus of the song. David lost himself completely in the song, as he'd done countless times. After working so hard to be impressive during the interview, singing was the one thing he could do effortlessly. He pulled back from the microphone and let his powerful voice fill the sanctuary naturally for the final rousing chorus.

> "You lift me to a highest place
> I see the beauty of your face
> My love for you will never stop
> Because you, You take me to the Mountaintop."

As he finished the song, a reverent silence hung over the sanctuary. Carissa, Pastor Rick, and Trisha walked up on the stage as he turned and put his guitar away. Pastor Rick was the first to speak.

"That was great, David! You really can sing."

"Very nice," said Trisha, smiling. "I love that song."

She loves that song, thought David.

Carissa had tears in her eyes again. "Wow. Oh, my heart! Wow. David, that was so, so — *Missional!*" Carissa, looked around, nodding at Trisha and Pastor Rick.

"Well, thank you. That's just such a great song," said David.

"How 'bout that sound system?" said Wayne.

"Oh, yes, very nice. Very nice, Wayne," said David.

As Wayne nodded approvingly, the doors opened in the back of the auditorium and a man walked in, a silhouette barely visible to David with the stage lights in his eyes. Trisha walked down the aisle to meet him, kissing him on the cheek. David felt instantly disappointed, though he knew someone like Trisha must have a boyfriend.

But as they walked into the light, David saw that it was a man in his sixties, thinning hair with a paunch, wearing dress pants and a pale blue golf shirt. This was definitely not Trisha's boyfriend.

"This is Bill Bain," said Pastor Rick. "He's our treasurer, and is also Trisha's dad. He's been around this church just about forever. I asked him to pick you up, David, and take you to your hotel for the night. It's been a long day for you. I'm sure you must be tired, and we want you rested for tomorrow morning."

"Sounds good." David shook hands with Bill and said goodnight to Carissa, Pastor Rick, Trisha and Wayne. He stopped by the boardroom to pick up his duffle bag. Bill was waiting for him at the main doors.

"How're you holding up?" asked Bill as they walked out to his car.

"Pretty well, I guess. Everyone's been really nice. And I really feel like I could contribute to the vision that Pastor Rick — "

"Hold it right there! Just relax. You don't have to impress me," said Bill.

"Oh. OK then."

"Well, listen David, I can take you to a hotel, but I have a perfectly good guest room at my house as well. Would you be OK if we saved the church a little money and you stayed at my place tonight?"

"Whatever you'd like. I'm easy. In fact, I admire your good stewardship. Pastor Rick must be so thankful to have a treasurer like you."

"David, first of all, I said you don't have to impress me. Second of all, Pastor Rick's opinion of me as a treasurer is a subject for another day."

David wondered what that comment could mean.

"I won't be an inconvenience for the rest of your family?" David wondered if Trisha lived there.

"No, it's just me. I'm a widower. It's no trouble at all."

Ten minutes later, they arrived at Bill's small bungalow. Bill offered David something to eat, but David declined out of politeness. Bill showed him his room.

"This used to be Trisha's room, but I turned it into a guest room when she moved out. I'll wake you up for breakfast and we'll be at church in plenty of time for you to get ready for the service."

"OK, thanks a lot." David wasn't sure whether he should call him Bill or Mr. Bain. He wasn't yet comfortable calling older men by their first names.

He sat down on the bed and wondered if it was the same bed Trisha used to sleep in. He tried thinking of something funny to say to Trisha the next morning about sleeping in her bed, but decided it would be far too creepy. He looked around the room trying to detect any signs of her. The room held no pictures or dolls or anything to suggest it had once belonged to a little girl.

David undressed and got into bed, reviewing the events of the day. He prayed earnestly. "Oh dear God, let this be it. I need this job. Please help me make them like me."

CANDIDATE

D avid heard footsteps coming down the hallway and then a knock at the door.

"Morning, David. Bacon and eggs OK for breakfast?" said Bill, through the door.

David was already awake. He'd slept poorly and had been wide awake for at least an hour, lying in bed praying anxiously, his mind alternating between imagined success or failure.

"Oh, sure, I'm easy," he said, already smelling the bacon.

He took a quick shower, dressed, and found his way to the kitchen where Bill had breakfast waiting, a plate of bacon and eggs for David, a rather unappetizing bowl of high fibre cereal for himself.

"Oh, you didn't have to make that especially for me."

"It's no trouble at all, David. Since my heart attack I have to watch my cholesterol. Besides, you wouldn't want my cereal. Believe me."

Bill said grace and they ate. David was nervous and had no appetite, but forced down his food.

"Do you think I'm dressed nice enough for church?" David wondered if his best khaki pants and plaid button-down shirt were good enough to impress the people of Lachance Community Church.

"Well, I think you look fine. Some of the older folks might not think so, but they've been complaining since Pastor Rick stopped wearing a tie. That was about five years ago. So don't worry about them. We better get going. Here, I'll just leave the plates in the sink. Let's go."

"David! Good to see you, welcome, welcome," said Pastor Rick. "This is Eric, our sound man. He'll get you set up."

David plugged his guitar into the cable on stage and sang into the mic. He played through the Tom Lindsey song, asking for minor adjustments from Eric. After meeting and praying with the team in a back room behind the stage, David took a seat in the front row, next to Pastor Rick.

At eleven o'clock, the worship team took the stage. Trisha sat at the piano, Inq was on bass guitar and Carissa stood up front singing. A teenager was on guitar, his face obscured by hair. A middle-aged man David hadn't yet met sat at the drums.

Carissa began. "Welcome, everyone to LCC this morning. We are so glad you're here and we just want to enter into His presence this morning because His presence is amazing and his presence is always amazing like His love, as just a gift to us when we are present here together as we seek Him in worship. Amen? Amen. Yes. OK, well please stand with us!"

David saw Pastor Rick rolling his eyes during Carissa's incoherent welcome. The drummer began clicking his sticks together to set the tempo. The band all came in together, but each member chose their own tempo. Even the drummer chose a different tempo than the one he clicked in. The music limped along like a horse whose four legs were each a different length. The lyrics appeared on two large screens over a digitally created abstract background image, usually late and often wrong. The opening line to the chorus of their first song read "We lift you up Jseus." David wondered what kind of church couldn't even spell *Jesus*? The congregation half-heartedly joined Carissa and together they endured three songs.

At one point during this opening set, as Carissa was talking about more of God's presence, Pastor Rick leaned over to David and said, "You can see why we need your help."

David felt bad hearing this. Everyone on the team was trying their best, and David was really trying to worship God despite the music and the nervous knot in his stomach.

Ushers appeared and passed the offering plate during a fourth song. Then Pastor Rick walked up on stage as the band left the platform. Pastor Rick put on a big smile and said "Good morning."

His mic wasn't on. Only the first couple of rows could hear him. He repeated "Good morning."

Still no mic. His mouth continued to smile but his eyes narrowed as they looked to the back of the auditorium where the sound booth was located.

"How about now?"

Still no mic, but the smile persisted. Lines were forming on his forehead. "OK, I'll just raise my voi — " The mic came on as he was shouting 'voice' and Pastor Rick's smile returned to his entire face, the lines in his forehead gradually fading.

"All right, well, I have someone very special to introduce to you. As you know, we've been looking for someone to become our worship pastor and we have our candidate here this weekend. Now, our bulletin says that his name is Josh Frayne, but his name is actually David Singer. We, uh, regret the mix up. Anyway, we've been getting to know Josh, I mean David, a little bit this weekend and we'd like you to hear from him as well. David, would you like to come up here? Let's welcome him."

David came up on stage, picked up and plugged in his guitar and stepped up to the mic as the congregation's applause died down. As David looked out over the auditorium he was surprised at how sparse the congregation was, perhaps a hundred and fifty people scattered around the five hundred-seat auditorium.

"It's great to be here. I've really enjoyed getting to know everyone. I'd like to sing a song for you called *You Take me to the Mountaintop* this morning. This song has really helped me connect my heart with God's heart. I hope you are blessed."

David prayed quickly, took a deep breath, and then began playing the introduction to the song. He tried to forget about the people who were sitting in front of him, evaluating him, weighing him on their scales. He sang for God and no one else.

He finished the song and the room was silent. As he collected his thoughts and surveyed his surroundings, the applause began. First one person in the back and then the entire congregation applauded.

"Thank you." David walked off the platform and took his seat, relieved. He was happy with how he sang — from the heart. He'd done his best and the rest was in God's hands. Or in the congregation's hands. He wasn't quite sure which.

Pastor Rick took the platform, thanked David, and said they'd expect to know very soon about the next steps for David and for

LCC. He then launched into his sermon. David tried his best to look like he was paying attention, but his mind raced with anxious thoughts. *Do they like me? What will I do if they don't offer me the job? Where will I sleep tonight?* He supposed that he could stay one more night at Bill's house even if he didn't get the job, and then they might offer to drive him somewhere. If not, he could use the fifty dollars from Dr. Franks to buy a bus ticket. He just didn't know where to.

Pastor Rick was reaching the high point of his sermon, summoning a tear as he told a story.

"There was a little girl who was very sick and needed a blood transfusion. But she had a very rare blood type and the only match was her little brother. And so the Doctor asked the little boy, 'Billy, would you be willing to give your blood to save your sister's life?' The boy looked up at the doctor, over to his parents, gulped and said 'I'll do it.' So the nurses hooked Billy up and took a pint of his blood.

"When they finished and the nurse was removing the needle from his arm, little Billy asked his mother 'When will it happen?' She replied, 'When will what happen, Billy?' He said 'When will I die?'

"'What do you mean, Billy?'

"'I mean, now that I've given my sister my blood, I'm going to die, aren't I?'

"And then Billy's mother's eyes filled with tears as she realized that Billy thought giving his blood meant he would die, and he was still willing to do it to save his sister's life. 'Oh, no Billy, you won't die. You won't die,' she explained as she hugged him tightly.

"Oh, brothers and sisters, how touching that story is, and yet, we have a beloved Lord and Saviour who did willingly give his life blood to save you and me. Let us pray."

As Pastor Rick prayed, David wondered what kind of sick doctor wouldn't explain to Billy that giving blood wouldn't hurt him.

After his prayer, Pastor Rick invited his listeners to recommit their life to Jesus.

David silently accepted that invitation. *Lord, whatever happens today, I'll follow you*, he prayed.

The worship team returned to the stage and played another song and then they were dismissed. Pastor Rick said grace for the potluck lunch as part of the benediction. He ushered David with him to the main doors of the auditorium to greet people as they left. David shook many hands and received many compliments. He couldn't tell whether they were genuine or simply given out of politeness.

Through the line of people exiting the auditorium, he noticed an elderly man, one of the only men in a suit and tie, looking at him intently. When the man reached the doors, David extended his hand and said, "Good morning."

The man looked at David's hand, pausing as if deciding whether to shake it. Then he shook it quickly.

"That song you sang never mentioned God or Jesus a single time!"

David was taken aback. "Oh? I suppose, yes you're right. I guess I never really noticed that. Um."

At this point a woman, obviously his wife, interjected. "Charley, don't be like that. Josh sang very nicely. We all know he was singing about God."

"Actually, it's David, not Josh," said David.

"Pardon me? The bulletin says your name is Josh, see it's right here." She pointed to her bulletin.

"I know, but they printed the wrong name."

"And I think you're the wrong person to be our worship pastor if you don't even know that your song doesn't mention the name of God!" said Charley. "Someone just hearing that song would think you're singing about your girlfriend."

Having grown up in church, David was used to the rudeness of church people. He smiled and tried to think of something positive to say. Just then Pastor Rick stepped in.

"Charley! Agnes! How are we doing this morning?"

"Just fine," replied Charley. "That was a good word this morning pastor, though I have concerns about the song that this Josh chose to sing to us this morning."

"Now Charley, you and I have talked a lot about the new church music. If we want to grow, we need to sing new songs. Don't you worry about things," said Pastor Rick.

"Well, we'll just see."

"Thank you, Pastor! Nice to meet you, Josh," said Agnes as she and Charley moved along.

"Don't worry about Charley," Pastor Rick said. "He wouldn't

have been happy unless you sang *Holy, Holy, Holy* and accompanied yourself on a real pipe organ. He's been sore ever since the first guitar showed up here. You hungry? You must be. Let's go get you something to eat before it's all gone and then you can spend some time pressing the flesh."

The last thing David wanted to do was press any flesh, but this was necessary if he was going to be a pastor. He steeled himself as he followed Pastor Rick into the church basement. He filled his plate with some egg salad sandwiches, baby carrots and ranch dip. Then he looked for a place to sit. Only two tables had empty chairs. One had Charley and Agnes and two other older couples. The other had a large Hispanic family. David chose the latter.

"Hello, I'm David, is this seat taken?"

Blank smiles. A mother and father and four children looked back at him. David sat.

"You speak Spanish?" said the father in a thick accent.

"I'm afraid not." said David.

"Español?"

"No, sorry."

The children were now giggling and whispering to each other. The mother just smiled.

"Guitar!" said the father, smiling and pretending to strum an imaginary guitar. "Bueno!"

David smiled and said "Guitar. Si, bueno." Then he began chewing on his egg salad sandwich while the family smiled at him.

"Hey!" said Trisha, taking the empty chair beside David. His heart began to race at the sound of her voice.

"I thought I'd rescue you. This is the Garcia family. They just emigrated from Honduras. They're very nice, but not much for English conversation. How'd you feel that went this morning?"

"Oh, it was good, I was happy with how it turned out. I don't think Charley liked it, though," David replied.

"Don't worry about him. You did really well."

In the pause that followed, David felt like he should say something. The only words coming to mind were, "Do you have a boyfriend?" And, "If not, will you marry me?" Instead, he mumbled a *thank you* and wondered why he was turning into such a puddle with her right beside him.

"I hope my dad didn't scare you off last night."

"Oh no, he was great. He made me bacon and eggs this

morning."

"Well, I'm glad you didn't have to eat his high fibre cereal." She laughed.

"Yeah, and I slept in your bed."

"Oh. I suppose you did." Trisha was no longer laughing.

David suddenly wished the floor would swallow him.

Pastor Rick was standing and loudly clearing his throat.

"Your attention, everyone. I have an important announcement to make. I've just met with the church council and we have decided unanimously to extend a call to David to be our worship pastor."

David was stunned. He wasn't expecting the decision so soon, or announced this way. The room filled with applause and sounds of approval. The Garcia family looked confused but eventually joined in the applause, turning and smiling at people around the room.

David stood and smiled, but couldn't figure out what to do with his hands, unsure whether to clasp them together, or wave or keep them at his side. The applause ended and David still stood, waiting for the weight of this news to sink in.

Trisha stood next to him and David snapped out of his stupor. She extended a hand to David and said, "Congratulations, Pastor."

Pastor? Not David? Pastor? It shocked him to be called *Pastor.* The word put distance between him and Trisha. He felt strange. This was everything he'd worked for since he was fourteen. Now he had it, but he still felt the same - insecure, timid and anxious. More anxious than ever.

The people began approaching David, shaking his hand, congratulating him, welcoming him to the LCC family. Eventually, Pastor Rick shook his hand and told him: "Bill will talk to you about some of the practical details. You just let me know if there are any snags, OK?"

After people began leaving, Bill approached David. "We should talk about the details of what we're offering. Let's head over to the finance office."

David followed Bill down a back hallway into a small room with an old metal desk. Stacking trays held invoices. A large tower computer and an old television-style monitor took up half the desktop. Bill sat at the desk, opened a manila folder, and motioned for David to sit in the chair opposite the desk.

Bill sighed "David, you understand that this is a small church, so I'm sure your salary expectations are somewhat measured. You need to know we are not doing well financially, but Pastor Rick really feels that it is important for our church to have a full time worship pastor in order to grow. The previous treasurer approved Pastor Rick's proposal to hire a full time worship pastor. I don't think I would've approved it, and honestly, I would've revoked the funding at our upcoming budget review meeting. But I can't change that now. It's certainly nothing personal. It's just a matter of numbers." Bill shook his head and rubbed the back of his neck. "In any case, what we are offering you is an eight-month contract that will take you through April. You'd work thirty-seven and a half hours a week at seven-thirty-five an hour. Take it or leave it. No negotiating. This is the only offer. I know the salary is probably insulting and I wouldn't blame you if you — "

" — I'll take it. Where do I sign?" said David.

Bill shook his head and pointed to the bottom of the page. They both signed the contract.

"Well, David, I do think you are a very nice young man. I hope for the best — for you *and* for the church. I really do. Maybe I'm wrong and this will all work out. Congrats and welcome aboard." Bill offered his hand to David.

"Thanks." David shook Bill's hand.

The salary was ten cents an hour over minimum wage, just enough so the church could deny they were paying him minimum wage. David didn't care. He knew how to live with little money. He'd rather be poorly paid doing what he loved than work a deep fryer at McDonalds. He knew Bill would've liked him to refuse the offer in order to save the church money, but David was happy to be employed, doing what he loved, what he felt God created him to do.

"After April, we will review your contract. Based on your performance and the financial status of the church, we will decide whether to renew. You can stay with me again tonight if you don't mind. I think tomorrow morning Wayne was going to take you out to start looking for a place to stay. Any questions about the contract?"

"When do I start?"

HUNTING

The next morning, David waited in Bill's living room until he saw Wayne's truck pull into the driveway. David went out to meet him as he walked up to the front door.

"Morning, David. Ready to go? You got some apartments to check out?"

"Well, I have one that looks promising. Let's start there. Two-forty-two Willow," David said.

David had searched Craigslist and found exactly one room for rent that met his requirements, being cheap and within walking distance to the church.

"OK, that's near the church. Let's go. I still have your boxes in the back of the truck, so if you find something, you can move right in."

They drove down Main Street and turned off on Willow, pulling up in front of number 242.

"You sure this is it?" asked Wayne.

"Well, yeah, that's what the ad said. I called this morning and the guy said he'd be home."

"Well, I'll say this, it doesn't look like it's too expensive. I'll wait here."

They both continued staring at the dilapidated one-story red brick house, the front door and window frames in need of paint, shingles dried out and curling up, lawn unkempt. David got out of the car and walked down the cement driveway, glancing at the weeds growing up between the cracks and the rusted white Chevy truck. He rang the doorbell and waited.

A raspy voice yelled "Hold on!" from behind the door.

A minute elapsed as David surveyed what used to be a flower

garden beside the porch. Through the front window, he could see a large flat-screen TV in the living room, opposite a couch and two folding chairs. A TV tray with several beer cans on it stood in front of the couch.

The door swung open and a thin man in his fifties appeared. Balding on top, long, stringy hair hung past his shoulders. He was wearing a Bud Light T-shirt, wrinkled as though he'd slept in it. He was still adjusting the belt on a pair of baggy jeans.

"You here about the room?"

"Yes, I called earlier."

"OK, come on in. I'll show you." The man led David down the front hallway, limping slightly. Though he was scruffy, he seemed friendly.

The lights were off, so David couldn't see much in the hallway, but the smell reminded him of the laundry room in the basement of the dorm back at school. He followed the man down some narrow stairs to the basement, through another door and into a sparsely furnished bachelor apartment.

"OK, you got your bathroom, shower there. Here's your cooking area, sink, hotplate and so on. Umm, this futon was left by the last guy, so you can use it if you want. It ain't much, but it's available."

David looked around the room and poked his head into the bathroom. *Serviceable.*

The man continued. "Yeah, the only thing it don't have is a separate entrance, but everything else you need is here. I've been renting it out for a little extra income. I got my disability pension and something from renting out the back lot to the bus company, but I started renting this room out for beer money, you know?"

David wondered how much Bud Light you could get for three hundred and fifty dollars a month. He looked out the rear window in the room and could see the tires and lower half of a yellow school bus. *This will do*, he thought. *At least to start.*

"I'll take it. What are the terms?"

"Like the ad says, rent is three-fifty a month, utilities included, and I'll need first and last month's rent up front."

David bit his lip.

"That a problem?"

"Well, I don't have it now, but I've just got a job and I should have it in a couple weeks, or as soon as I get paid. I can probably ask for an advance."

"Where you working?"

"Lachance Community Church"

The man stared at him blankly, a concerned look beginning to appear on his face.

"Have you heard of it?" David asked. "No? It's just off Main Street on Cedar Road. It's a red brick building."

"Oh, I thought that place was a funeral home."

"No, it's a church."

"Huh. You the minister? You seem kinda young."

"No, I'm the worship pastor."

"What's that?"

"I'm in charge of the music."

"You play the organ?"

"No, I play guitar. We play modern music. I lead the band and the music in the service."

"They pay you for that?"

"Yes."

"So is it part-time?"

"No, it's full-time."

"Well, what else do you do?"

David was starting to feel a little defensive.

"What do you do the rest of the week, like besides Sunday?" the man asked.

"Well, there's a lot, like I pick the songs."

The man just kept staring at him. David was trying to think of what else he might do during the week, but wasn't actually sure himself. "I think there's a lot of meetings and things. Honestly, this is my first job, so I'm not sure what all I'll be doing."

"Sounds like nice work if you can get it. I suppose if you're a church person, I can trust you not to stiff me on the rent. What kind of deposit can you manage?"

"I have fifty bucks I can give you."

"OK, that will do. When would you like to move in?"

"Well, my stuff is in the truck outside. I'd like to move in right now if I can."

The man shrugged. "Sure, what the hell. Oh... sorry. What the heck. I got a lease for you to sign upstairs."

They walked up the stairs and the man told David to have a seat on the couch. David sat there for minute staring at the blank TV.

The man returned with the lease.

"I changed the deposit to fifty bucks here and initialed it. You sign here."

David signed and then took out his wallet and handed over the fifty dollars. The man stared at David and didn't take the money.

"Is that the only money you got?"

"Well, yeah, actually."

"Well, I don't feel right about taking a holy man's last fifty bucks. Tell you what, hold on to that for now and we'll get caught up when you get paid. Just put in a good word with the man upstairs for me. Deal?"

"Well, that's very kind of you, sir. I'll see what I can do with the man upstairs."

He shrugged and shook his head. "I almost forgot. There's some rules. You can't cook any stinky food, OK?"

"I don't really know how to cook."

"OK. No smoking."

"I don't smoke."

"And no bringing around a buncha friends and making all kinds of noise."

"That's not a problem. I don't really have any friends." David, shrugged.

The man looked at him, shook his head, smiled and thrust out his hand. "Well you got one now. Chuck Weaver. Pleased to meet you."

David smiled and shook his hand. "David Singer. Nice to meet you Chuck."

"OK, let's get your stuff and see about you settling in."

FIRST DAY

David spent the rest of Monday afternoon exploring the neighbourhood, picking up some things for the apartment, revelling in his entry into responsible adulthood, if only some junior apprentice form of adulthood. He walked to the church and back. On the way back, he found a coffee shop and a corner grocery store where he bought generic brand peanut butter, white bread, powdered drink crystals, margarine, processed cheese, and Oreos. He brought them home and made himself two grilled cheese sandwiches for dinner.

The rest of the evening he spent noodling on his guitar and daydreaming, often about Trisha, wondering what she was doing. He was aching to get out his laptop and check Facebook and Twitter, but Chuck didn't have Wi-Fi, nor did Chuck seem to have heard of Wi-Fi when David asked him about it.

He looked forward with excitement to his first official day in the office, eventually putting away his guitar, lying down on his inherited futon and drifting to sleep. He heard Chuck's TV softly through the ceiling as he finally drifted off.

A ghastly shriek awakened David in the dark. He jerked up off the futon and fumbled around in the dark, unable to remember where he was. Light was now visible through the window, and then the unmistakeable growl and rattle of a diesel engine coming to life. One of the school buses had started right outside his window. David found his phone to check the time. Five thirty-eight a.m. He heard footsteps crunching over gravel as another driver came out to a bus, and then it also started up. David lay back on the futon, wide awake, listening to the school buses start and drive away, one every ten minutes until seven a.m.

On the way to church, David stopped at the coffee shop called "Beans of Production." He perused the posters with left wing slogans and Marxist imagery, all under the watchful eye of a Che Guevara mural that overlooked the menu. With a large black coffee in hand, he continued his walk to the church, arriving at eight-fifteen. The doors were locked, so he sat on the curb and drank his coffee. At eight forty-seven, a car finally pulled into the parking lot. David's coffee cup was empty, his bladder full.

A portly woman of about fifty ambled up to the front door. David stood to greet her, crossing his legs tightly together.

"Hi, I'm — "

"Don't tell me. You're Josh? I'm Rhonda, the church secretary."

"No, well, actually I'm David. David Singer."

"Oh. Can I help you? If you need to see a pastor, he'll be in later this morning. If you're looking for a handout, we don't do that. Try the Salvation Army downtown."

"Um, no, you see, I'm David Singer, the new worship pastor. It's my first day today. I was told to be here at eight-thirty."

"Well, I was told it was Josh who was the worship pastor. That's what I put in the bulletin."

"Well, there's been a mix up, and it's actually me. But, can we go in? I need to use the bathroom." David started to uncross his legs in an attempt to look relaxed. He quickly crossed them again.

"I don't see how that's possible. I know I put the right name in the bulletin. What happened to Josh?"

"I'm not exactly sure, but don't you remember me from Sunday?"

"From Sunday? Oh, no. I don't attend this church."

"You don't?"

"I'm Episcopalian." As though that explained everything.

"Then how are you... can we just please go inside?"

"Well, OK, but I'm going to call the pastor." Rhonda finally unlocked the front door.

David followed her into the church and urgently made his way to the bathroom. The paper towel dispenser was broken, so he wiped his hands on his pants and opened the door to leave. Rhonda was waiting for him right outside the men's room, startling David as he opened the door.

"I got a note that the paper towel dispenser isn't working," she said.

"Yes, it's broken."

"Can you put this sign on it?" Rhonda handed David a roll of scotch tape and a handwritten sign that read Broken. Do not use.

David complied with the request and then went back to the church office to return the tape.

"See, here. It says 'Josh.'" Rhonda held up a copy of the bulletin and showed it to David. "And here's Pastor's note. See, I didn't make a mistake."

"Well, no, but there was just a change. I'm a last-minute substitution, I guess," David said.

"Nobody told me. Nobody tells me anything around here, even though I'm supposedly the secretary. But that's—"

The phone rang. David waited as she took the call.

"Lachance Community Church," said Rhonda. "No, I'm not sure what is happening for the fall kickoff. No, I don't know of anything. I'm not sure why. I just work here. *My* church is doing a spaghetti supper on the tenth. Yes, I go to St. Peter's. Yes, it's at six o-clock and tickets are five dollars. All the money goes to our youth program. Well, that's fine, I hope to see you there."

She hung up the phone and looked back up at David. "Where were we? Oh, yes. I suppose you must be telling the truth. I mean, who would make up a story like that to try to get a job at this place?"

David wasn't sure if he was supposed to answer that question, but just then they heard the front door open and Pastor Rick walked in.

"David! I see you've met Rhonda."

"You told me his name was Josh. That's what I put in the bulletin. It wasn't my mistake."

"Rhonda, no, we found someone ten times better. Have you showed David his office? Get him set up on his computer, will you? David, I have some phone calls to make. What do you say we have lunch together? We'll leave at about twelve."

"Sure thing, Pastor," David said.

Rhonda handed him a manila envelope with JOSH written on it. "This has your computer stuff. Office is right there." She pointed her thumb over her shoulder to the door behind her.

David walked into his office and sat down at the small desk. He turned on the computer and opened the envelope as he waited for Windows to boot up.

"Salutations, Josh!

If you're reading this, it's because you got the job. Felicitations. You will have met me already this weekend. I am your humble IT guru and have prepared for your computer account needs:

Userid: JoshFrayne
Password: J05h4rayn3

Email address: josh@lachancecc.com
Email password: J05h4rayn3

Church Wi-Fi Password: J35u5

Email me with any questions or concerns.

Inq@AquaLungExp.com

David logged in using Josh's account. He already had two emails. The first one was from Inq, letting David know that he'd already set up a new account in his own name. The second was from Trisha.

To: josh@lachancecc.com
From: Trisha
Subject: Worship Info

David,

This is the email address they had for you, I assume you'll be changing it to your own name but in the meantime here's some info on worship ministries you should know. I've attached a Word document with our order of service template. It's pretty much the same thing every week. The worship leader just fills in the songs and emails it out to everyone before Thursday's rehearsal. We rehearse at 7:00. There are binders in the back room with all the songs we use.

Looking forward to seeing you Thursday.

Trisha.
Attachment: Service Template

David read the email several times. Each time, imagining Trisha saying the words 'Looking forward to see you Thursday.' He imagined her smiling as she said it, smiling and giggling after she said it, but the giggling didn't seem to match her character. He tried imagining her winking at him as she said it, but that seemed ridiculous. He acknowledged there was a slight possibility that he was reading more into that sentence than was actually there, but then went back to imagining what Trisha would sound like saying the sentence with the emphasis on different words. 'Looking forward to *seeing* you Thursday,' 'Looking forward to seeing *you* Thursday.'

Eventually, David tired of this and decided to choose the songs for his first Sunday. He walked to the back room, found one of the binders and took it back to his desk. He flipped through it, selected five songs, filled out the template and emailed it out to the team. The entire process took eleven minutes, including the walk from his office to the back room. He stared at the clock on the wall. Nine forty-one. He opened up Facebook and with great satisfaction, updated his profile with "Worship Pastor at Lachance Community Church." He wasted the rest of the morning on various social media accounts until Rick knocked on his door, poking his head in.

"Ready for lunch?"

"You bet."

"Then let's go!"

David followed Pastor Rick out to his tan Buick, parked right outside the front door under the carport.

"Wayne tells me you found a place to stay?"

"Yes. It's OK for now. It backs onto a bus company, so the school buses wake me up at dawn, but I guess I'll get used to it."

"Well, that's a perk! You don't need an alarm clock."

"Yes, I suppose so." David forced himself to laugh at Pastor Rick's joke. This was really the first time that David would get to talk to Pastor Rick. He wanted to impress him and learn from him.

"Pastor Rick, I haven't really had a chance to say this, but thank you for hiring me. It's been what I wanted to do since I turned fourteen."

"Oh, yeah, sure. Well, due to some administrative complications, which I won't bore you with, I had a very limited window of time to make the hire. When that Josh guy bailed on us, well, God knew, didn't he? Glad you're on board. And, here we are."

They pulled up to Smitty's Restaurant and sat in a booth. A waitress brought them menus and asked Pastor Rick if he wanted his usual. David ordered a bacon double cheeseburger. Pastor Rick leaned forward in the booth and looked across at David.

"David, do you know why I hired you?"

"Well, to be the worship pastor?"

"Yeah, yeah, but why did we — let's back way up. Something happened about a hundred years ago that completely changed everything for churches in this country. Do you know what that was, David?"

David thought back to his church history class and tried to recall what was going on in the early twentieth century. Somehow, the thoughts came to him. He slapped the table in triumph and blurted out.

"Yes! It was the schism between the theological modernists and the fundamentalists."

Pastor Rick looked across at David, mouth slightly open, blinked his eyes and shook his head.

"David, David, David. You aren't in Bible college any more. Those professors live in their own little fantasy world where things like that are actually important. You are now in the real world of ministry, OK?   So tell me, what happened about a hundred years ago that changed everything? I'm not talking just the church, but everything. In this country and the world?"

"Maybe you could just tell me."

"OK, fine. I'm talking about the invention of the automobile."

"The automobile?"

"Yes. The invention of the automobile. You see, before the car came along, people walked everywhere, including to church. So people would just go to the church in their neighbourhood. But once they started mass producing cars, and everyone had one, people started driving everywhere. And that meant that people could go to a church anywhere they wanted to, like on the other side of town. And they started doing that. People would drive past three churches to get to the one they liked better. So, you know what that brought into the church world?"

"Parking lots?" said David.

He got another blank stare from Pastor Rick and decided to stop trying to guess the answers to these questions.

"No, David. It brought competition to the world of churches. In order to survive, churches had to compete for a limited pool of churchgoers. At first, it was over preachers. The churches with the best preachers would grow. If your pastor wasn't a good preacher, your church would be in trouble. Then, it was Sunday school, then it was youth programs. But now? Now it is music. People want to have great music. So that's why we hired you."

"Well, why don't churches just grow by evangelism? Just bring in new people?"

"Well, David, of course we are doing that. It goes without saying. But that is long, hard work. And the fact is, that a new person coming in who is not a Christian, well, they don't serve, they definitely don't give, and it takes years before they start contributing in practical ways." Pastor Rick glanced around at the other patrons. "Now, don't get me wrong, I'm all for evangelism. But you compare that to getting a couple of families who transfer over and bring their tithes and their skills. Now that's a shot in the arm for any church. And you know what? I am not trying to steal sheep, not at all, but even if we just want to keep the people we have now, we can't fall behind the standards of all the other churches in town."

"I guess I see that," David nodded.

"And that's why we hired you. Our music is terrible, and it's your job to change that."

The waitress brought their food.

"I pay, so you pray," said Pastor Rick.

"OK." David bowed his head. "Lord, thanks for this food and bless our time here together, Amen."

Pastor Rick picked up a piece of his club sandwich and took a large bite. David thought about what he'd just been told as he put ketchup on his fries.

"Wow, that is really interesting, Pastor Rick. I've never heard that before. You're right. In Bible college, nobody ever talked about ministry like that."

"Oh, well that's not surprising. Most of those eggheads are out of touch with actual churches. You know, Joe Nascar-fan sitting in the pew on Sunday doesn't care about five points of Calvinism, but he'll walk out if the music is terrible."

"I have so much to learn."

"Well, sure, ask me anything."

"What are you reading these days?"

"Mmm. The Bible and the sports page," said Pastor Rick, between bites.

"Oh." David tried not to sound disappointed.

"Listen, David, there is one thing I can tell you about ministry, that I wish someone had told me when I was starting out, like you are now. And this has saved my bacon many, many times. This is so important."

The waitress came with the check.

"Oh, hold on, Doris, I'll pay it right now," said Pastor Rick. He pulled out his wallet and took out a credit card.

"Church credit card." He held it up for David to see. "This is one of the few perks of this job. The pay is lousy, hours are terrible, but it's nice to be able to pick up the check with this right here."

He paid the bill, they got up from the table and headed back to Pastor Rick's car.

"You were telling me the one thing about ministry?" David asked as they pulled out of the parking lot.

"Oh yeah, gosh, what was that?" They drove for a minute before Pastor Rick remembered. "Oh yeah, how could I forget? Always keep an extra shirt in your office at church. I don't know how many times I've been out for lunch like this and spilled mustard or barbecue sauce or something on my shirt. And then you have a meeting, or you have to preach. It can be very embarrassing. And then the other thing is to always wear black or dark pants. If you spill something on them you can't really tell."

"Oh," David said. "That is great advice. Thanks."

Back at the office, David reflected on his lunch with Pastor Rick. The best thing about it was the cheeseburger. There was much more to church ministry than he'd ever imagined. He couldn't decide what to make of Pastor Rick, though he wanted to like him and to look up to him. He mused alone in his office about this for about half an hour, but a heavy lunch coupled with a very early morning were more than he could handle.

"Whoa, there David. I'm gonna assume you were praying!"

Pastor Rick was laughing as David woke up, startled, jerking his head up from his desk, a gossamer strand of drool drooping between his chin and the desktop. He wiped his face with his hand, a face quickly turning hot from embarrassment.

"Oh, I'm so sorry. I shouldn't have ordered such a big lunch."

"Don't worry about it, I'd be lying if I said I never took a little siesta in my office now and then. But listen, I can't believe I forgot to tell you, we have our ministry council meeting tonight at seven and you need to report on your plans for the worship ministry and how we're going to turn it into the best worship ministry in the whole city. All right?"

"Oh, sure. I can do that. Tonight at seven. Got it."

David walked home, wondering what his strategy should be for having the best worship ministry in the city. As he entered the house, Chuck greeted him from the living room. Sports Center blared on his TV.

"Hey man, how was the first day of work?"

"It wasn't what I was expecting, that's for sure."

"Life never is!"

After two grilled cheese sandwiches and three Oreos, David pulled out his journal and wrote up some notes on his strategy for the worship ministry at LCC. He was out the door by half past six, back to church for the meeting.

COUNCIL

David fidgeted in his chair. He was twenty minutes early for the council meeting and sat opposite the conference room door. He didn't want to be late and wanted to observe people as they came in. He took out his phone to check Twitter, bouncing his leg, anxious for the meeting to begin. Pastor Rick was the next to arrive.

"David, you remember Wayne, of course."

"Hey there, professor! How's the college boy doing in the real world?" Wayne asked.

"So far, so good." David smiled.

"Good, good. Keeping out of trouble?"

"He better be!" Pastor Rick said.

Wayne and Pastor Rick laughed as they took seats next to each other opposite David. They stopped laughing as a matronly woman of about fifty entered the room. She was wearing a royal blue pant suit with shiny gold buttons, a paisley scarf and shiny black shoes with gold buckles that matched the buttons. She carried a binder in one hand and an orthopaedic seat cushion in the other. Beneath a thick layer of makeup, deep frown lines ran down from the corners of her mouth.

"Pastor, Wayne," she said, nodding to them.

"David, this is Jillian Moresby. She's in charge of women's ministry."

Jillian turned to David, her entire countenance changing from severe to jubilant. She put her binder on the table next to David, placed the orthopaedic cushion on the chair, and extended her hand. David stood to greet her.

"David! Welcome... oh, don't get up. Sit, sit, sit. So very nice to meet you. We're so glad that you're on board. Are you settling in?"

"Oh, yeah. I think so."

"Spencer! So glad you could make it," said Pastor Rick.

David looked up to see a man taller than himself, sporting a faux-hawk hairdo and spacers in his ears. He wore a tight T-shirt for a band that David had never heard of, brown corduroy pants, and a pair of Toms shoes.

"Oh yeah, well, I had to cancel a shift, but whatevs," Spencer said. "It's only money. Price of leadership."

"Spencer, you recognize David, our new worship pastor. David, this is Spencer."

"Hi," David said, smiling.

"Right. Yeah. Saw him on Sunday." Spencer didn't look at David. He pulled out a chair on the other side of the table, sat down and nodded at David before pulling out his phone. David noticed that Jillian's countenance had reverted to severity as she stared across the table in Spencer's general direction.

"Hello all," said a man with grey hair, wearing dress pants, short sleeve dress shirt and tie. He put his binder down at the head of the table and sat.

"David, I'm Gerald. I'm the council chair. Welcome aboard. You've met everyone?"

"Yes," David said.

"OK then. Let's pray and we'll dive into this agenda."

"I have an item to add to the agenda," Jillian said.

"Well, can we pray first?" Gerald asked.

"Of course. I just want to make sure I get on the agenda."

"You bet. We'll put Jillian's item in new business. Let's pray. Dear Lord, we thank you for this new ministry season here at Lachance. We pray for your blessing. We pray that we could see new things happening, a turnaround in our numbers would be such a blessing, Lord. Help us now as we work and plan together. In Jesus' name we ask it, Amen.

"Ok, then. Just so you know, David, I'm here representing the council, ministry reps are: you for worship, Spencer for youth, Jillian for women's, Pastor for everything else. Wayne is our property manager. First on the agenda is ministry updates for Worship and Youth. Spencer, why don't you start? Give David an example of how it's done."

"Oh, well, I'm only a volunteer. Since David's paid staff

shouldn't he go first? He's a professional," Spencer said.

"Spencer, David's been here for a couple days. You've been attending these meetings for two years. Could you just give your update?"

"Fine."

"And maybe give a little background for David, too, on what you do, etc."

Spencer's blank face looked across the table at David, then he pushed back from the table, tilted his chin up ever so slightly and began.

"As you all know, my official title is 'youth coordinator.' But what I really am is the architect of cultural essence for the next generation of Lachance youth."

Jillian sniffed loudly at the words 'cultural architect.' Spencer shot her a look but continued unperturbed.

"I craft the essence of weekly experiences for our youth in which they engage in deeper connection with God, missional endeavours, and redemptive visioning. We will continue our Friday gathering spaces and we are planning a retreat in October to Camp Cedarwood. We are currently experiencing huge growth in our spiritual depth and interconnectedness."

"What about attendance?" Gerald asked.

"We are on par with trends in overall church attendance."

"That's too bad!" Wayne said, laughing at himself. Pastor Rick shot him a look and he stopped.

"What are your plans for seeing some growth in numbers?" Pastor Rick asked.

"We expect that our programming decisions from last year are about to bear fruit. A change in mid-stream would be foolish. We are on the cusp of a real breakthrough. I won't change anything that would jeopardize that." Spencer glanced down at his phone, then shot a quick look at David. " Of course, if I had more time to devote to connecting one-on-one with the kids, and a budget for taking them out to lunch or coffee, that would help. But we just hired a new staff person, so I guess that's not going to happen."

"We've been through this before, Spencer." Pastor Rick said. "You're a valued member of this team, but we aren't ready to hire a full-time youth pastor. You get the gist, David? Why don't you give us an update on your plans for worship ministry?"

"Worship ministry is a key cog in any church," David began. He wasn't actually sure what a cog was, but he heard it at a leadership conference once and thought it sounded impressive.

"Anyone want a coffee? I'll go brew a pot. Excuse me. You guys continue," Spencer said, not waiting for anyone to respond.

"Seriously, you guys continue. I don't need to hear this part," he added as he left the room.

"Don't worry about him, David. He's a little bit — well never mind. But the youth think he's cool, even if he's not much for meetings. In any case, please continue," Pastor Rick said.

"Oh, sure. The first thing I want to do is to teach our music volunteers to worship from their hearts. On Sunday morning when they are leading the music, I just want them to be totally focused on worshipping God - an audience of One."

"Our attendance is trending toward an audience of one. That's why we hired you!" Wayne laughed again at his own joke.

Pastor Rick ignored Wayne. "David, that's really great. I heartily agree. Worshipping from the heart, high priority. But right now, the music is not good. It is a great distraction, and nobody can worship with that band hacking away up there. What are you going to do to solve *that* problem?"

"I think I need to begin with the heart, and from there we can move on to the hands, to the skills and techniques—"

Wayne cut him off. "David, I see what you got, with two different things here. The heart, which nobody can hear. And the music, which nobody wants to hear. You gotta decide which one to fix. Sometimes you need to be just like King Solomon, go ahead and split that baby right down the middle."

David paused, trying to understand what Wayne had just said.

"What Wayne means is that you need both. This is a both/and situation. We need to see an improvement in music. Immediately."

"Oh, of course," David said. "I'm sure that we'll see that now that I'm here. I'm sure we will see some improvement."

"Well, we expect no less. No less than a significant improvement, right away," Pastor Rick said. "Oh, and I almost forgot. Dress code. David, you need to make it clear that your team dress appropriately. No short skirts or yoga pants."

"Sure thing." David nodded. "I can do that."

Spencer returned to the room. "I started a pot. It'll be ready in a few minutes. I didn't miss anything, did I?"

Pastor Rick responded. "I was just telling David that we expect to see significant improvement, right away. We can't wait around two years before we bear fruit."

Spencer opened his mouth, hesitated. He looked stung by Pastor Rick's words, but held his tongue, instead turning to David and looking him in the eye for the first time.

"So, David, what's your plan for immediate, significant improvement?" Spencer tilted his head in mock supplication.

"Well, first of all, I think the drummer, Calvin, needs to use a metronome," David said.

"Oh, a metronome, Spencer said. "That's great. Great. I don't know who else could've thought of that."

"Well that's quite enough," Pastor Rick said. "We don't want to be bored with the details of metronomes and what not. Let's move on. Gerald, financial update?"

"Sure," said Gerald. "It isn't good, I'm afraid. We are down in our giving about twenty percent from last year, which was down from the previous year. We are behind in our budget by about thirty percent. But we have fewer people giving, and the people who are still giving are giving less. Bill has more in his detailed report. I won't go over it all, but basically if we don't turn things around... I don't know what. And we have new expenses. We now need to pay... well, staff costs are up."

Gerald glanced at David as he said this, then continued. "Now, I know we have a plan. But we need something to happen or we're going to be in deep trouble."

"Don't worry," said Pastor Rick. "I have faith, God has a plan for this church. Our best days are ahead of us. Things will turn around this year, I know it."

"I hope so. I hope so," Gerald said.

"We have faith in you, Pastor," Wayne added. "You will lead us through this season."

"Thank you, Wayne. Your positive attitude is an example for all of us. Now, how about a property update?"

"Nothing much to report except for the broken paper towel dispenser in the men's room. I've ordered a replacement. Should be here in six to eight weeks. In the meantime, we'll make do. And since most guys don't wash their hands after taking a—"

Pastor Dave loudly cleared his throat, interrupting Wayne. "That'll do Wayne. Well, that takes us to new business. Jillian? You had something?"

"I most certainly do have something. It is troubling to hear about attendance and finances, but there is another issue in the church. It is a total crisis. Immediate action is required or the consequences have eternal implications. Gentlemen, before I go any further I need to know that we are prepared to commit to a solution this very evening."

"Why don't you tell us what this crisis is first," Pastor Rick said.

"Tablecloths!"

"Tablecloths?" Wayne's eyebrows rose.

"Yes. Tablecloths."

Gerald, Wayne and Pastor Rick all had the same look of incredulity on their faces, but Spencer slowly sat back from the table and stood. "I think I'll get that coffee now."

"I think you should stay," snapped Jillian.

Spencer sat back down. Jillian continued.

"Allow me to explain."

"Please do," said Pastor Rick.

Jillian opened up her binder and took out a piece of paper. "I've written this down, so that I don't forget anything and to help me keep my composure."

Pastor Rick sighed, looked down and shook his head. "OK, Jillian. Let's hear it."

Jillian took a deep breath and began to read. "As you all may or may not know, we in the women's ministry at this church, strive to be a blessing, an oasis to the women of our community. We express the love of God on the tired and downtrodden women of this church through our gifts of hospitality. After a week of cleaning and toiling at home, changing diapers and doing laundry, we want these women to come and enjoy a meal in a pleasant atmosphere, for them to experience the love of God by being pampered. That means we certainly cannot serve them food on our old, scratched and stained folding tables. We require clean, ironed tablecloths."

"Don't we have tablecloths?" Pastor Rick asked.

"Yes. The women's ministry at this church collected money and bought a set of lovely white tablecloths which we launder at our own expense. We iron them and all that we ask of the church is a cupboard to store them in. Well, two weeks ago, Saturday, we had our ladies' fellowship breakfast. The executive team arrived at six o'clock in the morning to begin setting up. When I went to open the cupboard for our tablecloths, I was overcome with an unmistakeable stench. To my horror, I discovered our tablecloths were covered in vomit. After recovering from my initial shock, I was able to determine that someone had taken three of our tablecloths and used them to clean up vomit. They were drenched in it, and still damp. And then they had balled them up, still soaked with vomit and shoved them back into the cupboard, so that all the remaining tablecloths were either smeared with vomit or at least reeked of vomit. It was all we could do to get over our shock and horror to continue on with our preparations for the breakfast.

Jillian turned over the page, looked solemnly around the room and continued, "Thankfully, one of the ladies was able to run out to Walmart to get some disposable plastic tablecloths so that we could avoid having to serve breakfast on uncovered tables. But, the final result was cheap looking and garish. The only tablecloths available at Walmart were blue and white gingham and, well, Lorna Hopkins was in tears. She'd spent weeks working on centre pieces for the tables and they clashed with the blue and white gingham.

"Is this how we treat our hard-working volunteers, who provide their own tablecloths, clean and care for them, only to have them violated in this way? I should think not.

"I investigated what could have happened to the tablecloths, and I discovered that the previous night's youth meeting had included a pizza-eating and soda-drinking contest that resulted in a number of youths vomiting. This type of immature, irresponsible waste of food is bad enough, but to use our tablecloths to try and mop it up? I demand an explanation."

Jillian exhaled, looked up from her paper, first at Pastor Rick and then across the table at Spencer.

Pastor Rick rubbed his forehead with both hands, turned to Spencer, and sighed. "Well, Spencer?"

Spencer took a deep breath and looked at Pastor Rick, avoiding Jillian's gaze.

"Look. I admit this whole thing was very unfortunate. In youth ministry, you learn to expect a certain amount of vomit. It goes with the territory. Now, we had ordered too much pizza and I didn't want to just throw it out, so instead of actually being wasteful I came up with the idea of the contest. It was really fun, until Josh Harkin puked. And I had to act fast. All the cleaning supplies were locked in the supply closet and the paper towel dispensers were empty." Spencer looked up at Wayne and shook his head. "By the way they're always empty on Friday night and as we know, the one in the men's room doesn't work anyway. I had to come up with some way to clean up. While we were looking around, the smell made another kid barf as well. Anyway, the only thing we could find in the whole church that we could use was the tablecloths, so I don't know what else you'd expect us do to. So, yes, I was down on the floor on my hands and knees wiping up vomit with a tablecloth. I actually think I deserve some credit for that, you know."

"And for stuffing your vomit-soaked tablecloth back into the cupboards to ruin all the other clean tablecloths?" Jillian practically spat the words at Spencer.

"Well, I admit that wasn't the best idea, but after a night of intense ministry with the youth and being on my hands and knees mopping up barf, I wasn't exactly at my very best, OK? I told one of the kids to deal with the tablecloths... I guess he put them back in the cupboard. These things happen."

"So Jillian, what's the status of the tablecloths now?" Pastor Rick asked.

"The two that were used to mop of the vomit were ruined. The others have been dry cleaned and were saved."

"So where do we go from here?"

"Well, I think I deserve an apology, which I have yet to hear."

Pastor Rick turned to Spencer. "Spencer, that's quite a reasonable request."

Spencer looked back at Pastor Rick, shook his head and then turned to Jillian. "I'm sorry your precious tablecloths got ruined."

Jillian clenched her teeth, sniffed and tugged at her blazer by the lapels and sat straight up in her chair, eyes still locked on Spencer. "And I think this church needs a comprehensive policy on tablecloths."

"A what? O for crying out loud," said Wayne.

"It is unfortunate that it has come to this, but obviously common sense and simple courtesy is not sufficient to prevent this type of catastrophe, so we need to spell it all out. Storage, cleaning, ironing, authorized use, booking, and reserving them, and determining which tablecloths are suitable for which tables.

"And I think Spencer should be the one to write it."

"What? Forget that. Maybe Jillian should write up a

comprehensive policy on vomit," Spencer said.

"This is no joke," Jillian replied.

"Well there is no way I'm doing that. I don't have time for that. I have two jobs, plus volunteering at youth. Write your own policy."

David had been trying to remain completely still during this exchange. He looked around the room. Gerald was looking down at his binder. Wayne was sitting back and grinning. Pastor Rick's lips were pursed together, head shaking slowly back and forth as he looked between Jillian and Spencer.

Jillian broke the silence.

"If this policy is not written, then I have no choice but to step down as leader of women's ministry."

Spencer glared. "Well there's no way I'm doing it. I'll quit before I do that. I don't need this."

"Let's just hold on, take a deep breath, everyone. Nobody needs to quit over this," Pastor Rick said.

"Why don't you make David write the policy?" Spencer said. "I'm sure he has time. He probably needs something to do all day."

David resented the implication that he didn't have enough things to do, but he kept his mouth shut because it was true.

"That's actually not a bad idea," Pastor Rick said David, how about you write the tablecloth policy?"

"What? I don't know anything about tablecloths. And I'm not the one who ruined them. I don't have anything to do with tablecloths, I'm probably not the guy to write up the policy."

Pastor Rick glared at David. "Well, it might be good for you to learn. It will be a good exercise in the practical aspects of church life. Is that acceptable to you, Jillian? If David writes up a policy?"

"Yes, I suppose that will be fine. As long as all ministry leaders sign off on it." She looked straight at Spencer as she spoke.

"Sure, whatever, as long as I don't have to do it."

"OK, well, that's great. Problem solved. David, you can consult with Jillian on what needs to be in the policy and then get working on it."

"But Pastor Rick," said David, "Don't you want me to focus on improving the music? I really think that should be my focus, and not the table—"

" — David, I'll stop you right there. I've asked you to do it. We're a team here and we all help each other out. Is that clear? You wouldn't refuse to help out, would you?" Pastor Rick looked at him pointedly.

"Well, I guess not."

"Here, David. This can get you started." Jillian handed David a page from her binder.

It read:

Lachance Community Church Policy on tablecloths

Outline:

Purpose - The "why" of tablecloths

Use

Current inventory

Reserving tablecloths for an event

Cleaning

Storage

Reporting a tablecloth Problem

David read over the outline, looked back at Jillian and said, "Thank you."

"The whole thing shouldn't be more than ten pages. Twenty at the most," Jillian said.

"Well, glad that worked out. Any more new business?" Gerald asked.

There was an uncomfortable pause.

"Then let's call it a night," Wayne said.

"Great," Gerald said. "David, would you close us in prayer?"

"Oh, sure. Dear Lord, thank you for each one here and that they are willing to serve and lead their ministries. And we pray for this church, that you'll help us to get along and to grow and do your work. Amen."

After the meeting, David sat in his office, staring at the sheet Jillian had given him. There was a knock on the door and Pastor Rick stepped in.

"David?"

"Yes, Pastor?"

"David, you're new. So I'm going to be gracious about this, but I'm not happy. You're here to help me. Do you understand?"

"Yes," David said, though he didn't really understand.

"So, when I'm trying to keep the wife of our church's biggest donor happy, you need to help me."

"OK, now I see," David said.

"And listen, David. In general, whenever I ask you to do something, especially in front of other people, I am only asking because I am modelling servant leadership. But make no mistake, when I ask you, it isn't really a question. If I ask you to do something, your only option is to say yes. If that's not acceptable to you then we need to have a bigger conversation on whether you're the right fit for this church. Do we understand each other?"

"Yes, sir. Sorry."

"Glad we had this little talk. See you tomorrow."

"Goodnight, Pastor."

LEADING

David awoke to the sound of the first bus starting. One of the foam earplugs he'd begun using had fallen out of his ear. He lay awake and stared at the ceiling, considering how much had changed in the last week. He'd gone from penniless Bible college grad, illegally squatting in his old dorm room, to a fully employed religious professional. He'd received a small advance on his pay from Bill and was able to catch up on his rent and reactivate the data plan on his phone. At church, he was beginning to feel at home and was tinkering with the sound system.

Pastor Rick was still a mystery. David thought about the scolding he took on Monday night, and how on Tuesday morning Pastor Rick cheerfully greeted him as if nothing had happened.

After the fourth bus started, David climbed out of bed and got ready for work. Today was Thursday, and that meant he'd rehearse with the band tonight. He'd get to see Trisha.

"Welcome, everybody." David felt nervous. He hadn't led a rehearsal since university and that was with other students. Except for Sid the guitarist, these were all adults. He smiled and told himself he was a calm, confident religious professional. He realized they were all looking at him, waiting awkwardly. He'd been staring at Trisha, who was now looking at the floor.

"OK, let's gather around and begin with prayer. Any prayer requests?" David asked.

"Oh yes!" Carissa said. "My friend's uncle is a missionary in Guatemala and they have a boy in their village who is very sick."

"Do you know his name?" David asked.

"Oh, it was something Mexican-sounding, I think?"

"Sounds good. Any other requests?"

Silence.

"No other requests?" David paused. "Then, let's just pray as you feel led, then I'll close. Let's pray."

They bowed their heads and stood there silently for at least an entire minute. David wondered if he should just pray and get it over with. Then Calvin, the drummer, began.

"Dear God, we pray for this little boy with the Spanish name in Honduras - or was it El Salvador?"

"Guatemala," whispered Carissa.

"Right, that place. Anyway, God, you know this kid's name and what he needs, so be with him. And be with the missionary guy as well. And while we're at it, please be with all the missionaries. That's pretty hard work, so they need your help. And give us a good practice tonight. Yeah. Amen." Calvin's voice trailed off.

Another silence followed. David opened his eyes and looked at Trisha, closing them quickly when he realized Sid was watching him. He began to pray. "Lord, thank you for being here tonight. We want to honor you tonight as we practice. Help us to give you our best. Amen."

As soon as David said *Amen*, Sid had his guitar plugged in and was playing the guitar part from Van Halen's *Hot For Teacher*, loud enough that David had to shout at him to stop. Sid glared at him from behind his long, black bangs, turned the volume down on his guitar but continued to play the riff, scowling.

"Let's start with the first song."

Calvin clicked his drumsticks together, counting in the tempo. The entire band came in, ignoring Calvin's tempo. Even Calvin ignored his tempo. By the end of the introduction, they'd achieved a general consensus on tempo, though negotiations continued into the first verse.

They bashed their way through the verse, everyone playing as if they were wrestling for dominance but with no clear winner. Inq droned along on his bass while Sid played wailing string-bends which didn't seem to have any relation to the melody. When they got to the chorus, Calvin sped up and tempo negotiations began again with renewed vigor. Carissa was attempting vocal ad-libs far beyond her ability. David could see that Trisha was playing, but couldn't hear her keyboard over Sid's lead guitar. David knew he had trouble.

"Whoa, whoa, whoa, let's hold it there. Let's just stop there."

The band ground to a halt, all looking at David.

"Calvin, have you worked very much with a metronome?"

"Oh, I've heard of that. What is it again?" Calvin asked.

"It's a thing that keeps time, it clicks along at a constant tempo to help you stay in time. Do you have one of those?"

"Oh, I tried one once, but it didn't help. Stifled my creativity. I'm more of a, how do I put this, I'm a free drummer."

"A free drummer," David said.

"Free of talent," Inq said.

"Shut-up, Boethius! Nobody asked you," Calvin said.

Inq sniffed and turned away from Calvin, smirking.

Carissa chimed in. "Cut it out, boys!"

"Calvin," David said. "I think it would help us all if you focused less on being free, and more on steady time, you know? In fact, maybe all of us could. Let's all just try to play in time together and really listen. Just play the bare minimum, essential parts only? Why don't we start with just piano and light drums for the intro, then add bass for the verse and we'll all come in on the chorus. Let's try that."

They went through the song over and over again, David encouraged them that less is more, paring down and helping them break the habit of overplaying. *This is why I'm here, this is why Pastor Rick hired me*, he thought, as the band began sounding better. The music was improving and he was winning the respect of the band members. Even Sid was coming along, occasionally making eye contact with a single eye out from behind his hair.

David didn't have much to say to Trisha. She was a good pianist and knew her role in the band. David complimented her playing a few times. Each time he did, Sid would look at him with a wry smile that said, "I know what's going on." David ignored him.

They spent an hour and twenty minutes on that first song, polishing it until it sparkled. Then David realized they had to move on to the rest of the set. They began the second song, and everyone instantly forgot everything they had worked on over the last hour. But David patiently coached them along, and they started to sound more musical. All in all, a great rehearsal.

"Everyone, gather round. Pastor Rick asked me to talk about a few things with you, one of them being dress code."

Sid groaned.

"OK, first of all, modesty is very important. And no yoga pants. No sleeveless tops, no jeans, and no concert jerseys."

"No yoga pants. Got that Inq?" snarked Calvin.

"Calvin, if you insist upon insulting me then at least be creative," said Inq, unperturbed.

"We just don't want to cause any distractions. OK, team?" David hoped to regain control of the group. "Who'd like to close in prayer?"

Inq said "Let us Pray."

"Most Holy Triune Father Spirit and Son, we thank you for your servant David, for his perspicacity in musical direction and his willingness to share his gifts with us, lifting us to a higher plane of artistic endeavor. May we find beauty in simplicity, not burdening these songs with needless ornamentation, but rather serving them in simplicity, and with humility. Bless David as he leads us. Amen."

David was touched by Inq's prayer. He wasn't sure what perspicacity meant, but was touched nonetheless. They all said goodnight and went their separate ways home.

Friday was a quiet day at the office. David began working on his accreditation papers with the denomination, reading a very dull book on its history. He went for coffee with Pastor Rick, listening to him talk about a bathroom renovation project he was planning. David just listened quietly. He was too embarrassed to ask what grout was.

After coffee with Pastor Rick, he went back to his office and Googled "church tablecloth policy." He was surprised at how many results were returned. He downloaded some videos to watch at home where there was no Wi-Fi, and had lots to occupy him for the weekend. He checked a book on leadership out of the church library and tucked it into his backpack.

Friday evening was quiet. Chuck was still out when David went to bed, and he was awakened by the sound of him stumbling to bed sometime in the night. Saturday morning, there were still a couple of buses that woke him before eight o'clock, but he slept in anyway. After a late breakfast of scrambled eggs, he went for a long walk, exploring his neighbourhood. He strolled down Main Street and sat on a park bench next to the war memorial. He watched people driving past him as they rushed through their Saturday errands. *These people have lives*, David thought as he rose from his bench and began walking back to Chuck's.

At home, he watched some videos on his laptop, then tried to read his book on leadership, but it didn't seem to be written for the type of person that spent Saturday afternoons wandering around town wondering what to do. He was lonely, but he had a roof over his head, food to eat, and a job doing what he loved. *God is good*, he thought, *God is good*.

FIRST SUNDAY

Sunday morning. David rolled over in bed and the sunlight from his window caught his eye. It was the best night's sleep he'd had since moving to Lachance. Then he fumbled around on the floor for his phone, looked at it and gasped. It was ten seventeen. He jerked out of the bed. Through the window he saw the buses, parked and silent. It was Sunday morning. No buses. He checked his phone again. Three missed calls. He'd told his musicians to meet at nine-thirty for a sound check. He dressed as quickly as he could. No time for a shower or breakfast. He grabbed his guitar and began to run to the church, his guitar swinging wildly at his side, perspiration dripping down his temples, sides beginning to ache. He slowed to a fast walk, realizing he couldn't keep the pace, nor wanting to show up at church drenched with sweat. He reached the church at ten thirty-three and headed straight for the auditorium, where he heard the band rehearsing without him. They stopped as he arrived.

"I'm sorry, I'm so sorry I'm late. The buses didn't wake me up this morning," he said, embarrassed.

"Buses? What are you talking about?" Calvin asked.

"Well, never mind. Can we run through a song?" David said. Then he noticed Sid was wearing a Black Sabbath T-shirt.

"Sid, you can't wear that shirt. We talked about this." David blurted. He was already angry about being late.

Sid glared back at him. "I forgot. But I did remember to wake up and be here at nine-thirty."

"I called his mom and she's bringing him another shirt," Trisha said. "He can change before the service starts."

Sid didn't acknowledge this comment, but continued to glare at

David. Then he turned away.

"Thanks Trisha. OK, guys, let's run through a song."

They began playing their opening song. Sid's mother arrived with a plain black T shirt, leaving it on the amplifier beside him. Sid grimaced at her as she patted his shoulder. She mouthed "sorry" to David as she left the platform.

"Sid, you can change in my office," David said, wanting to offer some kind of olive branch to his angry lead guitarist. Sid stomped off toward David's office, silent, sullen, clutching the new shirt by the sleeve and letting it drag on the floor.

David and the rest of the band went backstage to pray for the service. Inq handed David a large cup of coffee from the pot in the corner.

"Looks like you could use this," he said.

Pastor Rick was already waiting for them, going over his sermon notes as they walked in.

"We thought you changed your mind about us," Pastor Rick said with a grin.

"I'm really, really sorry. The buses don't run on Sunday. I forgot to set the alarm clock. It won't happen again." David hated having to apologize to Pastor Rick in front of his team. He noticed Sid had returned in time to hear him apologize. Sid was shaking his head.

"Service starts in two minutes, we better pray and talk through the order. Do you have the orders of service?" Pastor Rick asked.

David flinched as he realized they were back in his office. "I'll go get them!" He bolted out the door, walking as fast as possible, smiling and nodding to people who were beginning to take their seats in the auditorium, balancing the coffee he still had in his hand, trying to look casual. He made it to the offices and leapt around Rhonda's reception desk and through his open door. He felt a tug at his shirt, then heard the fabric rip. His shirt tail had caught on the strike plate in the door frame and ripped from the bottom all the way up to the shoulder. He looked down in disbelief, seeing his soft belly spilling over his belt through the gaping hole in his shirt. His next thought was *Thank God for Pastor Rick's advice!*

He'd been disappointed that Pastor Rick's best advice for ministry was to keep an extra shirt in your office, but David was ever so grateful that he not only received that advice, but that he'd followed it. He set down his coffee, found the shirt in his desk drawer. It wasn't his favorite, but it would do — a white button-down that was a little too tight around the stomach. He furiously undid the buttons on the shredded shirt he was wearing and reached for the white one. In his haste, he knocked over the coffee cup, spilling its entire contents on the white shirt. He stood motionless as the knit cotton soaked up every drop of coffee, creating a large steaming brown stain. He tried to comprehend what just happened as the empty Styrofoam cup rolled to the edge of the desk and tumbled to the floor. His mind rebelled against what his eyes saw, trying to return to the moment just passed when the shirt was still clean and white.

"O Lord, help me," he said.

Then he saw on the floor, Sid's discarded Black Sabbath T-shirt. He picked it up, wondering how a loving God could let this all happen to him. He turned the shirt inside-out to obscure the graphics and stretched the small T-shirt over his chest and stomach, pulling it down to cover the gap between the bottom of the shirt and his belt. He grimly told himself *in an hour, this will all be over.*

He strode out of his office, through the foyer, into the auditorium and down the aisle of the auditorium, feeling the gaze of the congregation, the puzzled looks at his shirt, stretched tight with the tag hanging out in the back of his neck. Completing this walk of shame, he reached the front of the auditorium where the band was already on stage. He saw them staring at him, one by one, reacting with incredulity. Sid was the worst, his jaw slack and face filled with contempt. Trisha knitted her brow. Inq pursed his lips in thoughtful repose. Calvin laughing out loud. Carissa's head tilted quizzically to the side. Pastor Rick sat in the front seat, staring at him, his face turning red.

"What happened to your shirt?" Pastor Rick asked.

"I ripped it on the door frame."

"Don't you have a spare? I told you—"

" — Yes, I had a spare, but I dumped my entire cup of coffee on it."

"David, my goodness, well, never mind we have to start the service now. Did you bring the orders of service?"

In the commotion over his shirt, David had forgotten the orders of service, the reason he ran back to his office in the first place. He thought there was nothing left of dignity to lose, but another piece of it crumbled as he turned around and repeated the humiliating march back to his office to retrieve the orders of service. Walking up the aisle he could see people's faces as they reacted to his skin-tight, inside-out, undersized concert jersey, trying to make out what was on the other side of the fabric. Sid's mother looked particularly confused. He returned with the orders of service, handed them to Pastor Rick, then joined the band on the platform. He strapped on his guitar, thankful that it covered the gap where his stomach protruded out from the bottom of the shirt. He stepped up to the mic and said "Good Morning."

The mic wasn't on. People were looking at him, some craning their necks to the back of the room to look at the sound booth.

"Good Morning" he said again, still without the mic.

"Good Morning" he said a third, time, becoming desperate, but this time the mic came on and caught the "-orning."

"Let's stand together and sing."

They began the first song. David forced his mind to focus on the music and to forget what people were thinking of his shirt. He tried to hide himself in the music, his refuge through many difficult times in his life. Gradually, his embarrassment faded. His anger, frustration, and pride began to recede. The second song they got to was Tom Lindsey's hit, and David's favorite.

"Oh, You, You lift me to a highest place
Where I see the beauty of your face
My love for you will never stop
Because you, You take me to the Mountaintop"

All the anxiety of the morning began to melt away from David as he sang. He imagined himself disappearing into the lyrics of the song. He felt a presence near him, as though God's spirit spoke into his heart, telling him "I'm all you need."

David felt peace for a fleeting moment, but long enough to know it was real. The band finished their set and he sat down in the front row beside Pastor Rick, still glowing from the sense of God's embrace.

"David, you need to get your act together. You looked ridiculous up there. And that makes *me* look ridiculous." Pastor Rick whispered angrily, shattering David's sense of peace.

"I'm really sorry. I'm... I don't know what to say."

One of the deacons was making an appeal for the offering, explaining the current budget shortfalls. He was looking down at David and Pastor Rick, distracted by their exchange in the front row.

"Never mind, you gotta get back up there," Pastor Rick said.

The deacon was praying for the offering so David went back up to play an offertory, wishing he'd been able to explain himself to Pastor Rick. He played the song and then collapsed into his seat in the front row, exhausted from the ordeals of the morning. Pastor Rick took the stage, paused, looked back at the sound man, took a deep breath, and said, "Good morning." The mic wasn't on. Two *good mornings* later, it came to life.

Pastor Rick's sermon was a blur, David's mind racing over all the details of what had gone wrong, repeating to himself "if only" as he recalled each successive disaster.

Pastor Rick wrapped up his sermon and David led the band back on stage for the closing song. They finished the song, Pastor Rick gave the benediction, and David breathed a sigh of relief. He turned first to Sid.

"Sid, I need to explain."

Sid said nothing, one jaded eye looking out from behind his hair.

"I ripped my shirt on the side of the door, you know that metal thing that sticks out for the part of... well any way, I ripped my shirt really badly when I went back to get the orders of service. Then I had another shirt, but I spilled my coffee on that one. So I had no shirt to wear. Then I saw you left this shirt, so it was my only option. So that's why I'm wearing it. I'll wash it and return it to you."

Sid stared back at David for a moment.

"You can keep it." He turned away and began to pack up his guitar. The rest of the band had overheard his explanation to Sid, so David was relieved he wouldn't have to repeat it. He packed up his own guitar and retreated to the back room where he planned to stay until everyone left the church. He didn't want to be seen again in his ridiculous shirt. He sat quietly, reflecting on what he'd hoped for on this morning, and the painful contrast of what actually happened. He felt foolish, angry, and humiliated. *Pastor Rick must think I'm an idiot.* Tears welled up in his eyes.

Then the door opened.

Trisha came in and David sat up straight, rubbed his eyes and pasted a smile on his face.

"Umm, some of us head over to Broadway's for lunch after church. I just wondered if you'd like to join us?"

"Oh, yeah... I think I just want to go home, but thanks for asking."

"OK, I understand. And don't worry about the shirt. I think most people didn't even notice. And the music was really good. So, see you Thursday?"

"Yes, I guess so."

David waited in the back room until the stragglers left the auditorium. Once they were all gone, he went to his office, packed up his things, and got ready to leave. He decided to turn the shirt right-side-out since it would look slightly less ridiculous for the walk home. He locked up the church doors the way Rhonda had showed him and walked home, trying not to notice whether people were staring at his shirt and his exposed midriff.

When he got home he wanted to slip downstairs to his room past Chuck, but Chuck was waiting for him when he opened the door.

"Hey. Nice shirt! Sabbath rules!"

"Hi, Chuck. Well, it's not my shirt. I had an accident with my shirt and... I don't really want to talk about it. What a morning."

"Well if it makes you feel any better, I'd probably go to a church that played Black Sabbath. Anyway, you like football? If you're not doing anything we could watch the game. You don't have to stay down there in your room all the time."

David wanted to be alone. He didn't like sports and didn't know anything about football, but he didn't want to rebuff Chuck's invitation either.

"Sure. Let me get changed and I'll be right back up."

"OK. I made some nachos if you're hungry."

David changed into shorts and a T-shirt and returned upstairs to the living room. Chuck had a big tray of nachos and cheese on the coffee table in front of the couch, a couple of plates and some napkins.

"You want a beer? Or I got come cokes?"

"Coke would be great."

Chuck fetched a Bud Lite and a Coke from the kitchen, handing David the Coke. He ate some nachos and drank his Coke and listened to Chuck comment on the game, occasionally asking questions. It was nice to relax. By half-time, David began to see some humor in what had happened to him that morning. He even started chuckling.

"What's so funny?" asked Chuck.

"Oh, my morning. It was kind of crazy."

David told the entire story to Chuck, from sleeping in to the ruined shirts. Chuck laughed along with David, who started to feel better about the whole thing. They ordered pizza and watched the next game together.

When David finally went down to bed, he checked his phone for messages. He had an email from Pastor Rick.

Subject: Issues this Morning

David,

I'm not happy with all that went wrong this morning. I spent this afternoon dealing with complaints about you. Please see me in my office first thing tomorrow morning. Don't be late.

Rick.

PROGRESS

David was wide awake by six o'clock, the buses already rumbling to life and leaving the parking lot. He'd spent the night tossing and turning, playing out the meeting with Pastor Rick, trying out different strategies like a chess player predicting moves and countermoves. He prayed, asked the Lord for another chance. He remembered that in the midst of yesterday's debacle, wearing that ridiculous shirt, singing his worship to God, he felt a strange peace come over him. He now wondered if that had been something real or merely a psychological defence mechanism, a product of hormones and brain chemistry designed to protect a stressed animal. He wished for that sense of peace now as he began his walk to work.

"David, here's the thing," said Pastor Rick. "If you just embarrass yourself, well that's not good for you. But I've offered you this job. That means that when you embarrass yourself, like you did on Sunday, you embarrass me. And that's just unacceptable. Imagine how I felt, seeing you up there looking like that, knowing that everyone is thinking 'Oh, that's the young man that Pastor Rick chose for this job.'"

Pastor Rick leaned back in his chair, looked up at the ceiling of his office and shook his head. "Well, what have you got to say?"

"Like I said, I'm really sorry. I will be much more careful, and I won't let this happen again. I hope you can forgive me." David had chosen not to make excuses, but to simply throw himself at Pastor Rick's mercy.

"Forgiveness is fine. Let's put this whole thing behind us. But, I'm not going to forget about this and it better not happen again.

Understand?"

David didn't quite understand how these terms and conditions related to the concept of forgiveness. It wasn't like the forgiveness he learned about in Bible college.

"Yes sir, I understand."

"Oh, and talk to your sound man. Eric? Is that his name?"

"Yes, Eric."

"I'm sick and tired of my mic not being on. You need to fix it, fix him, or find a new sound man who can do the job. All right then. I'm glad we had this little talk."

Pastor Rick was smiling his mouth-only smile. David took it as his cue to leave. He returned to his office, slumping into his chair and wondering what he'd do with the rest of the day. He made his to-do list: plan the service, get two extra shirts for the office, practice. Maybe he'd do some reading. Thursday couldn't come fast enough. He'd see the band on Thursday. He'd see Trisha.

David arrived early Thursday evening so he could talk to Eric the sound man before rehearsal. Eric was setting up some microphones when David approached him.

"Eric?"

No response. Eric's back was turned

"ERIC?!?"

No response. Finally, Eric turned around. "Oh, David, I didn't hear you there."

"Really? I called out to you twice."

"Oh, well you know all those years I've spend in a factory with heavy machinery. My hearing isn't what it used to be."

"Eric, how do you mix sound if you can't hear?"

"Oh, I have a system, I learned from years of mixing sound in church. I just mix the band in rehearsal loud enough so I can hear them. But, I know that will be too loud for everyone else, so when the service starts I just turn the master volume down to the point that I can barely hear them and that seems to be the level that I don't get complaints that it's too loud."

"So, when you're mixing the band during the service you can't actually hear us?"

"No. That's how I know you're at the right level."

David considered what kind of through-the-looking-glass logic led to a half-deaf sound man mixing a band he couldn't hear. But he didn't know anyone else who could run the sound board, so he was stuck with Eric.

"Well, I wanted to talk to you about Pastor Rick's mic. It really needs to be turned on right when he gets on stage, before he starts talking."

"Oh, well he needs to talk first, so I know which channel he's in," replied Eric.

"What do you mean?"

"Well, when there's sound in the mic the little lights on that channel go up and down in the sound board, so I know that's the channel to un-mute. That's my system."

"OK, but don't you see how that would be a little frustrating for Pastor Rick?"

"He's never mentioned it to me. I've been doing sound for years. He must be used to it by now. I don't understand why this is coming up now."

"Eric, don't you know which channel his mic is in? Can't you just un-mute that channel before he gets up to speak?"

"Well, usually I know, depending on what channel I put it in. But I don't want to make a mistake and un-mute the wrong thing, so I just wait for the lights so I know it's the right channel."

"Listen, here's what I want you to do from now on. Always put Pastor Rick's mic in the same channel, label it with a piece of tape or something so you know which one it is, and un-mute it *before* he gets up to speak."

"David, can I ask you a question?"

"Sure."

"How long have you been running the soundboard in church?"

"I don't think that's really the point, Eric."

"Because I've been doing sound in this church since they built it, over twenty-five years ago. I kind of think I know what I'm doing."

David began to get angry. He felt his face get warm as he tried to find the words to say. "You... this.. If this happens again... Just try it my way. Can you try it my way? Please? Pastor Rick expects me to fix this, so can you please help me out? Yes, I'm sure you know way more about this than I do, but if I don't fix this for Pastor Rick, then I might not last here very long."

"Well, all right, fine. I normally don't let the people on stage push me around, but as a favor, I'll do it your way. You don't have to get upset." Eric turned back to the mic he was setting up.

David hated that he had been upset in front of Eric. Why hadn't he been able to win him over with reason and persuade him that this was better? Instead, Eric was doing this out of pity. And he still had to deal with the issue of having a half-deaf sound man who wouldn't listen to advice.

The members of the band began to arrive. First Calvin and Sid. David had Sid's Black Sabbath shirt, folded and in a plastic bag, ready to return to him.

"Sid, thanks for loaning me this."

Sid looked in the bag, recognized the shirt and smiled. "I said you could keep it. Looks good on you." He was smiling. Progress.

"Not really my size. Or my taste in music."

Sid shrugged, still smiling, and put the shirt in his guitar case.

Carissa arrived, her hair newly dyed red, resplendent in a coordinated designer yoga outfit. David calculated the cost of her outfit to be somewhere north of what he made in a week. She handed him a bag. David looked inside to find two dress shirts.

"I heard about your shirt incidents and when I was going through Bob's closet this week I found these shirts that he doesn't wear any more. I thought they'd probably fit you."

"Thank you, Carissa, that's very thoughtful of you."

David looked at the shirts, both Tommy Hilfiger and both looking brand new. He was touched that Carissa thought of him, but humiliated that she considered him a charity case. On the other hand, he'd never owned a single Tommy Hilfiger shirt let alone two, so that was nice.

When Trisha arrived, David felt a surge of nervous energy, a surge he was becoming accustomed to. He concealed his excitement at her arrival, projecting a casual air and saying a simple "Hello."

But his voice cracked as he said it and Calvin laughed. David cleared his throat, swallowed his embarrassment and called the rehearsal to order. They began with prayer, impersonal requests for various health needs or vague supplications for the church, nothing dangerous or intimate. David led a short devotional based on Psalm 19.

"The psalmist writes in verse fourteen, 'May these words of my mouth and this meditation of my heart be pleasing in your sight, Lord, my Rock and my Redeemer.' And so the state of our hearts must be as pleasing to God as the words to the songs we sing. Let's remember that as we work on these songs tonight." David tried his best to sound confident.

They worked through the songs for the week, hearing improvement over where they'd been last week. Calvin still randomly shifted the tempo throughout each song, but was more open to David's coaching. He even asked if David knew of a good metronome he should buy.

Sid still didn't smile, but he was attentive to David and played tastefully. Inq's bass playing was restrained and workmanlike and he showed only minor irritation at Calvin's tempo variations. Carissa sang enthusiastically, following David's lead. Trisha supported the music with well-timed chords. In the moments when David forgot about the desire to impress these people, he actually fell into the music, enjoying himself. Perhaps he really could do this. The rehearsal ended and David felt a sense that they had broken new ground together.

"I have an announcement," declared Inq, after David had closed the rehearsal in prayer.

He proceeded to hand out flyers advertising the return of "The Aqualung Experience" to the stage at Barrymore's, a week from Friday.

"I cordially invite you, my musical colleagues, to attend the triumphant return of 'The Aqualung Experience' to the stage. It would do me a great honor to have your presence."

"You gonna do any songs by Boethius?" quipped Calvin.

"Your attempted jocularity is neither necessary, nor effective. However, a discussion of the intersection between the themes of Boethius and Jethro Tull would be most edifying to all of us, I'm sure."

"Sure, I'd love to go, but I need a ride." David looked around the group, stopping hopefully at Trisha.

"Sure, I'll go," said Trisha. "I can pick you up, David."

David's heart exploded silently within his chest.

"No, I can get David," Calvin said. "I pass right by his place on my way to Barrymore's."

Calvin, you idiot, thought David.

"Sure, Calvin. That works too," Trisha said.

"Yeah, thanks Calvin," David said.

"Wonderful! I shall reserve a table for all of you," said Inq, delighted.

THICK AS A BRICK

David was looking forward to hearing Inq's band at Barrymore's. It wasn't so much Inq's band as it was to do something social. He'd discovered that the church had very few people his age, so opportunities for social engagement were hard to come by. He was hoping tonight would give him an opportunity to sit next to Trisha. He put on his favorite jeans and picked out one of the Tommy Hilfiger shirts Carissa gave him. Calvin picked him up at eight-thirty and they drove to the club.

"Hey guess what? I bought a metronome and started practising with it," Calvin said. "You know what I found out?"

"What?"

"I suck at drumming!" Calvin laughed at his own joke. "I guess I have some work to do. But I'll get there!"

"Yeah, you'll get there. You'll get used to it. It'll help a lot."

They arrived at the club and found the table Inq had reserved for them, directly in front of the stage. Carissa and her husband Bob were already there. David made sure that Calvin took the seat next to Bob, ensuring that Trisha would have to sit next to him.

Carissa introduced them. "Bob, you remember Calvin. And this is David, our worship pastor."

"Hey David. Say, I got a shirt just like that! Anyway, I normally don't let Carissa drag me to church stuff, but I don't mind going to something when there's beer involved!"

They exchanged pleasantries, the conversation difficult due to the volume of music blaring in the club. Trisha arrived, waved to everyone and took the seat next to David. He'd been longing to see her all day. Now that she was here, merely inches away from him, his yearning, rather than being satisfied by her appearance, exploded to the point that he could barely contain it. He turned to her and said, "Hey."

"Hey," she said back.

Then David turned to Calvin and asked him what kind of metronome he bought.

"The Aqualung Experience" took the stage. Inq smiled proudly at his friends at the table as he plugged in his bass. The rest of the band were men like Inq, aging rock and roll weekend-warriors, earnest in their pursuit of their music. The stage lights came on, the drummer played a roll on the toms and the flutist started into *Cross-eyed Mary*. The volume was deafening, eliminating any chance of conversation so David and Calvin ceased their discussion of Calvin's new metronome, leaned back in their chairs and listened to the music. David adjusted his chair so as to have a better view of the band, relocating himself a full quarter of an inch closer to Trisha. She didn't seem to notice. The band was good, that is, they played the music well enough. They had no time for showmanship, all their focus and energy devoted to concentrating on the material. The only acknowledgement of any audience at all were Inq's solicitous introductions of each song. The first set ended with *Thick as a Brick, Part One*, all twenty-three minutes of it, finishing it and bowing to a smattering of applause from the small crowd.

"Thank you for coming!" Inq said, beaming and proud.

They each complimented Inq's band. He pulled up a chair, said nothing and just smiled at them. David realized how meaningful and affirming it was to him that they were all here. David wondered how he could begin a conversation with Trisha. A simple phrase like *How was your day?* was inaccessible to his nervous mind until it was too late.

Calvin seized the initiative. "Hey Inq, guess what? I bought a metronome."

Inq huffed. "A sure way to eradicate the drama from your playing. A tool of the weak-minded musician."

Being firmly in the pro-metronome school of thought, David could not let this comment stand. "Every band on tour today is playing to a click."

"The tawdry circus-acts that lip sync amid lewd gyrations are hardly a model. That repetitive dreck is calculated to stunt the adolescent mind and conform it to the hive of bland consumerism. According to Boethius, 'Music is part of us, and either ennobles or degrades our behaviour' and I'm convinced that the un-fluctuating hammering of metronomic tempo is calculated to degrade the listener into an obedient automaton. I'll have no part of that. You can keep your metronome to yourself."

David wondered if Inq had rehearsed this rant or if that was how he talked all the time.

Calvin laughed, "OK, well if Boethius is against metronomes, that's good enough for me. Good thing I kept the receipt!"

During the debate about metronomes, Trisha had moved her chair to the other side of the table to talk to Carissa. Trisha was holding the fabric of Carissa's sleeve between her two fingers as they talked about her outfit. Bob was drinking his beer, staring into space. David looked across the table at Trisha and prayed for a chance to talk to her tonight.

Inq left them and joined the rest of the band on stage. Their second set was much like the first, continuing with Part Two of *Thick as a Brick*. But most of the band were into their third or fourth beer and tiring, evidenced by missed cues and overall sloppiness. They rallied for their closer, *Aqualung*, which they'd obviously played hundreds of times. Exhausted, they ended their second set much to everyone's relief. When they finished, Calvin approached the drummer and asked him about metronomes. He pulled one out of his equipment bag and showed it to Calvin. Then Calvin took a seat behind the drum kit and began playing. David saw this as his opening and walked over to Trisha.

"Looks like my ride is gonna be here for a while. Oh well."

"Yeah, he's looking pretty comfortable with those drums. Well, I could give you ride home," Trisha said.

A thousand suns exploded in David's mind, as he imagined winged cherubs flying circles around the two of them, showering them with rose petals. *I've loved you from the moment I first laid eyes on you. My greatest dream and fantasy is to live as husband and wife with you all the days of our lives, so yes, I would like a ride home with you, tonight and forever after, my love!*

"Sure," said David.

He followed her out of the club and down the street to where she was parked. David silently planned his opening line, perhaps something like, "How did you like the music?" Or would he ask her if she was hungry? Or was that too forward? The thought of rejection made him feel ill. He would begin by asking how she liked the music - safe territory, and if the opportunity presented itself, he would hint at his own hunger, read and react to her signals. A solid plan, not too risky, but with a huge upside. He imagined sitting across from her at a restaurant deciding whether to get the chocolate volcano cake or the créme brûlée. Perhaps, they weren't so hungry and would just share a dessert? *No, no, too fast, too soon*, he thought. They reached her car and he put his hand to the passenger door.

"BEER MONEY!" someone yelled from across the street. A figure staggered out of the darkness and crossed the street toward them.

"Quick! Get in," Trisha said.

David quickly got in and Trisha locked the doors. In her panic she couldn't get the key in the ignition. David sat beside her, frightened as the man crossed the street still shouting, "Beer Money." As he got closer, David recognized him. It was Chuck, very drunk.

"David! David, Beer Money Boy! I thought that was you! I gotta... I need to... can you open the window??"

"Holy Crap! You know him?" said Trisha, trembling.

"Yes, it's OK. I'm sorry. He's my landlord. He owns the house I rent a room in. He calls me 'Beer Money' because that's what he uses my rent for. It looks like he used a lot of it tonight. He's harmless. I'll talk to him."

David rolled the window down an inch. "Chuck, what's up?"

"David, I need your help, man. I gotta get home. But I lost my wallet. I got my truck down there but I can't drive like this and I can't call a cab. But then I SAW YOU! You can drive us *both* home! Unless you're drunk too. Are you drunk?"

"Uh, no, I'm not drunk. But I was going to—"

"You better drive him home, Pastor. It's the right thing to do. He might try to drive himself if you don't," Trisha said.

David knew she was right, but resented her for calling him Pastor. He was furious that his chance to be alone with Trisha had slipped through his fingers. Furious that he hadn't talked more to her when he had the chance. Opening the door, it occurred to him that he ought to say something meaningful, to express his regret and how he'd yearned for them to be together, but all that came out was "Goodnight."

"See you Sunday."

David closed the door and Trisha quickly locked it. She started the car and drove off into the darkness.

"All right, give me those keys," David said. "Let's go find your truck."

On the way home, Chuck slept in the passenger seat while David replayed his final exchange with Trisha in his head. He punished himself with thoughts of all the things he could have said to her. *Too bad, I was looking forward to talking with you. Too bad, I thought we might grab some dessert together. Too bad, as I was hoping that our time together tonight would start us down a path that would lead to marriage, a glorious honeymoon and a lifetime of wedded bliss and by the way I'm open to children.*

When they arrived home, David had to shout at Chuck to wake him up, then help him out of the truck and into the house.

"Oh, hey man. Thanks. Thanks. Here... I wanna give you something." Chuck pulled his wallet out of his pocket and offered David a ten-dollar bill.

"I thought you lost your wallet!" David said.

"Oh man! I thought... wait, I guess I didn't check. Well, here! Here!" Chuck waved the money at him.

"Keep your money." David turned and went downstairs, leaving Chuck leaning up against the wall, still waving the ten dollars.

THANKSGIVING

Out of the corner of his eye, David observed Pastor Rick's wife, Elizabeth Avery. She was in the front row, flint faced, determined not to acknowledge in any way what had just happened, what everyone had heard so clearly, as if the sheer force of her decision to ignore it would erase the incident from time and memory, making this Sunday like every other Thanksgiving Sunday. David had only ever had short conversations with her, shallow conversations about the weather or this or that church event, and yet he'd formed a detailed impression of her. She was guarded, concerned with her own dignity, always making a show of bestowing her approval upon people or things, as if her approval were quite precious indeed. She was ever in control, well dressed, though in a style a decade behind the times. She loved her husband and she hated Carissa Matthews.

David caught her scowling at Carissa on many occasions. Carissa and Elizabeth were a study in contrasts. Carissa unapologetically enjoyed all the accoutrements of the well kept suburban mom, with salon-dyed hair, designer clothes, nails, make-up, keeping trim and muscular from hours at the gym. Elizabeth coloured her own hair, made do with clothes from years past. Her stout frame said that she had neither the time nor the energy for the gym.

David had seen the two of them talking together many Sundays after service. Elizabeth would invariably ask after Bob, reminding Carissa of the one thing Elizabeth had that she didn't — a husband who was a Christian. And with a few well-chosen words, under the guise of spiritual sympathy, Elizabeth would pour vinegar in Carissa's open wound. David recognized this tactic. And he hated seeing it used against Carissa. As a child he'd been asked many times, "any word from your mom?" by people wishing to put him in his orphan place.

Carissa had been asking David if she could sing a solo since September. She had one picked out, a song filled with gratitude for God's creation and for his grace. David thought it would work well for Thanksgiving, Carissa was elated. She'd arrived at church that morning in an outfit that clearly overstepped the boundaries of Pastor Rick's dress code, but David could not bring himself to tell a woman nearly two decades older than he was that she was showing too much thigh. Her short skirt and sleeveless blouse were both form fitting, both in violation of the dress code. She had also dyed her hair red and tied it into two pigtails protruding cheerfully from the sides of her head. It all looked rather juvenile to David, but he knew he lacked a sense of fashion and assumed that Carissa knew what she was doing. He'd figure out how to handle the dress code issue later. It was too late to do anything about it now, and he couldn't imagine telling Carissa she couldn't sing her big solo.

She sang the solo right before the sermon, David and the rest of the band accompanying her. She sang well, from her heart. From the stage, David also noticed that Elizabeth's pleasant smile changed to a scowl whenever Carissa closed her eyes during the chorus of the song. They finished the song and the congregation responded with warm applause.

David looked over at Pastor Rick as he adjusted his wireless mic, which hooked behind his ear and protruded out to the corner of his mouth. As David set down his guitar he glanced back at Eric in the sound booth. Despite Eric's initial resistance to advice, he had responded well to David's suggestion that he mark down the channel for the wireless mic so that he could un-mute it before Pastor Rick began to speak. With some satisfaction, David observed Eric pressing buttons on the sound board, quickly muting the band and un-muting Pastor Rick's mic during the applause.

Unfortunately for Elizabeth, she was leaning into her husband and speaking directly into the mic as it was un-muted so that it broadcast her voice to the entire auditorium. "LOOKS LIKE A SLUTTY PIPPI LONGSTOCKING!"

The entire congregation gasped.

For a split second, as she realized what had happened, Elizabeth's eyes widened and she gulped. Then she slowly sat up straight, eyes locked on Pastor Rick as he ascended the stairs to the stage, recovering her composure. Pastor Rick smiled his mouth-only smile, surveyed the entire room, took a deep breath and launched into his sermon as if nothing was amiss.

After Elizabeth's comment, Carissa looked like she'd been struck with a tire iron. She put on a defensive smile and walked off the stage, to the back of the auditorium and out. She didn't return.

Elizabeth maintained her pose through the entire sermon as if nothing had happened. But when the congregation opened their eyes after Pastor Rick's closing prayer, she was gone.

After the service Trisha came to see David in his office as he was getting ready to leave.

"What are you going to do about this?"

"About what?" asked David, hoping it wasn't about what Elizabeth said.

"What do you think? About what Elizabeth said!"

David had exchanged pleasantries with many people after the service, and not a single one had brought it up. As if the church could collectively choose to ignore it. He was shocked to have it brought back to his focus so abruptly.

"Well, I don't know. What should I do?"

"I spent the entire rest of the service trying to console Carissa. She's *your* volunteer in *your* ministry. You have to do something."

"OK, I'll talk to Pastor Rick." David instantly regretted making this promise. Maybe he should just ignore it like everyone else.

"You better do something. You can't let them get away with this. Promise me you'll do something."

"I promise," David said.

"OK. We'll see." Trisha turned and left.

AFTERMATH

David arrived at work Monday morning filled with dread, still wondering how he would broach the subject of Elizabeth's hot-mic moment with Pastor Rick. It turns out he didn't need to.

"David, we need to talk about yesterday," said Pastor Rick, walking into David's office and sitting in the chair opposite him.

"Yeah. Sure, what about it?" David felt his palms immediately turn clammy.

"This is pretty delicate. I'm sure you heard some things that — well, I suggest a meeting with you, me, Elizabeth and Carissa. How about six-thirty on Thursday? Just before your rehearsal? Can you see if that works for Carissa?"

"Sure. What will we do in the meeting?"

"Well, if we all come in a spirit of grace, willing to apologize and forgive, everything will be just fine. I'll lead us. I don't think there's anything to worry about."

"Great!" David was relieved. He arranged the meeting with Carissa via email and she immediately accepted the invitation.

David paced nervously, waiting for Carissa to arrive for their meeting with the Avery's. He was beginning to feel sorry for Elizabeth, having to humble herself like this and apologize. David was surprised to be included in this meeting but figured that since it involved someone in his ministry area, the Averys wanted to make sure he was a witness to the reconciliation. Still, he knew this meeting would likely be highly emotional. He had stuffed a couple of tissues in his pocket just in case.

Carissa arrived right on time. She was covered head to toe, wearing black pants and a turtleneck, and a big ruffly scarf around her neck. Her hair pulled back in a pony tail. No resemblance to Pippi Longstocking at all. She and David walked into Pastor Rick's office together. Elizabeth and Pastor Rick were already there, Elizabeth sitting at the small round table next to Pastor Rick's desk. Pastor Rick rose to greet them. Elizabeth remained seated.

The four of them sat around the table, Carissa opposite Elizabeth, David and Pastor Rick facing each other. Both women looked down at the table.

Pastor Rick began. "Thank you all for coming. Let us pray: Lord, we thank you for your grace and mercy to us and we ask for your presence here with us to guide us in truth and in unity, Amen.

"Now, we are here to talk about something that happened last Sunday that was quite a distraction and our aim is to come to an understanding of just what that was and to move forward from it in unity. So, I'll begin by clarifying some things. On Sunday morning, even before the service, Elizabeth and I were carrying on a conversation about a matter that we were deeply concerned about and have been in prayer about. It's a confidential matter, so I can't tell you what it was, but it doesn't involve either of you two. Suffice it to say we were both deeply concerned.

"It was still on Elizabeth's heart during the service, and she was still speaking to me about it when my mic was turned on well before it should have been. The result was that some words from a private conversation, meant for only me, were heard completely out of context by the entire church."

David was confused. He couldn't believe what he was hearing. He looked at Carissa and Elizabeth. Both were still looking down at the table.

Pastor Rick continued. "Now, unfortunately for all of us, at the same time, Carissa, you were not dressed according to our new dress code. Now, I don't blame you for that. I'm sure you didn't realize it at the time. But because of your attire, some people may have assumed a connection between the words overheard in the sound system, and you. Now this is very important. I want you to understand that regardless of what some may think, there is no connection, between those words and you. Do you understand?"

Carissa looked up at Pastor Rick, then across the table at Elizabeth, whose eyes remained fixed on the table. She then looked at David, smiled flatly and turned back to Pastor Rick.

"If you say so, Pastor Rick. I understand."

David couldn't believe what he was hearing.

"Good, good, I'm glad we cleared that up," continued Pastor Rick. "Now in order for us to move forward in this area, we should look at how we got here. David, this is where you come in. Although I've asked you on numerous occasions to get my mic turned on at the right time, we are still having problems. This time it didn't just embarrass me, but it also embarrassed my wife. Secondly, David, by not clearly communicating and enforcing your own dress code, you've allowed Carissa to suffer embarrassment. Both things, unfortunately, come back to you. However, you're young, you're still new at this job. So I'm sure that if you can apologize for these two lapses in your leadership, we'd all be willing to forgive you and move on."

David couldn't believe what he was hearing.

"Wait — *I'm* supposed to apologize? What could you two have possibly been talking about that made you say..."

David trailed off, not wanting to repeat the offending words, for Carissa's sake. She was still looking down. Pastor Rick sat up and back from the table, growing taller in his chair, furrowing his brow, eyes fixed sternly on David.

He looked over to Elizabeth, who abruptly turned her head to him for merely a second. In that moment, David saw in her eyes a vast bolus of compacted rage that sapped his will to resist. He looked back up at Pastor Rick, who was breathing heavily through flared nostrils.

"Um, I'm very sorry to everyone here for my — lapses in responsibility. I won't let it happen again." David heard his voice speak the words, as if coming from someone else. He couldn't believe what was happening.

Pastor Rick's shoulders relaxed. The mouth-only smile returned to his face.

"Well, David, I'm sure we all forgive you and understand that you'll be working even harder not to let something like this happen again."

Pastor Rick stood, signalling the end of the meeting. Elizabeth hadn't said a single word. David and Carissa also got up. Elizabeth remained in her place, unmoving, unflinching, unassailable.

"Well, you two have a rehearsal to get to. I'm glad we could come together like this," Pastor Rick said.

David and Carissa walked out, and he wondered if she felt as baffled as he did.

David was still very distracted when he began the rehearsal, reeling from the meeting, angry and confused. How had he been the one that needed to apologize? It seemed terribly unjust. But he knew he had to focus on the task at hand. He escaped into the songs. When they got to *Mountaintop*, Tom Lindsey's song, David threw himself into it with all his heart, pouring out his anguish. He felt God's spirit filling him with peace as he did so. As disappointing as the evening had started, it was comforting to be doing something he was good at, something he could control, something safe. Until now he had avoided looking at Carissa but as they sang he glanced over and sensed that she was also finding peace through worshipping God.

They took a break midway through, and David saw Trisha and Carissa head to the back room alone. When they returned, it looked like they'd both been crying. Trisha looked angry, and for the rest of the rehearsal she was pounding her frustrations out on the piano. After the rehearsal, she followed David to his office.

"What happened?" she asked.

"I'm not even sure what happened."

"Carissa said that Elizabeth didn't even apologize!"

"No, she — look, I shouldn't be talking to you about this."

"I'm disappointed, David. You said you'd do something about this."

Just then Carissa appeared at David's door.

"Trisha, I'd like to talk to David. Would you give us a moment?"

Trisha turned and hugged Carissa and left, but not before she shot David a look filled with reproach and contempt. David's heart sank.

Carissa and David sat across from each other.

"Carissa, I'm not sure what happened in there. It wasn't—"

"David," she interrupted. "You shouldn't have had to apologize. I've known for a long time that Elizabeth doesn't like me. It's obvious. And I was very hurt on Sunday and was ready to leave this church. But I just can't. I've been trying to convince Bob to come with me to church for years. If I leave, he'll just say he was right about everyone here being a bunch of hypocrites. And tonight during rehearsal, when we were worshipping together, all of us, our little team, I love that so much. I won't give that up. It has been so good since you've come here, and I want to stay around and support you. I'm not going to let Elizabeth take that away."

"So then what are you going to do about her?"

"I'm going to kill her."

"What?"

"With kindness, dear. With kindness. I don't know what kind of pain she's been through that shrivelled her up like that, but I'm not going to give in to her. Besides, there's probably nothing she'd love more than to see me leave. I'm not going to let her win. I'm not going to let Satan win. I'm gonna keep on worshipping."

"But what about that crazy story about…" David wanted to tread carefully here. "…about why she said what she said?"

"That's between her and Jesus. I'll let him sort it out. Don't worry about me, David. And don't you feel like this is your fault. It wasn't. Let's just move on. OK?"

"Carissa, you're a better person than I am. You really are."

"Now, now, dear. Never mind that. We'll get through this."

David replayed the meeting in his mind as he walked home. Surely it wasn't possible for the Averys to keep pretending what happened didn't really happen. He also felt wounded, taken advantage of, that his superior had forced him to apologize, to make atonement for the sins of another.

Funny, that, he thought.

ADVENT

"It is the most important hour of the entire year for any church, David." Pastor Rick paced the floor of his office between his desk and the table where David sat, on this Monday morning in late November.

"We will have more people in our church building on Christmas Eve than any other time of the year. With the possible exception of a funeral for someone young, or someone really important. But those funerals don't really count, because you can't use them to promote your church. Not explicitly, anyway." Pastor Rick paused with a faraway look in his eyes. David wondered if he was seriously pondering how to use funerals for church outreach.

"But, back to what I was saying," Pastor Rick Continued, "Christmas Eve is extremely important because you have friends and family members here who were brought here as hostages, against their will. Every grandma and grandpa will drag their whole family here. We'll see people who only come to church once a year and we need to be ready for them! It is crucial, David, especially for us now, that we get this right. Our attendance is stuck, even moving backwards over last year's numbers. And our giving isn't good either. We need a momentum changer, and I think Christmas Eve has got to be it. David, you understand that this church needs to be on a solid financial footing if we're going to keep working together. Even though you and I got off to a rocky start, I've genuinely enjoyed having you as part of the team. But we're going to face some harsh budget realities next year if things don't turn around. So Christmas Eve has to be a home run."

"What did you have in mind?"

"Well, you can get the Sunday School kids to do something.

People eat that up. And the music has to be phenomenal. I'll preach a message and do an altar call. Then, I want to have a time for people to share a testimony or two. I want to show people how great it is to be a part of our church. I want to see lives changed right on Christmas Eve."

"How about we end with *Silent Night* and everyone can light candles?"

"That would be great, except that four years ago Wanda Sawatzky emptied half a can of hairspray onto her head before coming to church and she leaned into her husband Bert's candle and *poof!* Bert started smacking her in the head to try to put out the flames. He was really going at her, like he was enjoying it. I don't know what was worse, the sound of her screaming or the smell of burnt hair. Anyway, the board now has a strict no-flame policy. Too bad.

"Anyway, start putting together that service and we'll talk about it in a couple of days."

"Sounds good."

"Oh, and one other thing, David. That was big of you to apologize in our meeting last week. I know you were caught off-guard, but that's OK. You did what you had to do, that's the important thing. Also, I've asked Wayne to help with the microphone issue. He has an idea that he's working on. He'll let you know about it next week."

"OK, Pastor. I'll get to work on this."

David went home that night and sketched out his plan for the Christmas Eve service, thinking about some of the ominous elements of his talk with Pastor Rick. He knew his contract only lasted through April. It was already November, and there didn't seem to be any sign of growth or positive momentum for the church. Would he be able to make a difference? Would Christmas Eve be a game changer?

He pulled out his guitar and began to strum, aimlessly at first, and then he began to sing. He took great comfort in singing Tom Lindsey's *Mountaintop*. That song always moved him. He made a note to include it in the Christmas Eve service. He put his guitar away and turned in for the night with a prayer.

"Lord, give us success on Christmas Eve. Help me keep my job. Amen."

The next day, David entered the church auditorium to investigate the sound of a power drill. Wayne was on the platform, lying on the floor under the pulpit, adjusting a thick metal pipe that ran along the side of the pulpit from top to bottom.

"Hey Wayne. What are you doing?"

"Oh, David. Just in time. You can help me test this out. Pastor Rick asked me to help him out with a solution for his microphone problem. So I have created the world's first ultra secure foolproof hard-wired wireless system. Now look over here. I have the wireless receiver over here."

He walked toward the back of the stage and pointed to a small recessed cabinet. "The output of the receiver is hard-wired to the amplifiers driving our speakers. The beauty of this is that it bypasses the sound board completely so that Eric — or whoever you have back there — can't screw it up. This cabinet stays locked."

"So then how does the mic get turned on and off?"

"Well that is the beautiful part of my design. Look here at the pulpit."

On the top of the pulpit there was an opening for a key, next to a small orange indicator light.

"See, I ran the power through this secure switch, turned on and off with a key that only Pastor Rick will have. The orange light means there's power to the receiver, activating the microphone. You can help me test it."

Rick handed David the small wireless mic, David hooked it over his ear and turned on the belt-pack transmitter.

"Now here's the key. Turn the switch."

David turned the key. He heard a small *pop* and *hiss* through the speakers.

"Now say something. Test it out."

The only words David could think of were "slutty Pippi Longstocking,'" but he thought better of it and went with the generic "Check, one, Check, one, two, three."

The power went off in the entire auditorium.

"Dang it!" said Wayne. "Well I think I know what happened. I can fix it. Thanks for your help."

David went back to his office and spent the rest of the

afternoon checking Facebook and Twitter. Tom Lindsey tweeted that he'd be touring in the new year. Might he be coming somewhere near Lachance? He also found a blog post on Tom's web page that he would use for his devotional. He answered some emails and bided his time until he could go home at the end of the day.

He spent another evening on his own, eating his grilled cheese sandwiches, reading, looking at social media on his phone and noodling on his guitar, singing some of his favorite songs and then turning in, all to start again tomorrow. He had enough to keep him busy at church during the week, but that's all it seemed to do — keep him busy.

Sunday morning came, and David awoke to the alarm on his phone. He showered and dressed, ate a cup of yogurt for breakfast and began his walk to church. The sun was still below the horizon. Dark silhouettes of leafless trees loomed above him as he marched north on Main street toward the church. His coffee shop, Beans of Production, was closed.

He caught his reflection in the mirror-tinted front window of a twenty-four-hour gym and it startled him. He stopped and stepped toward the window. He'd gained weight since coming here. He needed a haircut, and he just looked so tired. He rubbed his eyes and face, smoothing out the skin around them to see if it made any improvement. Then he saw a man on the other side of the window running on a treadmill, laughing at him. David abruptly turned and went on his way, embarrassed. He was on his own treadmill. Sunday after Sunday, expending effort and energy without seeming to go anywhere.

God, why am I doing this? What's the point? Remind me. Show me why I'm here. He prayed as he continued to walk to church. He arrived and went into his routine to prepare the stage, check the setup, and tidy the cables. He tuned his guitar and thought about his team as they began to arrive. For each of them, it seemed they had full, busy, interesting lives and what they did on Sunday morning was just something extra. But for David, this was all he had.

After the soundcheck, Pastor Rick arrived. David felt his chest tighten. Since Thanksgiving, David had become wary of Pastor Rick, anxious that he would blame David for anything that might go wrong. David held his breath as Pastor Rick turned the key in the pulpit, engaging the power in the "hard-wired wireless." The speakers hissed warmly.

"Check, Hello. Good Morning. Well isn't that just the greatest thing?" Pastor Rick smiled his full-face smile.

"Sounds great!" David said, trying to be positive.

Pastor Rick smiled back at him. "There's nothing Wayne can't do," he gushed. He knelt down and ran his hand along the steel conduit that was bolted to the side of the pulpit, pushing and pulling at it and admiring its sturdiness. "Solid as a rock. Can't wait to try it out."

David and his team played the songs for the morning. The congregation sang along heartily. They were the same people who'd been there since David arrived. They were used to him now, comfortable with him, for the most part. The band was sounding good. They'd improved a great deal the first couple of months, but David wondered if they were now as good as they'd ever be. If this was as good as it would ever get. As they played *Mountaintop,* David sang the words to the bridge from his heart:

Everything I need, Everything I want, is to hear you say,
That you'll never leave, never let me go, come what may.

David prayed those words would be true of his own heart as they finished the song, knowing that in reality, his heart wanted many other things as well.

Pastor Rick took the platform, the keys to the hard-wired wireless already in his right hand. He slipped the key in the lock, turned it, smiled as he waited for half a second and then said, "Good Morning."

The words reverberated through the speakers, filling the room with Pastor Rick's deep baritone voice. He smiled his full-face smile and began his sermon. Pastor Rick spoke passionately that morning, as if the hard-wired wireless had inspired him, set him free to minister without worrying about technical issues. David wished he'd been the one to solve Pastor Rick's problem, not Wayne.

David was anxious about trying to impress Pastor Rick, to preserve his job. But deep down, he worried that if things didn't turn around for Lachance Community Church, no amount of impressing Pastor Rick could save him.

"How was work?" asked Chuck.

"It was OK." David smiled as he thought about the "hard-wired wireless" and how happy it made Pastor Rick.

"What's so funny?"

"Oh, just my boss, Pastor Rick. He always had trouble with his mic turning on at the right time. So one of the guys built him this foolproof, hard-wired switch that operates by a key. It's installed right into the pulpit so now when he gets up to preach he turns the key and starts it up like a car or something. It is wired through a steel conduit directly to the main amplifiers which are in a locked cabinet, so nobody can accidentally turn them off. It's really something. I've never seen anything like it. But, it makes him happy, so I guess that's good."

"Wow! I'd like to see that."

"Really? Well you should come to church some time." David immediately regretted the invitation, wondering what Chuck might think of everyone at the church, how they'd receive him, if anyone would talk to a bedraggled misfit who didn't know how to speak like a church person.

"Oh, no way. *This* is my church." Chuck pointed to the football game on TV.

"I gather with the faithful to watch every Sunday. We don't have wine and crackers. We have beer and nachos. I look forward to it all week. That's pretty much church, isn't it?"

"I think there's a little more to it. But I will have some of those nachos."

"Sure. I'll get you a coke."

Sunday afternoon football had become a ritual for the two of them. Since the "Beer Money" incident, Chuck had been especially kind to David. They would watch the early game and then order pizza to eat while they watched the late game. David would watch the game and keep Twitter open on his phone, occasionally repeating comments from fans about the play. He was beginning to enjoy watching football, but what he enjoyed most was just being with Chuck, someone he didn't need to impress.

At half-time in the late game, Chuck returned to the living room after putting away uneaten pizza and said, "Maybe I'll come sometime."

"Pardon me?" David wondered what he was talking about.

"Maybe I'll come to church. Hear you sing. You sound pretty good through the air vents. Be good to hear you with a band."

"Oh. My singing doesn't bother you does it?"

"No, not at all." Chuck shrugged. "I never had anyone in my house who played music or anything. It's nice."

They finished the game and David went downstairs. He pulled out his guitar and played and sang for a while, uneasy with the knowledge that Chuck could hear him, that Chuck was listening. He lay down for the night and prayed for his church, his team. He prayed that Trisha would notice him, he prayed that he could keep his job, and he prayed that if Chuck did come to church, it wouldn't ruin their friendship.

'Twas the night before Christmas.

Seven-year-old Ethan had been chosen by the Sunday school superintendent, the criteria being ability to take instruction, cuteness, and possession of an adorable yet still intelligible lisp.

"Then the thepherdth returned, glorifying and praithing God for all the thingth that they had heard and theen, ath it wath told them."

Then seven-year-old Ethan, wearing a bath robe, closed his bible and smiled at his parents in the first row. The entire church clapped enthusiastically for him and for the Sunday school children in full costume as they were ushered off the stage, Mary and Joseph, shepherds and sheep, wise men and a donkey.

Pastor Rick walked up on stage.

The church was full this Christmas Eve. David had enjoyed leading the opening carols. Everyone knew them and sang along heartily, Trisha accompanying on piano. He'd relaxed during the children's pageant and now he sat in the front row as Pastor Rick pulled out his key and turned the switch in the pulpit, looked out at the congregation with his full face smile and confidently said "Merry Christmas."

The congregation replied with a muffled "Merry Christmas" of their own. Pastor Rick launched into his sermon.

"Well, I'm sure we're all looking forward to opening our Christmas presents, aren't we? Especially the children here. I remember one special gift that I asked for when I was a child. I wanted an Evel Knievel wind-up motorcycle. I told Santa at the shopping mall, I told my Mom and Dad every day that I wanted it.

It had a rip cord that you'd pull and then Evel Knievel would ride his motorbike, doing wheelies and jumps and whatever else you could dream up for him.

"Finally, Christmas morning arrived. I opened my presents and you know what? I got my Evel Knievel toy. I was overjoyed. I played with it all day! My mom and dad had to pry it out of my hands just to get me to eat some turkey dinner. After dinner, I was helping clear the dishes when I heard the unmistakeable sound of the rip cord being pulled on my Evel Knievel motorcycle, followed by the even more unmistakeable screaming of my little sister. She came running around the corner, still screaming, Evel Kneivel's motorcycle gears irretrievably tangled in her long brown hair. While I was helping with the dishes, my sister thought she'd try out my new toy. Within half an hour my sister had short hair, I had a completely seized Evel Kneivel motorcycle engine, and we both had bitter tears in our eyes."

David looked around the auditorium as Pastor Rick continued. He missed his grandmother, but was grateful that he was beginning to feel like he belonged here. He was anxious about the service, especially since he'd been invited over to Pastor Rick's house for Christmas day. It would be much more pleasant if the service went really well.

Pastor Rick was winding up his sermon. "Now I thought that the gift I wanted was the perfect gift, that it would bring me joy and that it would last forever! But instead, it didn't last. It broke and everyone in my family ended up angry and upset because of that gift. Well tonight, I'd like to tell you about the greatest Christmas gift ever given. His name is Jesus, and He not only won't break, He will heal everything that is broken in your life and in my life. He will bring you joy and peace and love and forgiveness.

"If there is brokenness in your family, Jesus wants to make it whole. You see, when you accept Jesus, you become part of God's family. All of us who call Lachance Community Church home are part of God's family and we'd love to welcome you into our little part of God's big family."

Pastor Rick continued in this vein for another ten minutes, inviting people to receive the gift of Jesus in their hearts, to begin a new life with Him, because He can satisfy every need.

"Now David is going to come back up and lead us in a song that talks about how Jesus meets our every need. After that, we'll have a time of sharing. If you've decided to accept the gift of Jesus tonight, I encourage you to share that good news with us, or if you'd just like to share how being part of God's family has made a difference in your life, you can come up to the microphone in the aisle."

David went up and they all sang *Mountaintop*. The church regulars all sang along. A beautiful spirit filled the room.

Pastor Rick came back up on the stage. "If you'd like to share a word about what being part of God's family means to you, or a decision you've made, please come forward."

David sat down in the front row as Myrna Hoffmann shared about how the church cared for her when she had her hip replaced. Arthur Dodds was next, sharing about how his Friday morning men's breakfast was a real encouragement when he was unemployed last year.

"Are there any others who'd like to share?" asked Pastor Rick as Trisha played piano softly behind him.

David heard someone laboring up the aisle, a familiar cadence of steps he'd heard hundreds of times. He jerked his head back to see Chuck making his way up to the mic. In the darkness of the auditorium, David hadn't seen Chuck sitting in the back. He was astonished Chuck was even here, let alone coming forward to share at the mic. Instantly, he worried about what Chuck might say.

Chuck was shaking, just standing in front of the mic, hesitating. Finally, he began to speak.

"Hi everyone. My name is Chuck and tonight I decided to ask for Jesus to be part of my, or, oh gosh, I'm not really a religious person so I'm not sure what to call it. I just did the thing that the pastor here said."

The congregation laughed at this and then applause broke out through the room. This seemed to put Chuck at ease.

"None of you here know me, except for David there. I'm his landlord. He lives in the basement apartment at my house. Anyway, I was nervous about letting a pastor live in my house. It seems like most pastors I knew would just quote a buttload of Bible verses at you and make you feel like sh–"

Elizabeth Avery let out a shriek from the front row, partially drowning out Chuck's expletive. Dozens of people gasped. A few giggled. Pastor Rick grimaced and then his face quickly settled back to his mouth-only smile.

"Ay, sorry. Sorry. Anyways, David was different. He never really made me feel like that. And he could've. There was one night that I really screwed up. I had too much to drink and I saw David downtown with a girl and I think I scared both of them to death. But David took me home and he never rubbed my face in it, even though I deserved it. At night, most nights, I would hear him singing. And it got so that at nights I'd turn down my TV to I could hear him when he started. Then I'd turn the TV off and just listen. I'd look forward to it and it made me feel, I don't know, peaceful. So I came here tonight to hear David sing and to see what this place is all about. When I heard everyone sing that last song, it all just made sense. I..."

Chuck started to break down, taking a moment to compose himself.

"I done some bad things, I've hurt people."

Chuck paused again to fight back his tears.

"My life is messed up and I don't know how to fix it, so I figure it's time I try this Jesus thing. I know this church has its problems, but I wanna join up if you'll have me."

David's heart was bursting, his eyes wet with tears. He walked up to the platform and hugged Chuck, the congregation applauding warmly. David took his guitar and led the church in their closing song, *Silent Night*. Every line in the carol was loaded with fresh meaning, having just heard Chuck's testimony of Christ being born in his heart that very night.

After the service David had to work his way through a crowd of well-wishers surrounding Chuck.

"I'll see you tonight back at home," David said.

Chuck, still fighting back tears, nodded and smiled.

David exchanged many warm Christmas greetings with church families. As the congregation dwindled, he packed up his guitar and tidied up the stage. He walked back to his office when Pastor Rick called to him out of his office.

"David, come in here."

"Hey, Pastor. Great message. Great service. Great to see a full house. Man, I'm on top of the world."

"Oh, Yes. Indeed. Well you must be quite pleased?"

"Oh, I can't believe it! About Chuck, I mean. I had no idea he was going to come, no idea he was even here until he came forward. It's really amazing."

"It certainly is. It certainly is. And it's so, so interesting what he said, don't you think?"

"Well, I guess, so. You mean about trying the Jesus thing? Or the singing?"

David wasn't sure what Pastor Rick thought was so interesting.

"Oh yes, those things for sure." Pastor Rick cleared his throat. "I guess I mean what he said about our church. I found that very interesting. No, I guess what I really found interesting was that he knew about problems at our church."

Pastor Rick was smiling his mouth-only smile. His hands, until now folded together, were apart, palms facing up. "Now where would he have found out about problems at this church?"

"Well, I think maybe he just meant that he knew we aren't perfect. I don't think he meant anything specific."

"Specific? Like what kind of specific problem?"

"I don't know. I mean…" David fumbled for what to say.

"Do you talk to Chuck about the church?"

"Well, of course I do."

"So it seems to me he only could have heard about problems from you. Am I correct about that?"

"Well, I suppose, but I don't think there's any harm…" David's voice trailed off. He wasn't sure how to finish his sentence. He was getting the same sinking feeling from Pastor Rick he'd had in the meeting with Carissa and Elizabeth.

"Well, David, some senior pastors might be embarrassed to have a friend of the Worship Pastor's talk about church problems in front of a full house on Christmas Eve. But I'm not at all bothered by that. I'm really just more concerned. If you think there are problems, don't you think you should talk to me about them?"

"Of course. Of course I would tell you. But I don't really think there are. I'm happy here. I really am."

"David, if we can't trust each other, there's no hope for us to work together. I hope you understand that it is not acceptable for you to be telling your friends or anyone else for that matter about problems you think you see here. If you have an issue, you talk to me and to me alone. Am I clear?"

"Yes, sir. Yes"

The mouth-only smile slowly returned to Pastor Rick's face.

"One more thing, I know we invited you over for Christmas Day, but it would be a shame for your friend to spend Christmas alone, don't you think?"

"Well, yeah. I could ask Chuck if we wanted to join us."

"Oh no. David, don't trouble yourself. You don't need to drag him over to our home. You two just spend the day together at your place. I'm sure you have a lot to talk through with him. Sound good?"

"Oh, I understand. Yes. Sure, that'd be the best."

"All right then. I'm glad we talked. You have a Merry Christmas. I better get home. There's a yule log with my name on it waiting for me. You can lock up?"

"You bet. Merry Christmas, Pastor."

Pastor Rick grabbed his coat from a hook by the door and left David sitting in the chair, reeling, having crashed into earth after the euphoria of seeing Chuck surrender his life to Jesus. He sat there for a time, trying to quell the rising flood of rage and the despair that threatened to overwhelm him. When he felt the urge to cry, he stood quickly, hoping that action would stave off the tears. He walked methodically from room to room, turning off lights, one by one, checking that each door was locked. He returned to his office and put on his coat, hat and gloves. Walking out the front door, turning to lock it behind him, and pulling his coat tightly around himself against the wind and blowing snow, he turned away from the church and walked home alone in the darkness.

FOR UNTO US A CHILD IS BORN

David lay awake in bed until late that Christmas morning, imagining all the families from church with small children who were up at dawn. Thanks to the school buses, most mornings he was awake much earlier than the rest of the world. For once, it was nice to sleep in while the rest of the world woke up early. He heard Chuck stirring upstairs so he decided to rise and see how he was doing.

"Hey sleepyhead. Merry Christmas," said Chuck.

"Yeah, Merry Christmas. How are you doing?"

"Pretty good. I really can't believe about last night, you know. It's like a whole new — I don't know. I just used to think that this was my life. I made my bed years ago and all that was left was for me to sleep in it. But now it just seems like there's hope. You know? Like things can be better."

"You're right, Chuck. I'm so happy for you. Hearing you last night was the best Christmas present I could ever ask for."

"Oh, well that reminds me, I want to get something before you get going."

"No worries, Chuck. I don't have anywhere to go today."

"Really? I thought you said you were going somewhere."

"I did have an invitation, but then it didn't work out. But that's OK. I don't really feel like putting on good clothes and I don't have the energy to sit around and be nice to people all day."

"I hear you. That's pretty much my philosophy of life." Chuck laughed along with David.

"OK then, if you're not going anywhere, we can watch basketball and chow down. I got a couple steaks in the freezer I've been saving for a special occasion. You want coffee? I got some muffins too."

David sat down, touched at how happy Chuck was when he found out David would be spending Christmas day with him. Chuck brought out the coffee pot, two cups and a plate with two stale carrot muffins. David poured coffee for them both and started eating a muffin.

Chuck sat down, then quickly got up. "I forgot! Wait here."

He returned a minute later with a white plastic bag containing a large box. "Sorry it's not wrapped. I thought I had wrapping paper. I don't know why, since I can't remember the last time I wrapped a present, but here you go. Merry Christmas."

David opened the bag. Inside was a Wi-Fi router and modem. David was stunned.

"I got the Wi-Fi! The phone company has it all set up. You just need to plug this thing in and we're good to go."

"Chuck, I don't know what to say... this is so..." to David's great embarrassment he began to cry. The tears he'd fought off last night came in a torrent, originating from somewhere deep and hidden, a place where he'd locked away all the anxiety and pain and loneliness he'd been feeling ever since he came to Lachance, until Chuck's simple kindness broke the seal.

"Easy there, David. You OK?"

"Chuck, I'm sorry. It's been a pretty intense twenty-four hours. Weeks, months, I guess. This feels like the first nice thing someone has done for me since I got here. I know that's probably not true, but that's what it feels like right now. Wow! Sorry I'm such a mess. This is really nice. Thank you very much."

"Wanna plug it in and get it going?"

"You bet."

After half an hour of struggling with manuals and cables, David had it up and running. He felt a rush of joy as he opened a web browser on his laptop and saw the Google home page. No more staying late at church for the internet or nursing a coffee for hours at Beans of Production for the free Wi-Fi.

"So, do you have a Facebook?" Chuck asked.

David was surprised Chuck was interested in Facebook. Until now, he'd expressed no interest in the online world.

"Yeah, I'm on Facebook," said David.

"Can you show me? I'm kinda curious about it."

"Sure. See, here. There's me. And these are all my friends. See, this is Sid. He plays guitar at church. Looks like he got a new distortion pedal for Christmas."

David scrolled through pictures of family gatherings and Christmas presents.

"You can search for people on this?" Chuck asked.

"Yeah. You wanna see if someone is on here?"

"Linda Weaver."

"Is that a relative?"

Chuck nodded and, after a pause, said, "my daughter."

"I didn't know you had a daughter."

Chuck let out a long sigh, rubbed his forehead and looked up at the ceiling for a moment, then back at David.

"Yeah, well. She and I don't talk much. Is she on here?"

David typed her name into the search bar and the screen filled with Linda Weavers. David scrolled down the page slowly so Chuck could see them.

"Linda Weaver Schulz. Schulz is her married name, but that's not her picture."

A picture of a newborn baby wrapped in a pink blanket graced Linda's profile space. David clicked on the picture and scrolled down through several photos of a young couple at the hospital after the birth of their baby. David looked back at Chuck leaning over his shoulder and saw tears forming in his eyes. Chuck was slowly shaking his head, biting his bottom lip.

"I didn't even know," he finally said.

Chuck came around from behind the couch and sat down in his chair, let out a sigh, continuing to shake his head.

"I haven't been much of a father. I haven't been a father at all. Her mom and I divorced when she was little. Her mom kicked me out and, well, I drank a lot. I was mean. I deserved it. But I was... I don't know. I was terrible to be around."

"When's the last time you talked to her?"

"I didn't exactly talk to her. She sent me a letter a couple years ago saying she was getting married and that I shouldn't come to the wedding. That if I tried to, there'd be some guys making sure I couldn't. So I parked down the block from the church in my truck. I saw her show up in her white dress. I don't even know who walked her down the aisle. I waited until I saw them leave the church and then I went home and got drunk. That's the last time I saw her."

"Chuck, I'm sorry. I'm really sorry." David didn't know what else to say.

"Can you get phone numbers from there?"

"It depends on what a person shares. Let's see. Looks like she shared everything. There's her phone number. You gonna call her?"

"I don't know. It's probably hopeless."

"It can't hurt to try," David said.

Chuck looked at the phone sitting in its cradle on the end table beside the couch.

"It's hopeless," Chuck repeated.

David picked up the phone and handed it to Chuck, who took it and held it limply on his lap. David set his laptop beside Chuck and pointed to Linda's phone number on the screen. Chuck looked like a lost child as he stared back at David.

"You want me to dial?"

Chuck looked down at the phone, then back at David and nodded. David took the phone, dialed Linda's number and gave it back to Chuck.

"It's ringing," said Chuck.

David could faintly hear a click followed by a man's voice saying what sounded like *Merry Christmas.*

Chuck took a deep breath and sat up as he responded.

"Yeah, Merry Christmas to you too. Is, um, Linda there?" Chuck stared out the window as he talked. David couldn't make out what the man on the phone was saying.

"It's Chuck... yeah, Linda's dad."

The line went silent. Chuck looked from the window to David as they both waited. Chuck was slowly shaking his head. Then David heard a voice on the phone, but it sounded like the man.

"Would you just tell her-Hello? Hello?" Chuck looked back at David as he set the phone down on the armrest. "Hung up on me. I guess that was her husband. Told me Linda didn't want to talk to me and not to call again. Like I said, hopeless."

Chuck sat quietly on the couch, looking at the floor. David didn't know what to say. They sat together in the living room without speaking. David thought about his own mom, about whether she was alive or dead, and wondered what she'd be thinking about today if she was alive. After several minutes David broke the silence.

"Well at least she knows her dad was thinking about her today. That's something."

"Yeah, that's something," said Chuck. "Can I see those pictures again?"

"Sure."

David put his laptop on the coffee table and they sat next to each together on the couch scrolling through Linda's profile, all the way back to her wedding pictures. Chuck didn't say a word. After scrolling through them for a second time, Chuck sat back and slapped his knees with both hands.

"Can you believe that? I'm a grandpa! Dang! Well, enough moping around. The basketball game starts soon. Nachos?"

"Nachos," David nodded.

They spent the rest of the day watching TV together, while David gorged himself on social media. Christmas dinner was steak and potato chips in front of the TV, watching *Die Hard* until Chuck fell asleep on the couch and David cleaned up the kitchen and went down to his room.

LEADERFEST

David braced himself as he heard Pastor Rick's footsteps coming toward his office. David had come in early the first morning after the Christmas break and sat at his desk with his door closed. He wanted to avoid Pastor Rick after what happened on Christmas Eve. David hadn't slept the previous night, hounded by anxiety, unable to predict how Pastor Rick would treat him.

He was about to find out.

"David!" Pastor Rick said as his hand reached the doorknob, opening the door and practically jumping across the threshold. He was grinning, eyes wide open and almost out of breath. David gathered his arms around his chest and pushed back in his chair as far from the door as possible.

"Guess what!" said Pastor Rick.

It took David a moment to realize that the man wasn't angry. He was excited. David's fear slowly turned to confusion. He made no reply.

"C'mon, guess! Oh never mind, you'll never guess. Here it is." Pastor Rick stepped right to the edge of David's desk, leaned over it and said, "We're going to Leaderfest!" He pumped both his fists in sync with the 'Leaderfest.'

David flinched. "Oh! What is Leader... fest?"

"It's only the greatest live-via-satellite inspirational leadership event in history!"

"Oh. That's great, I guess. Sounds fun."

"David, you have no idea. It will rock your world. I think it might be just the thing we need. And it's a God-thing. You probably know that the budget is pretty tight, but I go way back with the pastor at The Flow where they're hosting it. They had two people cancel and he gave me their spots."

"At the what? *The Flow*? What's that?"

"Oh, they used to be Ebenezer Baptist, but what a terrible name. Can you imagine trying to invite someone to Ebenezer? About five years ago, when they built their new building they re-branded and became 'The Flow.' Much more exciting. I wish we could have a cool name like that. But never mind."

"So what is this thing?"

"They bring in the best leaders from everywhere. CEO's of companies, army generals, celebrities. Not only Christians either. And they really care about the diversity angle too, so there's always at least one black guy. Usually he's pretty hilarious. It's awesome. It's next Thursday. I'll email you the details."

Then he left, cheerful, as though nothing unpleasant lingered between them. The Christmas Eve fiasco was ignored, denied, banished from memory. David realized he actually did want to talk to Pastor Rick about how he was feeling and about their relationship. Maybe Leaderfest would teach him how to approach this type of thing.

David's head was down looking at his phone, checking Twitter as he cut across the parking lot toward the Leaderfest breakfast kickoff. He didn't seen the car wheeling into the open parking space in front of him. The bumper of a gleaming, new, Honda Civic grazed David's knees, the shock of the near miss enough to send David reeling backwards, landing hard on the wet grass and soaking the seat of his pants.

"Dude! Look up from your phone! I almost killed you. You OK?" asked the driver.

"Yeah. Fine." David, still stunned, picked himself up off the grass, twisting his head around to get a look at his wet butt.

"OK. Cool." The Civic's driver hardly looked back as he rushed toward the building, leaving David standing still and staring at the car that had almost broken his legs.

David had left the house at six-thirty, taken three buses and walked the last two miles to reach the suburban campus of "The Flow." He thought about what it would be like to drive a new white Honda Civic. He made a quick calculation, that between his meagre wages, student loans and living costs, he might be able to afford one in a decade or so.

He dreaded arriving here and spending the day in crowded rooms with people he didn't know, pretending to enjoy himself. And now he had a wet butt to ensure his continued misery. He thought about turning around and taking the three buses back home and crawling into bed, but decided that was not an option. Explaining his absence to Pastor Rick would likely be worse than Leaderfest itself.

"You're at Table Eight with the other worship and music guys! Over there!" said a preternaturally perky woman at the registration table. She handed David a tote bag filled with his conference notebook, an official Leaderfest note-taking pen and some other promotional material. He made his way toward Table Eight where seven other men already sat, engaged in lively conversation. David took the remaining chair, which was facing away from the stage and the screen at the front of the room so he'd have to twist around to see what was happening once the program began. He placed his cold, wet butt into the seat and listened to the conversation around the table, wondering whether it was more polite to keep listening or interrupt to introduce himself. Mercifully, a voice over the PA interrupted them as it welcomed everyone to the breakfast.

"Welcome to the Leaderfest kickoff breakfast. My name is Dean Goodwin and I'm the lead pastor here at The Flow. We are *thrilled* to have you all here for Leaderfest!"

At the word 'Leaderfest,' the room erupted into applause. In the back, some men started chanting "Oo! Oo! Oo! Oo!"

"You guys settle down in the back! They're crazy, aren't they?" said Pastor Dean, to laughter throughout the auditorium. Dean looked around Pastor Rick's age, but that's about all they had in common. Dean was tall and athletic with broad shoulders. He had shiny black hair that would've done a newscaster proud, blue eyes and a telegenic smile that he flashed regularly. He wore a well-fitted blue dress shirt with the sleeves rolled up. A large shiny diver's watch adorned one wrist and a gold bracelet hung loosely around the other.

Dean continued. "We love the excitement, but we wanna keep it real. We all have struggles. Yes, I know, it's true. So we're gonna accelerate right into some authenticity time. I'm sure you've all introduced yourselves, so as we wait for breakfast to be served, let's go around and everyone just share one issue you're struggling with. OK? You guys cool with that? OK. Let's Pray. 'God, we are so glad you're here with us at The Flow for Leaderfest and we are here to maximize our capacity as leaders. But hey, you know we struggle too. So help us keep it real. Yeah. Keepin' it real is what it's about. Yeah. So, thanks for this food and give us a great day at Leaderfest. Amen."

David's anxiety grew as he tried to think of a struggle to share. He could share how he was afraid of Pastor Rick, how he could be unpredictable, capricious, vindictive and manipulative. Or how he constantly felt like he was a complete fraud, making everything up as he was going along and that any day now he'd be found out. Or maybe how he was falling deeper and deeper in love with Trisha, but the more intense his feelings became, the more paralyzing was his fear of rejection. Or maybe how he felt trapped in a job filled with frustration that was nothing like he thought it would be, but he continued because he needed the money and couldn't think of what else he would do.

"I'm Josh Frayne and I'm the Assistant Worship Director for Junior High ministries here at The Flow." It was the guy who nearly ran him over in the white Honda Civic. And David thought he recognized that name. Then it came to him. Josh Frayne was the guy that was supposed to candidate at Lachance. Josh was their first choice. And now, here he was — Assistant Worship Director for Junior High? Junior High needed a head worship director of its own, and that director needed an assistant? And the junior high assistant worship director's salary could pay for a new Honda Civic? Lachance didn't even have a Junior High group. This was a different world.

"So what I'm struggling with is that we got some used Mac 250 moving lights for the youth cave, but out of the ten we have, it seems like there's always a couple that aren't working and my lighting designer is always freaking out because we don't have all the movers working. I'm trying to tell him to relax and that some youth groups don't even have moving lights. I think he just feels undervalued because we got used ones instead of new ones. It's great that he's really passionate, but just trying to help him stay positive, you know?"

All the other men around the table nodded in agreement. David did not know what it was like to struggle with a lighting designer.

At his church, lighting was still controlled by a set of four rotary dimmer switches on the back wall of the auditorium. His only lighting issue was the Sunday when one of the ushers leaned against the back wall and turned two of them off.

"How about you?" Josh turned to David, not seeming to recognize him as the person he'd nearly run over earlier that morning.

"My name is David Singer and I'm the Worship Pastor at Lachance Community Church. I guess I'm struggling with recruiting new team members." Innocuous, believable, betraying no weakness. The trifecta of safe prayer requests.

"Lachance!" A look of recognition registered on Josh's face. "I was... oh, guys this is actually funny. I had an interview there and totally forgot about them when I got the job here. Then like a month after I started working here, they called expecting me to come and candidate that weekend! Oh man, the pastor was ticked. But, hey, it all worked out for the best, right?"

"Sure," said David, smiling a mouth-only smile.

The rest of the men around the table shared their so-called struggles, carefully calculated to reveal how great they were. One of the men was struggling with the "explosive growth" in their youth group, another with demands of managing the upcoming worship recording that the church was producing. Every one of them worked for The Flow. David couldn't stand it. He felt so inadequate as their prayer time turned into an inverted bragging circle.

Breakfast was served and as conversation continued around the table, Josh turned to David. "Hey guess what? You like Tom Lindsey?"

"Of course. I love him. *Mountaintop* is my favorite song."

"Well, I'm so pumped. It hasn't been announced yet, but he's extending his tour and he's coming to The Flow! He's gonna be here in this building! And as part of the contract, our worship teams get to hang out with Tom after the concert! Is that sweet or what?"

On one hand, David was thrilled that Tom Lindsey was coming to town. On the other hand, he had one more reason to hate Josh. That undeserving, privileged brat was going to get to meet Tom Lindsey.

"That's great! I'm really happy for you," he said.

"Yeah, well it's all hush-hush until it gets announced, but Tom should be tweeting out the new tour dates some time today. Then we get to announce it and tickets go on sale! Yeah, not only do I get to hang out with Tom Lindsey himself, we're gonna make big bucks for hosting the concert. Like, thousands! I might be able to get new moving lights after all!"

"LADIES and GENTLEMEN" It was Pastor Dean again, from the stage. "I'd like to invite you all to a little celebration just before we get the 'leader-festivities' under way. As you know, God has truly blessed us here at The Flow and we've just completed construction on our brand-new atrium, so please exit through the south doors and join us for the grand unveiling! I'll see you there in five minutes!"

Everyone in the hall got up from their tables and made their way like a herd of cattle through the doors in the back of the room, toward the atrium. The atrium was open and bright, floor to ceiling windows on one side, about forty feet high, through which the morning sun shone, blinding them. In front of the windows, they could all see Pastor Dean's silhouette, standing behind a podium on a small stage that had been set up for this occasion. In the middle of the atrium was some kind of structure, about thirty feet high and thirty feet around, encircled completely by a black shiny curtain.

"Welcome to our new Atrium at The Flow!" said Pastor Dean's silhouette. "Oh, is the sun in your eyes? Well let me just take care of that." He pointed somewhere toward the back of the room and nodded. A set of semi-opaque blinds were electronically lowered down in front of the windows, obscuring the glare yet leaving the room bathed in natural light. They could now make out the features of Pastor Dean's face. He was smiling broadly as the crowd applauded.

David reflexively joined in the applause and abruptly stopped when he realized he was clapping for window coverings.

"Thank you! Thank you for that. Yes. But that is not all. Let's be quiet and use our ears here," said Pastor Dean, putting his hand to his ears.

A mechanical sputtering emanated from the behind the curtain in the middle of the room, and soon water could be heard flowing and splashing. After a few seconds, the curtain was released, dropping dramatically to the floor, revealing an enormous fountain. The base was a sunken oval pool. Out of this pool rose a flagstone mound, fifteen feet into the air. On top of this was mounted a steel and glass cross, with a steel crown of thorns, or rather, barbed wire. Water spewed out from behind the top of the cross, down through the crown of thorns, the length of the cross and out of the two sides of the cross. It continued down the flagstone mound in multiple rivulets to the pool below.

David thought he heard a voice behind him murmur "*Hideous!*"

The crowd applauded wildly.

"I know what... Now, now, if I can just..." Pastor Dean was trying to speak over the applause. "I know what you're thinking! Yes. I know. Then answer is YES! It is designed to facilitate baptisms! See the stairs right there on my left. Yeah!" At this point Pastor Dean's face took on a more earnest look. "We, at The Flow are so glad you could be here for this unveiling. I wonder if I could put my old friend Rick on the spot and ask him to lead us in a prayer of dedication? Rick Avery, everybody. Let's welcome him up here!"

A few of the rowdy guys hooted "Rick, Rick, Rick!" but soon gave up when nobody else joined in. Pastor Rick slowly made his way up to the platform.

"Well this is something else, Dean. Who would've thought we'd be here doing something like this when we were both studying Greek twenty years ago? It might not have happened if I didn't loan you my course notes!" A polite chuckle went up from the crowd. "OK, let's pray. 'Lord, we are astounded to see what is possible when your people put their faith in you and give their resources to your work. And so I pray that you would use this new space, this new fountain for your glory! Amen!'"

After a hearty chorus of *Amens* and a round of applause, Pastor Rick and Pastor Dean posed for pictures. Pastor Rick flashed his mouth-only smile and Pastor Dean flashed his telegenic newscaster smile. Then the crowd made their way through the atrium into the auditorium for the first session. Classic rock music played over the PA and a huge video screen showed promotional slides for books and videos available for purchase after the sessions.

David picked up a flyer from the seat pocket in front of him and leafed through it. It advertised several church ministries. The men's ministry was called 'Bro at the Flow.' Their missions group was called "Go with the Flow." Women's ministry was called "Beauti-Flow." Everything was meticulously branded and coordinated. It made David nauseous. His wet bottom irritated him, so he slipped out to the bathroom to air things out. If nobody was there, he might even dry his underwear with the hand dryer.

David walked to the back of the auditorium, out the doors to the atrium. Once in the bathroom he gave up on the idea of drying his underwear on the hand dryer. Someone was already in there. Another man, a little older than David, was at the sink washing his hands. David just went to the sink, leaned over and stared into the mirror, contemplating whether he should text Pastor Rick that he was feeling ill and begin his long bus journey home.

"You OK? Is 'Leaderfest' getting to you already?" The other man asked.

"Pardon me? What do you mean?"

"Oh, I guess I find 'Leaderfest' a bit much sometimes. How about you? Is that why you're hiding in the bathroom like me?"

"I'm not really hiding. Its just that I fell on the wet grass coming in and my pants are wet. It's not comfortable for me to sit."

"That's terrible. You want to dry them off? We have a dryer here you can use. Come with me. My name's Brett. I'm one of the youth staff here."

"Oh. You have a dryer? That would be great. My name is David. I'm the Worship Pastor at Lachance Community Church. Nice to meet you, Brett."

David followed Brett out of the bathroom and down a hallway and up a flight of stairs to a room Brett unlocked. Inside there was a large commercial washer and dryer and shelves with towels, tablecloths and various other linens. The tablecloths reminded David that he'd yet to complete the tablecloth policy. He hadn't even started it. Brett took a large terrycloth robe down from one of the shelves and tossed it to David.

"Here, you can put this on. We use them when we have baptisms."

David put on the robe and then took off his damp pants and underwear and threw them in the dryer and started it.

"So, how long you been at Lachance?"

"Started in September."

"Is it everything you thought it would be?"

"Not really. I thought it would be more... I don't know exactly. I thought it would be more spiritual. But it's just... I don't know. There's a lot more hassle than I thought there'd be."

"I hear you. I've been here for five years. I thought I'd be changing the world when I came here. I thought I'd be meeting with youth, discipling them, praying with them, leading kids to Christ. But instead, I'm a recreational activity coordinator for rich suburban white kids. I spend more time arranging for gluten-free snacks than I do praying."

"Yeah, I know what you mean. I spend most of my time doing stuff I'm terrible at, and that I hate. And the stuff I'm good at, well, I don't have much time for it," David said.

"Why didn't anyone tell us that before we got into ministry?" Brett laughed and shook his head.

"Do you get along with your senior pastor?" David asked.

"I report to the Director of Youth Ministry who reports to the Executive Pastor who reports to the Senior Pastor. So Pastor Dean, he barely even knows my name."

"Maybe it's better that way."

"Uh oh.. How's your relationship with your Senior Pastor?"

"I'm scared of him, to tell you the truth. I think he wants me to turn our church into a place like this. But we just aren't... we don't have the money or the people or anything. I don't even think the people at our church want to be like this. I don't know what he wants. I'm not sure I'm cut out for this."

"I hear you. After a couple years here, I sort of made peace with the way things really are. I stopped fighting it and just did what they told me to do. Now I'm married and we are expecting a kid. I need this job and don't know what I'd do if I quit. So... here I am, spending my days trying to find the best gluten-free pizza."

The dryer chimed and Dean opened the door. "I'll let you retrieve your underwear, if you don't mind."

David laughed as he pulled his clothes, now warm and dry, out of the dryer. He slid them on under his robe, then took off the robe and tossed it in a hamper next to the washing machine.

"Thanks a lot. You have no idea."

"No problem. It was nice to actually help someone."

"Can I ask you one more thing?" David said.

"Sure, anything."

"Do you guys have a tablecloth policy I could see?"

"You're kidding, right?"

"I wish I was."

"Man... I'm gonna pray for you," Brett said.

They exchanged phone numbers and email addresses and made their way back to the auditorium.

An enormous screen on the stage displayed a live feed from Hickory River Church, located just outside of Nashville. A band made up of studio musicians played a medley of popular worship songs. The video feed alternated between wide shots, showing the light show and thousands of people writhing along to the music, to tight shots of the musicians flawlessly performing. It was a galaxy away from what David experienced on Sunday mornings at Lachance. His reaction wavered between inspiration and depression, finally settling on the latter.

The band finished and the lead pastor of Hickory River Church took the stage. He looked like a CEO of a Fortune 500 company, blue dress shirt, no tie, sleeves rolled up, a two-hundred-dollar haircut and a thousand-dollar smile. He looked like an older, richer version of Pastor Dean.

"How'd you like that band? Yeah!!! I guess they're OK. Yeah, I'm just kidding. Those guys are amazing! Well, I just love this time of year at Leaderfest, where we all get to come together, thousands of us here at Hickory River and thousands more at our hundreds of satellite sites throughout the country and around the world. And we get to become better leaders. Because we are it, people. The church is God's only plan - and y'all have been entrusted with leading the church. Yeah... Yeah... Let that sink in. Let. That. Sink. In."

He continued in this vein for another forty minutes, saying obvious things, repeating them sotto voce, then yelling the same thing. He maintained a nearly hypnotic hold on the audience, both on-site in Nashville and in the auditorium of The Flow.

The session ended, and an emcee announced the different breakout sessions that would occur before lunch. There were seminars on different kids' ministry, youth ministry, web streaming and satellite church models among them. David chose to take the backstage tour of The Flow. He was morbidly curious to find out just how far behind the state of the art he was back at Lachance.

The tech tour was led by the "Technical Pastor" of The Flow.

He'd been a tour manager for various Christian bands and was now in charge of production at The Flow. They began in the tech booth at the back of the auditorium where he rattled off a list of pieces of equipment, pointing at them as he did so. Each piece of gear was accompanied by a price tag. David's mental tally reached half a million dollars before he lost track, and gave up hope as well. How could Lachance ever compete with a place like this? Why would anyone attend Lachance when this hi-tech cathedral of worship-tainment was a short drive away? They moved on to the video system. David stared at one of their four cameras, each costing more than double his annual salary. The Flow estimated that over a hundred thousand people watched them on Sunday mornings during their broadcast of services. A thick cloud of despair formed over David as he finished the tour.

The afternoon sessions featured a Harvard professor, a young woman who started a ministry to ex-cons, and a very theatrical black preacher who was as comfortable quoting scripture as he was making "white" jokes. Through it all, David wondered what he was doing there and how any of it related to his struggles at Lachance. He ran into Pastor Rick as they were leaving the auditorium after the final session.

"David, are you fired up? Man, I am fired up. I have a million ideas. We are going to turn things around. I just know it. You want a ride home?"

David was hoping to have some alone time on the bus ride home, but knew it would be rude to refuse the ride.

"Oh, yeah. Sure. That'd be great."

They headed out to the parking lot, Rick greeting several other pastors on the way out with hearty handshakes and back slaps.

As they pulled out of the parking lot, David was trying to think of positive things to say about the conference.

"Well, what'd you think?" Rick asked.

"Oh, well it was really impressive," David said. Non-specific, positive, safe.

"What impressed you the most?"

"Gosh — it's kind of hard to—"

"Yeah, that's not a fair question. There was so, so much! But you know what? I am ready to lead." Pastor Rick gripped the steering wheel with both hands. "It's been a tough season for us, but I think I have a way for us to get back our momentum. Say, are you Twitter?"

"Am I what? Do you mean am I on Twitter?"

"Yeah, whatever. You Twitter?"

"Yes, I use Twitter, if that's what you mean," David said.

"I took a workshop on social media. We need our church to Twitter. Can you Twitter me this: 'Awesome!'"

"You want me to tweet the word 'Awesome?' Why? How does that—"

"Because today was awesome! That's how it works," insisted Pastor Rick.

"But, I don't really think—"

"C'mon David, in the time you've been talking we could've Twittered a thousand new people. The potential is huge! Huge!"

"Um, OK. There. I did it." David pretended to type something on his phone.

"Great! Maybe tomorrow you can get me set up a Twitter. We'll talk more tomorrow. I'm sure you have a lot to process after such an amazing day. I have the answer to our problems. I'm sure of it. I'm sure of it."

They rode together in silence for a few minutes, David feeling like he needed to break the awkward lull.

"So how long have you known Pastor Dean?"

Pastor Rick's face tightened. David regretted asking.

"He and I were in Bible college together. We both came out here together to Lachance. He was at Ebenezer Baptist and I started at Lachance. That was *twenty* years ago. They changed their name and moved way out here to the suburbs. So, all the rich people leaving town to move out to the suburbs started attending The Flow. More importantly they started giving their offerings to The Flow, so today they have money to burn. Did you see that fountain?"

"Yeah, it was..." David caught himself before he said "hideous," wondering whether Pastor Rick might have liked it.

"Unbelievable," said David.

"Yeah. I mean, I'd never get the funding for something like that. I can only dream."

David inwardly breathed a sigh of relief.

"But that may change soon if things turn out as I hope they will! Here we are. Have a good night. We'll talk about some big plans tomorrow."

David was not looking forward to hearing about the big plans.

"Looking forward to hearing about your plans! Thanks for the ride," said David, smiling his mouth-only smile.

PLAN

"It's the fourth quarter David, and this church needs a touchdown in a very bad way. I couldn't be more serious. Our season is over if we don't pull this off. OK? Are you with me?" said Pastor Rick. He'd been pacing back and forth in front of the whiteboard on his office wall as David sat at the small round table.

"Of course, Pastor. I'm totally with you."

"Good, good. I need to know that. Now, I'm going to let you in on some church business that not everyone knows. Because you need to understand how important it is that we succeed. But you cannot, I mean you absolutely cannot tell anyone about this. Not anybody, understand? Not even your landlord, *whats-his-name.*"

"Chuck."

"Pardon me?"

"My landlord. His name is Chuck," said David, wishing he hadn't mentioned him.

"Right. Well don't tell Chuck."

Yes sir. Not a soul."

"So, this renovation that we completed last year. The way we structured the mortgage means that we have a balloon payment of eighty thousand dollars due in May. If we don't, if we can't make that payment…" Pastor Rick trailed off and stared out the window, grim-faced.

"Then what?"

Pastor Rick shook himself and looked back at David.

"We must make that payment. That's all. That's all you need to know. But you also need to know that we basically have no money as a church. Our offerings aren't covering weekly expenses and we hardly have any cash reserves. David, you understand you must not repeat any of this to anyone, right?"

"Right. So, what are we going to do?"

"David, I was feeling hopeless until we went to Leaderfest. And there, I was inspired by what is possible when people are excited about a vision. Look what they did at The Flow! That building, that new fountain! They aren't any smarter or better than we are. We can do that too. But we need a new dream for this church. And I have it, David. I have it! Do you know what it is, David? Do you know what it is?" Pastor Rick was standing across the table from David, leaning toward him with his hands on the tabletop, fingers splayed out.

"Uh, I don't know. Why don't you tell me?"

"Web streaming!"

"Web streaming? How does that help?" David instantly realized his reaction did not please Pastor Rick. He shrank back in his chair as Pastor Rick reared back and pointed his right index finger at him.

"You are small-minded just like the rest of this church. You can't see beyond whatever is right in front of you." Pastor Rick turned around and picked up a marker on the ledge of the white board and furiously scribbled WEB STREAMING in large letters. The green marker he was using ran out of ink when he reached the A in STREAMING. He threw down the dead marker and finished the word with a blue marker, and then underlined it twice.

"Web streaming! See?" Pastor Rick pointed at the whiteboard. "This is our chance to get up in the big leagues with churches like The Flow. They spent millions on getting their television ministry up and running, but now, thanks to the miracle of the internet, we can reach more people over the Internet than they do on TV. And because it's on the Internet, it's all free!"

He wrote FREE on the whiteboard and circled it.

"Are you sure it's that simple?" David asked.

"Yes, it's that simple. I went to a workshop at Leaderfest and the guy there explained how you do it. And he said it doesn't cost anything."

"But how does it help us pay the mortgage?"

"They really don't prepare you for ministry in Bible school, do they? OK, I will spell this out. We need to have a huge special offering to raise the money for the mortgage payment. But nobody likes to give unless they're excited." Pastor Rick wiggled his hands and rolled his eyes along with the word *excited*. "A special offering for a mortgage payment is not exciting. But a special offering to help us reach a billion people over the internet? *That's* exciting! *That's* what we need! *That's* the new dream."

Pastor Rick leaned across the table again. "Here's what we're gonna do. We're gonna launch our web streaming ministry on Easter Sunday, when we have more people in church than any other Sunday. Then, on that Sunday, we're going to have a special offering to prepare our church for this new worldwide Internet ministry. And *that's* how we get the money."

David could feel that knot in his stomach again. "But is it right to ask people to give for web streaming if we use the money for the mortgage?"

"Look, there's a principle about money that they don't teach you in Bible school. Money is fungible. You know what that means?"

"Fungible? No, what does that mean?"

"It means that money over here," Pastor Rick held his left hand up and shook it in the air, "is interchangeable with money over there," he said, now raising his right hand and shaking it in the air. You can use it for anything you want. It's like, a legal, financial concept. You can look it up. Besides, if we don't make this payment and the church closes down, there won't be any web streaming. It's really all one and the same."

"Is that what'll happen if we don't make the payment?" David asked.

"Hey, I didn't mean that. That was just an example to prove my point about the money. And you remember, this stuff is not to be repeated anywhere. Got it?"

"Right, absolutely," said David. The knot in his stomach began to twist and churn as he grasped how desperate the situation really was for Lachance Community Church. "So who's going to get this web streaming thing going?"

Pastor Rick looked at him incredulously. "Why, *you*, of course! Who else?"

"Me? I don't know the first thing about web streaming."

Pastor Rick began pacing in front of the whiteboard again. His breathing accelerated and then he wheeled around on one heel, leaned over the table, grasped its sides with both hands and looked directly at David.

"It has to be you, David! Who else? You are young and you are tech savvy so you will figure this out. Everything depends on this. Go find your Google and look it up and make this happen. Do you understand? DO. YOU. UN. DER. STAND?"

The knot in David's stomach tightened even more. He didn't understand how he would make this happen. He didn't understand how it would help the church.

"Yes sir. I understand."

Pastor Rick continued leaning over the table toward David, though his eyes drifted up, staring into the distance. He stayed there, not moving for half a minute.

"Is that all?" David asked.

Pastor Rick let go of the table, slowly stood upright, walked back to his desk and sat in his chair. He leaned back and looked up at the ceiling.

"Just one more thing. It has to be Hi-Def. Nobody will take us seriously if it isn't in Hi-Def. That's all," he said, still looking at the ceiling.

David got up from his chair, left Pastor Rick's office and quietly closed the door behind him. Rhonda gave him a concerned look as he walked past her. She'd obviously heard Pastor Rick's raised voice through his door. David walked past her, into his office, closing the door behind him. He sat down at his computer, opened Google and typed "free church web streaming."

David spent the rest of the week learning everything he could about web streaming. He was still confused about frame rates, compression formats and video codecs, but one thing he knew for sure was that this endeavour would be expensive. Saying that web streaming was free was like saying that driving on the roads is free. It's free as long as you already have a car and can pay for gas and insurance.

For Lachance Community Church to begin web streaming, they'd need to purchase a new computer with the right kind of video card, upgrade their Internet service, acquire a Hi-Def video camera with the right kind of output, and subscribe to a video streaming service. This would cost several thousand dollars to start up, plus at least an additional hundred dollars per month. David wondered how he'd explain this to Pastor Rick, who was determined to believe anything involving the Internet was free.

David felt certain there would be no web streaming, no mortgage money, and no job for him once Easter came and went. He consoled himself with the fact that at least he'd have some experience when looking for his next job.

FLOOD OF GOOD NEWS

David stared at the two Tom Lindsey tickets pinned to his bulletin board. In just a few days, he'd be listening to Tom Lindsey. The entire worship band was going: Inq, Sid, Calvin, Carissa, and most important of all, Trisha. David had collected their money and purchased the tickets. He prayed he would be able to sit beside Trisha during the concert. He imagined them, side by side, hands raised as they listened to Tom Lindsey. Their hands might even brush up against one another as they sang together, and then they'd look into each other's eyes and both realize that their love was ordained by God himself.

David's reverie was interrupted by the sound of Pastor Rick's car pulling up to the church. David had to tell him about how much it was going to cost to get web streaming up and running, and he wanted to get it over with quickly. He'd come up with the cheapest plan possible to start a web-streaming ministry for the church, but it was still going to cost a few thousand dollars. He arrived early at church that morning and waited for Pastor Rick to arrive. When he heard his car pull up, David left his office to catch Pastor Rick as he entered the foyer.

"Pastor Rick, can we talk this morning? It's important."

"Sure, sure, David. My door's always open. You know that."

David followed Pastor Rick into his office and took a seat at the round table. Pastor Rick hung his coat on a hook by the door and sat down at his desk.

"What's on your mind, David?"

David said a quick silent prayer and took a deep breath. Just then Pastor Rick's phone rang.

"Hold on, David, let me take this."

David exhaled and tried not to look annoyed.

"No way! Are you kidding me? Dale, that is unbelievable! What must they be doing? Oh man, I wouldn't want to be Dean Goodwin today! That thing was his idea! Oh man, oh man. Yeah! Oh my. Yes, Well, pride goeth before a flood!! Dale, that's incredible. Oh man. Oh man, Yeah, thanks for calling me. OK, see you later." Pastor Rick hung up the phone and looked up at David with a grin.

"Guess what!"

"No idea," David shrugged one shoulder.

"That was Dale. He just heard from one of his contractor buddies. Remember that huge fountain at The Flow?"

"Yeah."

"Well I guess last night one of the valves or something got stuck and the thing overflowed and flooded their new atrium. It all drained down into their sanctuary — carpet, dry-wall, all ruined! They'll be closed for weeks dealing with this! And they still might have mould! Oh man! I can't even think... whoa. I mean, you just have to wonder what God is teaching them. I guess old Dean's luck finally ran out. Yikes!" Pastor Rick was laughing and shaking his head.

"That's terrible," David said.

"Oh, yes, of course. Yes, it *is* terrible. Very bad. I feel awful for them." Pastor Rick's countenance changed from mirthful to serious.

"Hey, the Tom Lindsey concert is supposed to be there on Friday! That's only two days away! What are they going to do?" said David, concerned about his plan to sit next to Trisha and brush their hands together.

"Not our problem." Pastor Rick shrugged.

"Wait, maybe we could have the concert here!" David said.

"I don't know about that. Most of the time those things are more trouble than they're worth."

"No, this is a God-thing! I know it! The reason I came in here was to tell you that before we can start our free web streaming ministry, we'll need to spend a couple thousand dollars on a new computer and a video camera."

Pastor Rick was paying close attention to David now.

"But I was talking to Josh Frayne at The Flow, remember him? Josh Frayne?"

"Oh, yeah. That little jerk. What about him?"

"He said the church was gonna make thousands by hosting that concert. We could host the concert and use some of that money to start up the web streaming, and the rest of it toward the mortgage payment!"

Pastor Rick's eyebrows rose. "Huh, maybe that's worth a try."

"Just leave it to me, Pastor Rick. Leave it to me."

"Ok, David. You got it. Go ahead. See what you can do. Say, is Tom Lindsey on Twitter?"

"Oh yeah! He has thousands of twitter followers," David said.

"Do you think he'll tweet about our church?"

"He might."

"Yeah, the guy at the social media workshop said that one way to leverage it is to get other people to tweet about you to their followers. It would be great if Tom Lindsey tweeted about us! Anyway, go ahead and see what you can do, David."

"You bet!"

David rushed back to his office. He opened Tom Lindsey's web site and clicked on the booking inquiries link where a dialog box opened up. He began typing:

> Hi, I'm the worship pastor at Lachance Community Church in Lachance. You were supposed to have a concert at The Flow this Friday, but they had a flood and now you need a church to host. We can host here. We aren't quite as big as The Flow, but we're available. Email or call me if interested. David@lachancecc.com.

David clicked on send. Seven minutes later he got a response.

> To: david@lachancecc.com
> From: info@tomlindsey.com
> Subject: Friday
>
> Call 316-555-2049.
>
> Thx.

David's eyes widened as he read the message. This was really happening. He called the number from his cell phone.

"This is Paul," said the voice on the other end of the phone.

"Hi, this is David at Lachance Community Church..."

"Right. What's your capacity?"

"My what?"

"Capacity! How many do you seat?"

David was taken aback by Paul's abruptness.

"Well, like, five hundred max, I think," David said.

"Five hundred? Crap. We'll be lucky to break even. Pews or chairs?"

"Chairs."

"Can you remove them?" Paul asked.

"Not really, they're bolted to the floor."

"Crap. We've sold sixteen hundred tickets already. Well, that'll be my problem. Listen, I'm gonna email you our contract and the tech rider. You need to print, sign, scan, and send it back to me right away. Got it?"

"Wow, yeah, you mean you'll have the concert at our church? That's awesome!" David's heart was pounding.

"Yeah, awesome. Just sign the contract and then the tour manager will be in touch," Paul said.

"OK, Will do. Does that mean I get to hang out with Tom Lindsey?"

"What? Oh yeah, for sure. All that is in the contract and the rider. Check your email."

Paul hung up before David could ask anything else. Thirty seconds later, David was printing up the contract. It was thirty pages long and David didn't understand most of it. He did manage to find the section of the rider that mentioned how the worship leader from the hosting church would have the opportunity to meet Tom Lindsey after the concert. After reading this section, David signed the contract, initialed each page, scanned it and sent it back to Paul.

Josh Frayne, eat your heart out, thought David. *I'm gonna meet Tom Lindsey.* David began singing *Mountaintop* in his office. His door opened. It was Pastor Rick.

"So, what's going on?"

"We're having the concert here. I just signed the contract," David said.

"All right! Good work, David. You know, I wondered how things were gonna work out with you, but I like seeing you take this kind of initiative. It's only a bonus that we stole it out from under The Flow! It feels good, doesn't it?"

David grinned back. "It sure does."

LOAD IN

The next morning, David arrived at church at quarter to eight. He had another email from Paul telling him that the crew would arrive shortly after eight. A large cube van pulling a large trailer pulled up to the church. A gruff looking man around thirty, all dressed in black, climbed out of the truck and met David at the door.

"Is there a loading dock?" he asked.

"What? A loading dock? No."

"OK, let me look around."

The man stepped around David and began walking through the foyer toward the auditorium. David followed him and turned on the lights for him.

"Crap." He said as he looked around the room.

David stood there in silence, unsure of what to say.

The man turned to him. "This is gonna be brutal. What's the nearest door to the stage?"

"The main front door."

"Figures. So where is everybody?"

"What do you mean, everybody?" asked David.

"The load-in crew. Where's the load-in crew?"

"Shouldn't you know that?" David said.

The guy stared at David at moment. "You're kidding me, right?"

"Um, not really, no."

"It's in the rider. Did you get the rider?"

"Yes, but—"

"In the rider, you're supposed to have a crew of ten people to help with load-in and load-out. Where are they?"

"I guess I missed that. I could try to call some people?"

"For crying out loud. We did a show last night, drove all night to get here, and you have no help ready. Great. I had two hours of sleep in the last two days and that was in the truck. And now we've got another eighteen-hour day ahead of us and you didn't read the rider. Great."

The other two men had come into the auditorium. One of them was walking on the stage. He called out to David.

"Where's the power hook-up?"

"You mean the outlets? There's two in the floor and two on the back wall," David answered, glad he finally had something helpful to say.

"No, no, no, no. The power hook up. Direct to the panel."

David stared blankly back at him, wondering if this was one of the things he didn't understand from the rider.

"Don't tell me you don't have one!"

"I don't even know what that is," David said.

Now all three of the men were staring at him and shaking their heads. David began to perspire. The first man pulled out his phone.

"Yeah, Paul. Chris here. Total gong show. No load-in crew. No power hook-up. No clue. I haven't slept in two days and I've had it with this crap, Paul."

He looked up at David and realized he was listening, so he turned away and walked toward the stage, continuing his conversation as he went. After five minutes on the phone with Paul, he came and talked to David.

"Here's the plan. You and the guys will unload the gear. I'm going to try to rent a generator we can put out behind the stage and run power in off that. That will come off your rental fee. Got it?"

"Yeah. OK. Whatever it takes." David nodded.

Three hours later, David sat in his office, door closed. His whole body ached from unloading and setting up the lighting and sound gear. His left shoe and sock were off and he was staring at his purple swollen pinky toe, the result of dropping an amplifier case on it. At least the gear was loaded in. It would all have to go back in the truck at the end of the night, but he was sure he'd be able to convince concert goers to stay after and help with that.

A knock came on the door and David gingerly put his foot

down behind his desk. "Come in."

A trim man wearing jeans and a tight-fitting black t-shirt entered David's office. His hair was one of those "carefully messy" cuts and he wore an earring in each ear. Following behind him was a young woman, close to David's age. She wore black jeans, a black T-shirt, round wire-frame glasses and jet-black hair. Her left arm was covered by a tattoo of intertwined roses that originated above the edge of her sleeve and reached down to her elbow. David was staring at her tattoo when the man began to speak.

"Hey, David, is it? Tyler Glass. I'm Mr. Lindsey's personal assistant. Great to meet you. This is Amy. She does merch and is the official tour factotum." The words came out in rapid-fire fashion, not even stopping to breathe.

Amy shook her head at the word 'factotum.'

"Factotum?" said David.

"Yes. From the Latin 'fac' which means 'do', and 'totum' which means everything. She does everything. Logistics, email, social media, merch, fan relations. Whatever we need. Isn't that right, Amy?" Tyler said.

"I'm a gopher," said Amy, ignoring Tyler.

"Oh, nice to meet you both," David said.

"Gotta go over some deets with you, OK? Good news. Found a generator, being delivered as we speak, final cost quite reasonable, you'll still come out ahead, I'm sure. Good? K? Secondly, need some tables for merch setup. Four of them preferably three by eight. One each for CDs, T-shirts, Sponsor Kids and Autographs. Where are they? It was in the rider. Did you read the rider?"

"Oh, yeah. I did read it. I'll get the tables."

"Also can you direct me to Tom's dressing room?"

"Sure."

David got up from his desk and was instantly reminded of his throbbing left pinky toe. He stumbled, sat back down and gingerly slipped sock and shoe over his foot. He stood again, tested the foot, and winced. Tyler and Amy watched him in puzzled silence.

"I had a little accident earlier. Sorry."

Tyler and Amy shrugged and then followed David as he limped down the hallway to a Sunday School room David had set aside for Tom's dressing room.

"Well this is dreary. But I guess it will have to do. Fine," Tyler said.

"When does Tom get here?"

"Mr. Lindsey won't come until just before the show. And when he does arrive here, it is imperative that no one speak to him or approach him. Understood? And where is the nearest bathroom?"

"Down the hall, two doors down."

"Nobody uses that bathroom once he arrives. Got it? And stage access, also down there? OK. Nobody allowed back here at all. Got it?"

"Sure, I guess so. But, like, nobody can even talk to him? Like even just say, Hi?"

"Listen, what was your name again?"

"David."

"Right. Listen, David, Mr. Lindsey loves his fans so much, and loves meeting them so much that if we allowed them any access to him before the show, he would spend all his time and energy being with them. And then he wouldn't be at his best when showtime came. And everyone who bought a ticket to come tonight deserves to see Mr. Lindsey at his very best. This way, everybody wins. I know it seems harsh, but I don't make the rules. We really are excited to have this opportunity to partner in ministry with you. It's just the business. That's all. OK? Great! You can show Amy the tables."

David left the room and hobbled back to the foyer, Amy following him. She seemed slightly embarrassed by Tyler's manner.

"This your first time hosting something like this?" she asked.

"Isn't it obvious? I feel like I don't know what I'm doing. Here are tables. You need four?" David asked.

"Yeah."

David helped her move them into place in the foyer. She wanted the child sponsor table to be the most prominently displayed.

"I think it's great that Tom is helping promote child sponsorship. I mean, I'm sure it means he sells less of his own merchandise because people decide to sponsor a kid instead."

"Well, yeah, I suppose. But the truth is, he gets a hundred and fifty bucks from The Child Hunger Foundation for each kid that gets sponsored at one of his concerts. So it's actually the biggest money maker on the whole tour."

"A hundred and fifty bucks?" David was shocked. "That doesn't seem right."

"I don't make the rules. That's just the business. Probably most of these kids wouldn't get sponsored in the first place if it wasn't for Tom's concert, so look at it that way. Everybody wins." Amy waved her hands in mock celebration.

"But shouldn't you be upfront with people about where their money is actually going?"

"I don't make the rules. It's just the business. Besides, kids get sponsored, Tom's tour gets paid for, fans feel like they're doing a good deed. Everybody wins," she said flatly.

"I guess so."

"Can I have your cell number if I need anything else?" Amy asked.

They exchanged numbers and David helped her finish setting up the tables.

By five o'clock, the church was humming with activity. A construction rental company had delivered a generator the size of a minivan to the church. It was positioned in the back of the church parking lot near the rear door. The power cables weren't long enough to make it down the hallway to the stage door, so the gruff sound man had made a hole in the wall with a hammer to pass the cord directly to the stage. When David protested, the sound man told him, "Next time read the rider. Besides this is easy to patch up. In fact, you should probably leave the hole for the next concert."

David told himself there'd be no next concert if it was up to him.

Presently, David was being interrogated by Paul about the capacity of the auditorium.

"So, if people don't actually sit in their seats, we can get maybe a thousand people in here, you think?"

"That's not really safe, is it?"

"There's nobody from your church who works for the fire department, or the city, is there?"

"Not that I know of."

"OK, that's good. We'll just figure out what to do when people get here. Leave that to me. Things are coming together. We're in good shape, I think. Well, actually it's a total disaster! But... Rock-n-Roll! You know what I'm saying?" Paul laughed.

David wasn't finding it humorous. As Paul continued to talk about the tour, David wondered how this night was going to turn out. He was worried about all the people they were trying to fit into the church, about explaining the hole in the wall to Pastor Rick and wondering how much the generator rental was going to cost. He wondered if there would be enough money left over to cover the cost of the equipment he needed to start the web streaming.

"So I think that's it. I gotta get some other stuff done," Paul said.

"When does Tom get here?"

"Oh, Mr. Lindsey will arrive right before the show starts. But don't worry. He'll be here."

"And I get to meet him? After the concert?"

"Yes! And he's really looking forward to connecting with you."

"He is?" David was embarrassed by the swell of emotion sweeping through him as he thought of Tom looking forward to meeting him.

"Oh yeah, of course. Mr. Lindsey loves connecting with the local worship pastors. I mean, you guys are such a big part of his ministry. If you weren't leading his songs in church, he wouldn't be where he is today. Just the church copyright royalties he generates make much of this ministry possible. You are part of the Tom Lindsey team. Don't forget that, David. You make this all possible."

David was exhausted already, before the concert even began. He was a little surprised at what he was learning about the business side of ministry, but was able to convince himself that it really was the best for everybody. In any case, he looked forward to meeting Tom Lindsey. What a great opportunity. He thought of the smug worship pastors at The Flow, and how much they'd like to be trading places with him now. It felt good. He was part of the Tom Lindsey team. He would have a chance to see and interact with greatness up close tonight. And despite the things he wasn't comfortable with, the money would help him get the equipment he needed for the web streaming, and to save Lachance Community Church. It was worth it, he told himself. It was all worth it.

CONCERT

People started arriving and lining up outside the church doors a full two hours before the show was to start. Word had spread that tickets had been over-sold, so people were anxious to get in. Paul reassured David that everything would be fine. David chose to trust him. At a quarter to seven, a black Lincoln Town car from a car service arrived and pulled around to the back door. David watched from his office window as Tyler rushed out to open the door. Out stepped Tom Lindsey, in the flesh. A wave of nervousness and excitement washed over David. Tyler led him in the back door. Tom would be doing his sound check shortly, so David slipped into the auditorium.

Tom walked to the stage and held his arms out at his sides as one of the crew members came to him with his guitar and put it on him. Tom walked up to the mic and spoke.

"Check, 1, 2, Check-a-chick-a how's it soundin' boys?... Man, this place is kind of a dump. Is this the best church we could find? It's tiny. Are we gonna break even tonight? How are we, ready for a song?"

David tried not to take his comments on the church personally.

The band had been on stage waiting for Tom. The drummer launched into *Mountaintop*. Tom sang the first two lines and then said, "Are we good?"

The reply came from the back of the room where the sound board was setup.

"All good. Thank you, Mr. Lindsey."

Tom held his arms out as before and the crew member removed his guitar. Without another word, Tom returned through the door at the back of the platform and disappeared.

David went back into the foyer where he ran into Pastor Rick.

"Everything set, David?"

"I think so. Paul says we're in good shape."

"I see they brought a generator. I guess it's gonna be a powerful show!" Pastor Rick laughed at his own joke.

"Yeah, well we didn't have the right kind of electrical hookup thing so they rented it. It will come out of our end."

"Oh. How'd that happen?"

"It's my fault. It will be a few hundred bucks, but we should still come out ahead by a couple thousand dollars, I think."

"I guess if that's the worst thing that goes wrong tonight we're in pretty good shape. I knew you could handle this. I'm looking forward to a great concert!"

"Yeah, me too. I can't wait for it to start so I can finally relax. Plus, I get to meet Tom after the concert. He loves to meet local worship pastors when he tours!"

"Really? That's great. You're meeting right here?"

"Yes, he's using the pre-school Sunday School room as his dressing room. I get to hang out with him there for a bit after the show."

"Well that's just great! I'm happy for you."

After the sound check, the doors opened. The first few hundred people pushed their way into the auditorium and occupied every seat. By some miracle, Paul managed to squeeze all but a couple hundred people inside. Every square foot of floorspace was occupied. To those who didn't make it into the auditorium, Paul offered T-shirts and CDs as compensation. Failing that, he signed the back of their ticket and gave them an address to mail it to for a full refund. Many of the fans were irate, but most accepted the explanation.

At a quarter to eight, David was standing in the back of the auditorium as the lights went down. A nervous murmur emanated from the crowd. Suddenly bright lights shone directly into the crowd, blinding everyone as the band began the thunderous opening to Tom's debut single *You are my Rock*. David's pulse quickened as he anticipated seeing Tom Lindsey and hearing his voice sing out the thunderous opening lines. This was going to be awesome.

Someone was shaking his arm and calling his name. Paul had a hold on David's arm and was dragging him toward the door. At first David resisted, but Paul yanked his arm so hard it hurt. David was out the back door of the auditorium just as he heard Tom Lindsey's vocals begin the song.

"What is it now?" David felt agitated to be missing the opening of the concert.

"You have a problem. And don't give me that look. You're here to work, not listen to the concert. I was looking all over for you."

Paul was angry and still had a grip on David's arm.

"What is it?"

"The toilets are overflowing!"

"The toilets?"

"Yes. There's crap everywhere in both bathrooms. You have to DO something. There's a thousand people in here and we need working bathrooms."

"Well, what am I supposed to do?"

"It's *your* church! You are in charge! Fix it! Call somebody! Do something!" Paul gave David's arm a shake before letting it go.

David turned toward the back of the foyer where the bathrooms were. He saw two women running out of the bathroom with their hands over their noses, screaming. He froze. What was he supposed to do? Mop. He better mop up the mess.

He ran down the hallway toward the custodial closet. One of the guys from the truck guarded the hallway where Tom's dressing room was. He called out toward David as he ran toward the closet. "You can't come down here." "Get outta my way!" David screamed as he pushed the man's outstretched arm aside. "And you should help me too. We have an emergency."

"Nah *You* have an emergency. I gotta stay here."

David grabbed the mop and bucket, ran back to the bathrooms, and banged on the ladies' room door.

"Anybody in there?" He didn't wait for an answer but went in. He'd never actually been in the lady's room. It was a lot nicer than the men's room. It had wallpaper and there were fake flowers on the counter between the sinks. An inch of dirty water swirled around the floor. In one of the stalls, the toilet was still running and overflowing onto the floor. A woman came into the bathroom, saw David standing there and screamed.

"Sorry... these toilets aren't working. There's another bathroom in the basement," he said.

She backed out without saying a word. David's skin began to crawl from the smell and from sheer panic. Water had made its way to the door and was streaming into the hallway. His mind raced, trying to figure out what to do. Then he remembered Wayne, contractor and all-around church fix-it man. He pulled out his phone and called Wayne. As it was ringing, he walked to the door of the bathrooms and held up his hand and waved off another woman wanting to enter. David checked the men's room and was horrified to see the toilets overflowing there as well.

"Wayne here, who's this?"

"Wayne, it's David. I'm at the church and all the toilets are overflowing! What do I do?"

"What? What's going on there? *All* the toilets?"

"Yes. All the toilets! Can you come here and help me? The Tom Lindsey Concert is happening and there's like a thousand people here and the toilets are flooding!"

"I can be there in about half an hour. The septic must be clogged. Here's what you gotta do. First, shut off the main water. You know how to do that?"

"No! I'm a pastor, not a freakin' plumber!" David shouted.

"For crying out loud! You're a grown man, you should know how to shut off the water!"

"Wayne, just tell me what to do, you can lecture me later!"

"OK, go down to the utility room. You know where that is? Right in the back, there are some pipes. There's a big valve, you can't miss it. Turn it off - clockwise. Got it?"

"I'm on my way. Stay on with me."

"I'm getting in my truck. I'm on my way. I'll keep you on speaker."

David walked back down the hallway toward the utility room. He gave a murderous look to the man guarding the hall, who stepped aside and let David pass. He found the room and fumbled for his keys to open the door. Thankfully, his master key worked.

"I'm in. I think I found it." David put his phone on speaker, set it on a shelf of cleaning supplies and tried to turn the valve. It wouldn't budge.

"It won't move!"

"Yes it will, use your muscles."

David wrapped both hands around the faucet and cranked with

all his strength. Finally, it started moving and David turned until he felt it stop hard. His hands felt like the skin had been ripped off.

"I turned it all the way. Will the toilets work now?"

"What? No, the toilets won't work now! You need water for toilets to work. That just stops the overflowing. You need to see if you can unclog the septic. Grab the shovel in the janitor's closet and a flashlight. You need to go outside to the tank access and open it up and have a look inside."

"What? I don't know what you're talking about. What's outside?"

"The septic tank access! Don't you remember the first day I met you and drove you to Lachance? I explained everything about septic systems to you. Don't you remember anything I told you?"

"Well, excuse me, but NO! I don't remember. Just tell me what to do."

"You need to head out to the back. On your left, you'll find a round cement access cover with a steel handle on it. You need to remove that lid and try to see what's blocking the pipe. Sometimes you can just tap the inlet pipe and clear the crap around it and it will start flowing again. I've done it a few times. Trust me."

"There's no shovel, just a rake."

"A rake is fine. Just get out there."

"I'll let you know when I find the lid thing."

David ran down the back hallway. He could hear the concert through the walls. The singing of the crowd was as loud as the band. Seething with rage, he kicked open the back door, turned on the flashlight and scanned the ground for the septic system lid. He found the lid, set down the rake, and pulled on the handle with one hand. It didn't budge.

His hand burned with pain, still raw from shutting off the water. He set down his phone and the flashlight and used two hands, to no effect. He squatted over the access cover, pulled on the handle with both hands, arms, legs, back, all straining. Finally, the lid moved up a few inches. About to lose his balance, David let go of the lid and it settled right back down into place. His right hand was scraped and bleeding. He swore under his breath, but at least he knew he could get it moving. He tried again., This time, it came up easier. He pulled and slid the lid off to the side of the hole. He retched as the odor from the tank hit him like a punch in the nose. He fumbled for his phone.

"Wayne, you there?"

"Yeah, I'm here."

"I got the lid open. It stinks like crazy."

"Yeah, well, what do you expect? Now, here's the trick. There's an inlet pipe that you need to unclog. Just loosen everything around it with the rake until it starts flowing again. You got it?"

"I think so."

David stood over the tank and looked down at the layer of dark scum. He located the inlet pipe, then looked behind him for the rake. He took one step toward where he thought he left the rake. He felt the stab of the rake's teeth through his injured left foot and realized the handle was now rapidly swinging up through the darkness, directly at his head. He jumped sideways and the rake handle harmlessly swung past him to the left. His feet, however, did not find the ground, but instead passed directly through the opening of the septic tank.

David's every muscle snapped taut as he realized he was chest deep in liquified excrement. His nose and eyes burned. Both of his arms were outside of the hole. He reached out and tried to lift himself. The ground was loose, and he couldn't find anything to grip. His feet were stuck to the bottom of the tank, mired in sludge. He tried to call out, but he was shivering violently, gagging whenever he tried to draw breath.

Trying to call for help would be pointless with the music from the concert so loud, even through the walls of the church. The liquid had fully soaked through his clothes, almost up to his armpits. David waited. He looked up and saw the stars in the night sky. He could hear Tom Lindsey talking now, introducing the next song. Then he heard the opening chords of *Mountaintop* that he'd listened to hundreds of times, that he himself had played hundreds of times. The crowd roared as it recognized the song, then quickly fell silent to listen to Tom sing out.

"You lift me to a highest place
I see the beauty of your face
My love for you will never stop
Because You, You take me to the Mountaintop"

David began to cry. Angry, resentful tears welled up in his eyes and he began to sob. Then he heard a gurgling sound coming from the inlet pipe in front of him, a rush of air as the clog in the pipe gave way. A torrent of water, urine and excrement rushed through the pipe, against David's chest, rising up, splashing up over his shoulders into his face. The level rose higher. David gagged and coughed and flailed his arms, trying to get away from the deluge. After what felt like hours, the flow slowed to a trickle. The level fell back down to below his chin, but he was soaked head to toe, stunned, motionless, helpless.

David heard a truck coming, saw the beams of the headlights through the steam rising over his head from the septic tank. He could hear the door open.

"What the hell happened. I mean heck happened? What did you do, how did you... what on earth?"

Wayne knelt and reached out his hands toward David, then pulled them back when he saw David's slimy hands. He looked around, found the rake, and extended it to David. David grabbed on to the teeth of the rake with his sore hands.

Wayne pulled. The rake slipped through David's hands. He was sure his hands were cut and bleeding now and he was too weak to hold on. Wayne went back to his truck and came back with a rope. He made a large loop on the end and fed it around David's back, under his arms. David fell limp as Wayne pulled him up out of the hole.

David got up on his hands and knees and then slowly stood. His left shoe was still lodged in the sludge at the bottom of the tank.

"Oh man, this is bad. We gotta get you cleaned up. Oh man, this is bad. Are you OK? What happened?" Wayne asked.

David was hurting, freezing, gagging, mortified, embarrassed, soaked, and enraged. The smell still made him retch, between sobs. He was still crying. He hated that most of all, crying in front of Wayne like this.

Wayne looked embarrassed to see David like this and turned to peer into the hole. "Good news. It looks like you cleared the blockage, but..." his voice trailed off. "Holy crap, we gotta get you cleaned up. Get in the truck"

David slowly walked toward the truck. With each step, the liquid dripped and oozed down his torso and legs. He reached for the door.

"What are you thinking?" Wayne reached around David and slammed the passenger door shut.. "I didn't mean inside the truck. You gotta ride in the back. I can't let you sit inside like that."

Suffering yet more indignity, David climbed into the back of the truck next to some lumber and leaned up against the tool case mounted near the cab.

"Don't touch that! Just... don't touch anything. We'll go to my shop and clean you up. Do me a favor and duck down in case a cop sees you and pulls me over. I don't wanna get a ticket."

The concert still reverberated through the church walls, Tom Lindsey and his fans oblivious to David's ordeal. David thought of ending it all by jumping out of the moving truck, but figured they weren't going fast enough to kill him. He stayed down, enduring every bump in the road, shivering in the filth. After what seemed like hours they reached Wayne's shop, a small corrugated metal building illuminated by a single bright lamppost. Wayne pulled up in front of it and stopped.

"You can get out," he called as he opened the large garage door and went inside. David struggled to climb out of the back of the truck. His whole body screamed in agony.

Wayne came back out of the garage holding a hose. "Take your clothes off."

"What?"

"Look, you gotta get outta those clothes. I got a shower in the shop you can use, but the clothes have to come off first. I'll hose you down out here."

Something inside of David broke apart and crumbled, and it was as though David's consciousness detached from his body. He watched himself struggle to remove his stinking soaked shirt, pulling it over his head, smearing more putrid liquid over his face, inducing another fit of gagging. He observed his hands unbuttoning, unzipping his pants and removing them, tossing them away on top of his shirt. He watched his remaining sock and his underwear come off and be tossed with the rest of his clothes, until his body stood there shivering and naked, hands folded in front of him, as if there were any shame left to cover.

"Listen, I'm sorry about this," Wayne said as he turned on the hose. A jet of freezing water hit David's body and consciousness snapped back into his brain. He jerked and writhed until Wayne came closer to make sure he'd thoroughly rinsed him off.

"OK, the shower's this way. I got some coveralls and a pair of rubber boots you can borrow. They're on the hook outside the door. Take your time."

As the hot shower began to warm him up, David started to feel like himself again. He scrubbed and rinsed and scrubbed again, rinsing eyes, ears, and everywhere there might still be some residue of filth. The cut on David's hand stung. His toe throbbed. David finished, dried off with paper towels and put on the coveralls. They were ridiculously large on him. The rubber boots were also too big. He felt like a sad circus clown, coming out of the bathroom.

Wayne was waiting for him "Well, that's better. How you doing now?"

"Better. Thank—"

But before he could say 'you', he vomited. Then the floor came up to meet him and everything went black.

When David came to, he found himself in the passenger seat of Wayne's truck as it pulled out of the driveway of the shop. "Where are we going?"

"I'm taking you to the hospital. You need to see a doctor, man. You need some antibiotics or something," Wayne said.

"No, take me back to church. Now."

"What? You need to see a doctor. No, I'm taking you to the hospital. You just took a swim in liquid sh–"

"SHUT UP, WAYNE! TAKE ME TO THE CHURCH! I can go see a doctor tomorrow. After all I went through I am NOT going to miss my chance to meet Tom Lindsey. So help me God, Wayne, you take me to the church right now. You understand?"

"OK, OK, but if you get dysentery, don't go blaming me. You understand? Do you have any clue what happened to you tonight?"

"Wayne, nothing happened to me tonight. You understand? This never happened. It never happened. You understand? No one can know. You keep this a secret. Just take me back to church. I am going to meet with Tom Lindsey so help me God, just like this never happened. You understand?"

Wayne looked over at David for a moment, then slowed down the truck and made a U-turn.

"I might have already told some people, out of concern for you, David. So it might be too late for keeping secrets. But whatever. We'll go back to church."

When they arrived, concertgoers were flooding out the doors. David had missed the entire show. Wayne drove over the curb and onto the grass, up to the side door to avoid the jam of cars exiting the parking lot. David got out of the truck and gallumped in his oversize boots and coveralls through the side door and to his office. He got puzzled looks from everyone who saw him but David chose to ignore them.

Once in his office, he changed into a fresh pair of pants and pulled on one of the spare shirts he now kept in his filing cabinet. He even had some old sneakers in the drawer to replace the rubber boots. He left his office and Trisha came running across the foyer. She was wearing rubber gloves and holding a bucket.

"David! Are you OK?"

"I'm fine. Why? What's with the gloves?"

"Wayne called my dad. He said you, um, had an accident. Dad came right away. He texted me and we've been trying to clean up the bathrooms. Are you OK?" She took off one of her gloves and reached out to touch his arm. David fought back tears.

"I'm fine," he said through clenched teeth, unable to look in her eyes.

"Have you seen a doctor?"

"I'm going to see Tom Lindsey." He turned and walked away from her, afraid he'd begin crying again if he stood there any longer, her hand on his arm. He got to Tom's makeshift dressing room where one of the guys from the truck stood by the door.

"When do I meet Tom? I'm ready now."

"Whoa. Yeah. Wait here, I'll see." He poked his head through the door, said something David couldn't hear. There was a reply, and then he turned back to David. "Wait. A few minutes."

David needed a few minutes to compose himself. He was still seething with anger. Anger at falling in the septic tank, anger at his humiliation in front of Wayne, which was bad enough, but that Wayne called Bill and now Trisha knew as well. He was angry that he'd not heard any of the concert, but now he had a chance for something even better: a chance to meet Tom Lindsey. He was not going to lose this, too.

BRUSH WITH GREATNESS

The man at the door held up one hand to David as he opened the door a crack and looked inside the room. Then he opened the door all the way open. "They're ready for you."

"Thanks." David took a deep breath and entered. Tyler and Amy were sitting at a table in the middle of the room.

"Where's Tom?" David asked.

"Oh, don't worry, Mr. Lindsey will be joining us soon. Have a seat, David. While we wait for Tom, I have an exciting opportunity to discuss with you." Tyler motioned to a chair opposite himself and Amy.

"That's great, but when does Tom get here?" David asked.

Tyler ignored the question. "David, I've been talking to people around here and they tell me you are a very gifted worship artist."

"Really? Wow. That's really nice." Finally, something from this nightmare event was going right.

"In fact, the way people talk about you, and from what I pick up from you, your confidence, intelligence, and presence, well... it wouldn't surprise me if you became the next Tom Lindsey."

"What? Wow! I had no idea! Well I guess I had *some* idea, I mean, I do believe that God has given me a gift, but really, the next Tom Lindsey?" David tried not to blush.

"In fact, you remind me very much of a young Tom Lindsey, the one who just a few years ago was a worship leader at a church a lot like this one. And you know what started him on the path to where he is today?"

"No, I don't," David said.

"He started writing songs. David, I bet that you write songs. You do, don't you, or at least I'd bet that you want to write songs.

Am I right?"

"Absolutely! I mean, I only sort of noodle around, but man, I would love to be able to write songs like Tom," David said.

"David, I'm amazed. Hearing you say that, well, you sound exactly like a young Tom Lindsey, before he got where he is today, by writing great worship songs. Well, David, what if I told you that there was a way for you to accelerate that song writing process, so that you could start writing great worship songs as early as this week? Would you be interested in that?"

"Of course I would," David said.

"I knew you would be, David. And that's why I am really excited to offer you an exclusive membership to the Worship-XT network. It stands for Worship Extreme Toolkit. This is a brand-new resource kit and network to help you craft powerful worship songs just like *Mountaintop*. This system combines a state-of-the-art song composition heuristic software modeller, with a database of today's most popular worship lyric formulations. Using the simple and elegant user interface, you simply enter your chords, your melody contour and lyrics, and within seconds, Worship-XT produces a rating out of a hundred on your song, along with suggestions on improving any non-compliances within your song. You don't even have to read music. It's that easy. And you become a part of the Worship-XT community."

Tyler produced a glossy brochure from a satchel beside his chair and slid it across the table to David.

"Wow. Well sure, that sounds amazing. I've never heard of anything like this, how does it work? Can you really write a worship song with a computer program?" David asked.

"It is very sophisticated technology, for sure. But just let me tell you this, David. We entered *Mountaintop* into Worship-XT, and do you know what its score was? It scored ninety-nine out of a hundred. Ninety-nine. So, obviously Worship-XT recognizes greatness."

"So Tom Lindsey wrote *Mountaintop* with the Worship-XT?" David asked.

"Many songs, just like *Mountaintop* have been written with it," Tyler said.

"But not *Mountaintop*?"

"David, I assure you that if Tom Lindsey were writing *Mountaintop* today, he'd be using the Worship-XT. Now David, would you like to sign up for the Worship-XT? We can do it right now, it only takes a few seconds and then you are on your way to becoming the next Tom Lindsey. What do you say? I just need a credit card and off we go."

"Well how much is it?" David asked.

"Before I answer that, consider this, David. A top ten worship song can bring in thousands of dollars a month in royalties from airplay and church copyright licensing. And, whenever a song scores over ninety out of hundred on the Worship-XT scoreboard, I receive an instant notification to review that song, where I can pitch it to Tom Lindsey. Do you know how much in royalties you would earn if Tom Lindsey recorded one of *your* songs on his next album?"

"How much?" asked David.

"A lot! So David, how much do you think something like that is worth?"

"Oh man, I don't know."

"Just two hundred and ninety nine dollars..."

"What? Two-ninety-nine? Oh man, I'm sorry, Tyler, but I just can't swing that. I'm barely scraping by."

"David, think of all you're getting for only two-ninety-nine per month," Tyler said.

"Per Month? Oh man, that's totally out of the question! I'm sorry. No way."

"David, the price will never be this low. I can only offer you this price because you hosted the concert. Once we leave tonight, this price won't be available any more. You know, a lot of guys have their church cover the subscription price. You can sign up with me now, and then talk to your church about covering the cost. How about it?"

David was reminded of one of the few vacations he took as a child with his grandmother. She'd received a phone call telling her she won a free week at a lakefront resort. It turned out to be a time-share condominium sales scheme. He and his grandmother had to attend daily high-pressure sales meetings that lasted for hours.

"Look, Tyler. As much as I'd like to, there's no money to pay for it."

"Well, one option is for us to take the money you earned as the hosting venue and put that toward your subscription. How about we do that?"

"We need that money for something else."

"David, you know the guys at The Flow are really excited about starting their subscription. Now, they aren't getting the same deal you are, as host church, but really, David, do you want to miss out on what they're getting? Don't you deserve the same?"

David looked down at the table, then across at Amy. She'd been sitting motionless with her eyes down at the floor during the entire meeting.

"The answer is no. I'll just have to write my songs the old-fashioned way. When do I get to meet Tom?"

"Well, David," Tyler said. "What Mr. Lindsey really loves is connecting with young worship leaders who are serious about their craft. And he will be *really* impressed if I tell him that you've signed up for Worship-XT. So, how about it?"

"The answer is no." David slid the brochure back across the table to Tyler.

"David, I probably shouldn't do this, but because I'm so impressed with your potential, I can offer you the first month for free with your twelve month commitment," Tyler said.

"No. No. No! Now, am I gonna get to meet Tom Lindsey or do I have to go find him myself?"

Tyler exhaled and looked down at the table. He picked up the brochure and returned it to his satchel. "Wait here. I'll be back with Mr. Lindsey." Tyler got up and left the room.

David looked across the table at Amy. She looked up at him and shrugged.

A minute later, Tyler returned with Tom Lindsey, who had changed into a tracksuit and ball cap. He was looking at his phone as Tyler placed a chair at the end of the table for him to sit in. He sat down, still looking at his phone. Tyler sat back in his chair opposite David, who was staring in awe at his idol.

Tom Lindsey was still looking at his phone.

David was mentally rehearsing what he would say, about what a great role model and inspiration Tom had been all these years, how *Mountaintop* had given him hope in some very desperate times, and how honored David felt to partner with Tom in ministry like this.

"Mr. Lindsey, there's someone I'd like you to meet," Tyler said.

David took a deep breath. Just then the door to the room burst open. David turned around to see Pastor Rick barging into the room. He looked back at Tom Lindsey, who finally looked up from his phone to see who was there.

"Hey everybody, I'm Rick Avery, Senior Pastor here at Lachance Community Church. We are so, so glad to have been able to host you tonight. Great job, everybody. And Tom Lindsey, welcome, welcome, welcome!" He marched over and began pumping Tom's hand while he talked. "You know, the mountain song is our favourite song here at Lachance. We just love it! Now, things are really exciting here at our church. In fact, we are about to launch live web-streaming on Easter Sunday in just under a couple of months.

"And Tom, I know you are very big on Twitter, and I thought it would be really cool if you could make a tweet on Easter Sunday about our web stream! Boy, it would mean a lot to us. So, I just wrote it down here."

Pastor Rick released Tom's hand and reached into his pocket. "'Check out what I'm watching,' with a link to our web site. I wrote it on this yellow sticky note, so you can just leave it in your day timer for Easter Sunday. So, what do you say? It would be pretty cool if you did that, hey?"

Pastor Rick was holding the sticky note out to Tom Lindsey. Tom didn't take it, but rather looked over at Tyler and shook his head. After holding his hand out for a few seconds, Pastor Rick set the sticky note down on the table in front of Tom.

"I'll just leave this right there for you. Again, great job you guys!" Pastor Rick backed away from the table and left the room.

David looked back at Tom Lindsey, who was now standing up.

Tyler spoke next. "Mr. Lindsey has a plane to catch, so that is all we have time for. Amy, grab our things and I'll meet you in the van."

David sat in his chair, stunned as he watched Tom and Tyler walk out together. Then, with a jolt, he rose from his chair and bolted out of the room, determined to speak to Tom. He sprinted down the hallway, out the emergency exit to the back of the parking lot just in time to see the Lincoln Town Car pull out onto the road and drive away.

David's rage returned. He went back inside the church to the room where they'd all met. Amy was still inside, packing everything up in a roller suitcase.

"What was all that about?" David asked.

"What can I say, David? I'm sorry. I don't make the rules. There's nothing I can do about it. It's just the business." She left the room.

David slumped down in the chair at the end of the table, where Tom Lindsey had been sitting. Anger continued to swirl inside him. He realized how exhausted he was, and then his nausea returned. He lurched to the corner of the room toward the wastebasket. He fell to his knees, grasped the basket with both hands, and closed his eyes as his stomach heaved violently.

Nothing came up. His empty stomach wrenched two more times before his body slowly relaxed. He opened his eyes and looked down in the wastebasket. It was completely empty, except for Pastor Rick's crumpled up sticky note.

David got up and walked back to the foyer in a daze. Bill, Trisha and Inq were there, still cleaning. Trisha came right up to him.

"How was your meeting with Tom Lindsey?"

"I don't want to talk about it," David said, through clenched teeth.

"Oh, so, not good?"

"I didn't even get to talk to him."

"What? Why not? You were in there a long time."

"They tried to sell me a computer program to write worship songs, then Pastor Rick barged in. Then it was over. I missed the whole concert. I didn't get to talk to Tom Lindsey. I don't know what just happened."

Inq chimed in. "Well you didn't miss much of a concert if you ask me. The music simply lacks the intricacy and adventurousness of progressive rock. Dull stuff. In any case, I think we've done as much as we can with the bathrooms for tonight."

"Well thanks for helping out with that," David said.

Trisha reached out and touched David's arm again. "I'm sorry tonight didn't turn out how you wanted."

David looked at her and forced himself to smile. They put away the cleaning supplies and left together, Inq offering to drive David home.

When David got home, he took another shower just to be on the safe side. Then he sat in bed, remembering what it felt like to have Trisha touching his arm. Then he reached over the nightstand for his laptop, opened it up and Googled "symptoms of dysentery."

SERMON PREP

The next morning David rose and inspected himself in the mirror for signs of dysentery. Finding none, he stepped into the shower. He could still smell the remnants of the previous night's disaster as he rinsed his hair. He washed it three times just to be safe.

He walked to church to find Wayne and Pastor Rick talking in the foyer. They stopped when they saw David, and then continued in hushed tones. David went to his office, took off his coat and sat in his chair. Pastor Rick arrived moments later.

"You, uh. You OK? Wayne told me what happened."

"I think so."

"Have you been to see a doctor? Wayne said you didn't want to go last night."

"No, I haven't been. I think I feel fine."

"Well, listen. It's your call if you want to go to a doctor. But, hey, listen… if you do, it's probably a good idea if you don't mention anything about it happening at work. I mean, it just creates a whole lot of extra paperwork that can be a real hassle. You know what I mean? And it's not really like what happened was part of your regular duties, so it really wasn't a workplace incident. You know what I mean?"

"You want me to lie?"

"No, no, no, David, that is not what I'm saying. Just, if they don't ask, you needn't mention it, that's all."

"Got it."

Pastor Rick sounded relieved. "Good. Well, I'm glad you're feeling all right. Oh, one more thing."

"Yeah?"

"Next week, the Missus and I are going to Florida. My in-laws have a time-share down there that they can't use... anyway, I'd like you to preach next week. You up for that?"

"Uh, yeah. I'd love to."

David was surprised to be asked to preach. Pastor Rick guarded his pulpit vigilantly. He felt honored that Pastor Rick considered him worthy of taking his place in the pulpit.

"That's great! We don't really have the budget to bring in someone from outside. So if you preach, it saves us the money for an honorarium."

"Oh. Well, I'm glad I could save us some money." David's heart sank, even as bitter thoughts formed. *Why should I be surprised?*

"OK. Thanks, David. Things are looking up!"

For you, they are. For you, thought David. After last night, Pastor Rick was more concerned about the hassle of a workplace accident than he was with David's well-being. And he only asked David to preach to save money. David felt like the hired help.

Still, he was intrigued by the opportunity to preach and thankful for a week of respite from Pastor Rick while he was away in Florida.

David spent the rest of the day trying to figure out how to web stream the services for free and to come up with ideas for his sermon. He was unsuccessful on both counts, but knew he still had time to figure these things out. He packed up his knapsack, put on his coat, and got ready to go home. In the foyer he saw Trisha. The sight of her lifted him out of his funk. He took a deep breath and put on a smile.

"David! How are you? I mean, really. How are you?" said Trish.

"Oh, I'm OK. I feel fine. What are you doing here?"

"Oh, I forgot my sweater here at the concert last night. Have you been to see a doctor?"

"No, but I don't feel sick at all. I'm fine. Really."

David realized this would be the perfect opportunity to ask her out to dinner. Conditions were perfect. If she had plans and said no, there'd be no embarrassment. He was just on his way to get dinner and it would only be polite to ask her to join him. If she said *yes*, oh, if she said *yes*, to have an hour, or even more, alone with Trisha. What would he say? What would they talk about? He realized he had been staring into space for several seconds now, playing out these various scenarios in his mind.

"Um, David?"

"Yes." This would be the moment. He'd take this opportunity to ask her to dinner, casually, comfortably, at ease. "You wanna go grab a coffee?"

Oh, why did you say coffee? It's five-thirty. You coward!.

"Uh, well, sure. Beans of Production? I can drive."

"Sounds good. I really need a coffee."

I am so dumb, David thought. *Why did I say that?* On the way, he tried to salvage his earlier bumbling and upgrade their coffee to dinner. "Actually I'm kind of hungry too, now that I think of it," he said.

"They have sandwiches there. And soup, I think," Trisha said.

OK, thought David. A compromise. Technically, they were having dinner together, although it was just a light dinner, at a coffee shop.

They ordered sandwiches and coffee. Trisha was first with her wallet out and insisted on paying. They sat down at a corner table. As he prepared to bite into his sandwich David saw that Trisha was silently saying grace. He quickly set his sandwich back on the plate and said his own silent prayer.

Dear God, thank you for this food and please make Trisha love me. Amen.

Trisha began the conversation "So David, how is it going? Last night must have been horrible. But how are you doing? It's been, what, five months? How do you like ministry? How do you like Lachance?"

"Oh, it's great! It really is my dream job. I mean, everyone has been great. Pastor Rick is great, the congregation, the people in worship ministry. They're all just... great."

He didn't have the nerve to tell Trisha that she was great. And hated himself for lying about everything being great. It wasn't great. It was terrible.

"Really? I guess I'm kind of surprised to hear that. Isn't it hard? The church isn't doing so well. We seem to be getting smaller. I don't know." She looked down and picked a tomato out of her sandwich. She lifted the sandwich for another bite, then lowered it and looked up at David instead. "Carissa told me about the meeting with Pastor Rick and Elizabeth. I don't know how you manage."

David had hoped that meeting was forgotten. He regretted lying about things being great. Trisha saw right through him.

"Well. Yeah. That was strange. I guess I just haven't really thought about it much."

"It was horrible! How could he blame you? It's obvious what was really going on. How do you put up with it?"

"I pray a lot." Also a lie.

"Hmmm... That's great, David. You are really strong." She reached across the table and put her hand on his arm. David began to melt. He felt a rush as though he were floating up to the ceiling.

And then the dam burst.

"It has been really brutal. I never know what Pastor Rick wants. He wants things that I think are crazy. I feel like I can't do anything right. This has turned out nothing like what I thought it would be. I thought that by getting this job, I'd be home free. I mean, what I love the most is to sing and lead worship. That's what God made me for. At least I used to think that, but now I just don't know. The harder I try, the harder it gets. And Pastor Rick wants the impossible. I'm so..."

David had said too much. He was about to say *I'm so lonely*. But stopped himself.

"I'm going to need a vacation soon." Not a lie, but nowhere near the deep truth.

"David, you're doing a great job. Things have gotten a lot better since you came. I'm glad you're here. I really am. And so is everyone else. Don't be too hard on yourself."

"I just don't know how to... I don't know. I just work and go home and watch TV with Chuck. I don't have a life."

"I know what you mean. I know exactly what you mean. And you know what? I think I found what's missing. It was right in front of me. Right in front of me."

She had a far off look in her eye as she continued. "Maybe your missing piece is right in front of you," she said, still looking out the window.

What was this she was saying? Was this a veiled confession of her love for him? His heart began to race, the rush of euphoria rising again.

"Do you think so? Right in front of me?"

She laughed. "Don't look at me like that! David, I'm just saying that was my experience. Your experience might be totally different."

David just continued to look at her. She was so beautiful, so close, so full of wonder, yet so unobtainable. It was excruciating.

"Well, I better get going. I've got tests to mark and lessons to plan. I can drop you off at your place."

"Sure. Thanks."

David could hardly remember what they talked about on the short trip back to his apartment. She was describing something from the concert. He listened, drinking in her very presence, trying to slow down time to stretch this moment as long as he could. He thanked her for the ride, smiled and waved as she drove off, watching her car all the way to the end of the street until it was gone. Then he strode up the walk to the door, singing to himself,

My love for you will never stop,
Because You, You take me to the mountaintop

The buses again woke David just before six. He sprang from bed, well rested having sank into a deep and satisfying sleep the night before, carried there by memories of his dinner with Trisha and thoughts of their future together. What else could she have meant by "looking right in front of him?" The tender touch of her hand on his arm to show her concern, her care — dare he even think — her *love* for him? He replayed every minute of their dinner together as he showered. Bouncing out, he checked his face in the mirror for spots, rashes or other signs of dysentery. He found none.

Perhaps there was good that could come out of the disaster at the concert after all. Falling into the septic tank had been the catalyst for Trisha to discover and express her true feelings for him. If the result was to bring him and Trisha together, then it was worth it. He'd be willing to fall into a thousand septic tanks if that's what it took to win her love.

He poured his cereal and fantasized about what married life would be like with Trisha. He imagined pouring two bowls of cereal. Sitting down together and talking about their plans for the day. He envisioned her smiling back at him, reaching her hand across the table to hold his arm. His cereal was soggy by the time he shook his head and came back to reality.

He sang all the way to work, not caring about the strange looks from school children waiting for their buses. Upon arrival at work, he was still full of joy.

"Good morning, Rhonda," said David, loud and uncharacteristically cheerful.

She looked sideways at him. "What's the matter with you?"

"God is good!"

"Do you have a fever?"

"Oh, just a new perspective on life. Hope and joy and goodness. I'm just... I can't describe it. But I have a sermon to write. Hold my calls!"

"Someone would have to actually call for you," said Rhonda.

"First time for everything, Rhonda!" David walked past her to his office. He sat down at his desk, took out a pad of paper, and began scribbling down ideas for his sermon the next week. Yesterday he felt flat, used, pessimistic. But this morning he was inspired. He would give a message of hope. How even in the darkest circumstances — Joseph in the Egyptian jail, Daniel in the Lion's Den, even Jesus dead and buried in the tomb — even in those circumstances, hope and joy broke through and victory was won!

He pulled down his hermeneutics textbook from a shelf and thumbed through it as he worked his outline, alternatively pacing around the room, practicing sermon fragments aloud, and rushing back to his desk to make revisions and write down any particularly dazzling turns of phrase to ensure they'd make it into his final script. The hours passed. He had his plan for the sermon.

He wondered about the next step in his relationship with Trisha. She'd very delicately hinted at her feelings for him, but the next play had to be his. He would need to be bold. A marriage proposal would certainly be too bold, he thought, and besides he had no money for a ring. That would have to wait, but he fully expected God would be faithful and provide for a ring when the time came.

Perhaps a real dinner out together. He could ask to borrow Chuck's truck and pick her up. They could go someplace nice, where you didn't line up at the counter to order. Not too nice though. He wouldn't want to appear to be trying too hard. In fact, perhaps a bona fide date was too much too soon. Then it hit him. He would ask her if she wanted to have lunch with him after church. He could then explain to her how he had looked right in

153

front of him and found the joy of his heart, the joy of his life. Or, perhaps that was too forward. What if she had plans for lunch? Oh, the possibilities for failure. He could say, "I wanted to talk to you about something. Are you doing anything for lunch?" Perhaps that would work. The "wanting to talk about something" would pique her interest. A smart move. If she had plans, then it would be only natural to ask about dinner, or dinner some other night. He could settle for coffee, he supposed, but wouldn't use coffee as his opening bid. Boldness was called for, and bold he would be.

Over the next few days, David finalized his sermon. In fact, all his other responsibilities were sidelined as he focused on his sermon and his plans with Trisha. Every day, he practised in the empty auditorium. He'd been given the keys to the hard-wired wireless microphone system. He practiced with the mic on, testing each inflection of his voice through the loudspeakers. He practised raising his voice, his mock whisper, making his voice crack with emotion. The sound of his voice booming through the auditorium was intoxicating. No wonder Pastor Rick loved preaching so much. It felt good.

He read through his script multiple times, almost memorizing it. And he had the perfect finale to the service. David himself would lead the closing song. Pastor Rick was a great preacher. He knew all the tricks, but he certainly couldn't lead the closing song. David had heard Pastor Rick sing, and he was terrible. Carissa would lead the opening songs and then David would lead the closing song after his sermon.

He explained the plan to the worship team at their Thursday night rehearsal. They all agreed it would be powerful to have David lead them in singing *Mountaintop* as their closing song. Rehearsal went well, the team members were all working their hardest for David's sake, to make Sunday a success.

After rehearsal, Inq encouraged David. "I expect a highly impactful Sunday, David. To think that you, the preacher, are also leading the closing song. We will experience nothing less than perfect alignment between word and song. I am grateful to be a part of it."

"Thanks, Inq. I'm looking forward—" David was interrupted by a squeal.

Carissa and Trisha were talking in the corner. Carissa had

screamed at something Trisha had told her and given her a hug.

"Girl talk," said Inq, rolling his eyes.

"Oh, yes. Well, thanks for encouraging me. Pray for me, too."

"Of course I shall, without ceasing, my dear boy."

David looked over at Trisha and Carissa. Trisha was continuing to talk to Carissa in hushed tones. He could only surmise that Trisha was talking to Carissa about him, about their dinner together. He decided to play it cool and just put away his guitar and tidy up the stage. By the time he was leaving the auditorium, Trisha had left and Carissa was putting on her coat.

"David!" she called, beaming at him.

"Yes?" David tried to seem oblivious to what they were talking about.

"I just think it's great that you can preach. And thanks for asking me to lead worship!"

"Oh, you're welcome. Umm, anything else?"

"Um. No. Just... I really think Sunday will be great. Great," she said, smiling at him.

David thought she must have been sworn to secrecy by Trisha.

"Well, great. Thanks. Thanks for everything. You and Trisha were certainly excited after rehearsal tonight," he said, providing an opening for Carissa to divulge the contents of their conversation.

"Oh, yes. You know. Girl talk! Goodnight!" She turned and walked out the door.

You're a good friend, Carissa, thought David. *You can keep a confidence*. But David was sure that all would be out in the open very soon. Very soon indeed.

Saturday night, Chuck was upstairs watching a basketball game on TV as David paced below in his room, practicing his sermon. He was having trouble focusing on it, and was more nervous about how he would ask Trisha to lunch or dinner. This time would be different. He wouldn't lose his nerve or fumble his words. He had a plan.

Sunday morning, while the band was warming up, he'd casually tell Trisha he'd like to talk to her about something and ask if she could see him after church. This was a low-risk way to ensure the conversation happened. It would also commit him to follow through and ask her out.

Then, after the service when he and Trisha talked, he would say that he's hungry and why don't they grab lunch together? He'd still be depending on her to drive, which was not ideal, but it would get them to a restaurant together. He'd suggest the Italian restaurant downtown since it wasn't frequented by churchgoers and they wouldn't be interrupted by anyone they knew. If she had lunch plans, then he'd have to fall back on asking her to dinner. He'd suggest that evening or a night that would work for her. It would have to be casual, saying something like "well, hey, it was fun to go for dinner the other night. How about dinner tonight? Or what night is good for you?" This was riskier, putting himself out there.

And what if she rejected him? What if he had somehow misinterpreted the signs? He told himself that was impossible. He had been observing her, studying her from the day he arrived in Lachance and had detected a difference in her over the last couple of weeks. She wasn't so sad, there was a lightness that was new. He just had to play it right. He just had to be bold, and not be overcome by nerves. His plan was sound. He had to trust it.

After a final run-through of key portions of his sermon, he poured himself a glass of milk and went upstairs to unwind in front of the TV with Chuck.

"Hey... you goin' crazy? You been talking to yourself all night," Chuck said.

"I feel a little crazy. Just making sure my sermon is ready for tomorrow. I've never preached for real in an actual Sunday morning church service, so I want it to be good. I want to be ready."

"Well I'm looking forward to it. I'm sure you'll do great. I could never get up in front of a bunch of people and talk for that long. Hey, check out this play."

Chuck pointed to the TV as the sports highlight showed something from a basketball game. David pretended to be impressed. "Wow. That looked really difficult," He sat down on the couch and drank his milk, pretending to be interested in a discussion about which players were overrated.

"Guess what," said Chuck.

"What?"

"My daughter Facebooked me. She said she'd be willing to meet sometime next week."

"That's amazing! I'm really happy for you, Chuck. How do you feel about that?"

"I'm really nervous. Would you, could you pray about that?"

"Yeah. You bet. Yeah. How about right now?"

"Oh, I'd really appreciate that."

Chuck turned off the TV and bowed his head.

David prayed. "God, thank you that Chuck's daughter is willing to meet with him. I pray you'd give Chuck peace about this and that you'd continue to bring healing to their relationship. I pray the meeting would go really well and that they'd continue to get together more and more. In Jesus' name we pray, Amen."

"Amen," Chuck echoed.

"I'm happy for you. You can pray for me, too. I'm nervous about tomorrow."

"OK. Like, right now?"

"Sure."

"I never prayed out loud before," Chuck said.

"Just tell God what you're feeling, ask him for what you want. And then say *amen*. That's all."

"All right, here goes. Uh, Dear God. David is a really good guy, and I hope he preaches the best damn sermon you ever heard! Amen. How was that?"

"Well, that was good. Typically, though, we don't swear during our prayers."

"Oh, Sh..." Chuck caught himself before completing the expletive, then continued, "I mean shoot! Sorry. Should I do it again?"

"No, that was fine. I'm sure God knows what you meant. Thanks for praying for me. Tomorrow's a big day for me. I better get some rest. Goodnight."

"Goodnight."

A HEARTBREAKING SERMON

David was the first one at church on Sunday morning. He arrived early enough to run through his sermon from the platform, with the hard-wired wireless mic system. He stumbled in a few places, but he was certain that the presence of an actual audience would sharpen his mental focus and prevent such stumbles during the real thing.

Now he paced back and forth up the aisles of the auditorium thinking about Trisha, the exact wording, tone and inflection of what he'd say to her. He was startled from his meditation on Trisha by her actual presence. He almost ran right into her as she came through the doors of the auditorium.

"Whoa, look out David! All ready for this morning?" she asked.

"Oh, I think so. I think so."

David froze for a moment and then realized this was his opportunity for the first step of his plan to be sprung into action. He took a breath, said a quick silent prayer, reminded himself to appear casual, and then spoke.

"Say, that reminds me. I wanted to talk to you about something. Can you come and talk to me after the service?"

"Oh, sure. Good luck this morning. I mean, I'm sure you'll do great. And I'll be praying for you."

"Oh, thanks Trisha."

Success. The appointment after the service was set. David congratulated himself on thinking quickly, having been startled by Trisha's arrival and yet pulling off step one of the plan with such aplomb, surely a sign of good things to come.

The rest of the band arrived, each one expressing their support and encouragement to David in their own way. Even Sid said it would be nice to not have to listen to Pastor Rick for a change.

The band rehearsed their set. Carissa was in fine form. Then David ran through *Mountaintop* with them. It was the best they'd ever sounded, it seemed to David, each member of the team pouring their heart into the song. They were all pulling for David, he could tell. He permitted himself another moment of self-congratulation, recalling what they had sounded like when he first arrived back in the fall and how far they'd come. *Leadership, that's the difference,* he told himself.

He surveyed the room. Sid and Inq were tuning up, Carissa and Trisha had retreated to a corner for a private conversation. David had little doubt that Trisha was telling Carissa about his request to talk to her after the service. Everything was coming together. Finally, he was beginning to experience what success in ministry felt like. *Thank you, God,* he prayed silently. People were beginning to arrive, filling in the seats. David went to the back room to pray with the team before the service. They were all in the back room except for Carissa and Trisha. As they stood to pray, the two women rushed in, apologizing for being late. Trisha slid in next to David.

Inq spoke first. "David, ordinarily you are the one who approaches the throne of grace on our behalf, but on this auspicious morning, I think it more appropriate that one of us should pray for you, as you lead us into God's word. May I have that honor?" Inq bowed slightly as he finished.

"Oh, of course," David replied.

"Well then. I suggest we hold hands as a symbol of our unity."

Sid and Calvin groaned, but complied. Calvin pretended to spit in both of his hands before taking Sid's and Inq's hands into his. But the rush of euphoria surged through David again as he reached out and took Trisha's left hand into his right. Her hand was small, delicate, soft, her fingers curled around his hand, gently squeezing. David told himself to remember this moment, the first time they held hands. He imagined the two of them as an old married couple, reminiscing about this moment.

Inq began to pray. "O Gracious Heavenly Father, Creator and Redeemer of all things. May your Spirit guide our friend and brother David this morning as he preaches from your holy word. May you speak to us powerfully through him. And may you also do a wonderful work in Him as he ministers. We thank you for David and ask that you shower him with an abundance of grace, mercy and love. In the glorious name of Jesus we ask it, Amen."

Everyone followed with an "Amen."

What a prayer! thought David as he reluctantly released Trisha's hand. He made a mental note to ask Inq to pray a benediction on him and Trisha at their wedding.

The service began with Carissa leading the band and the congregation in three songs. David sat in the front row, unfamiliar with the feeling of being led rather than leading. He sang along half-heartedly, distracted and nervous. Bill came up and made an appeal for the offering, putting a damper on things, saying that the financial situation for the church was quite tenuous and suggesting that everyone sacrifice a little more. Carissa then led another congregational song as the offering was taken up.

David took the platform while they were singing the last chorus. He wanted a seamless transition from the singing to the preaching, so he took the hard-wired wireless microphone system key out of his pocket, put it in the ignition switch on the pulpit, turned it on and listened for the warm hiss of the microphone coming to life. As the last few lines of the song were being sung, David looked out over the congregation and smiled. There were the Garcias, hands raised and faces beaming as they sang. Charley and his wife were sitting together, dutifully standing with the rest of the congregation but certainly not singing. Bill was sitting in his usual spot, third row on the left. There was even a new guy sitting in the fourth row by himself. *A good omen*, thought David as the last chords rang out. He took a breath and said, "let's pray."

As the congregation bowed their heads and closed their eyes together, Carissa and the band quietly left the stage and walked down to their seats.

"Lord, open our ears this morning, to hear what you have to say to us. Anything that is of me, may it be forgotten, but what is from you, may it penetrate our hearts."

David had heard another preacher pray that once and thought it sounded really humble, so he decided to use it. He continued, opening his eyes to arrange his papers on the pulpit. "May you receive the glory and honor and may we be made more into the image of your Son, Jesus, in whose name we pray. Amen."

The congregation mumbled an *Amen*.

David looked up from his notes and froze.

He blinked, swallowed, blinked again and tried to comprehend what he saw. Seconds ticked by. He began to sense the congregation becoming uncomfortable as he stood behind the pulpit, mute as a statue. Everyone had their eyes on him, except for Trisha and the new guy sitting in the fourth row. They were seated side by side, gazing at each other, not at David. Someone in the back coughed. The church still stared. One of the Garcias said something in Spanish. David felt a bead of sweat roll down his left temple.

David quickly disregarded the possibility that this wasn't what it seemed. He'd been so very, very wrong. Trisha wasn't in love with him. It was this other guy. She wasn't at all interested in him. She'd just felt sorry him. It wasn't love. It was pity. The room began to spin. He grasped the pulpit with both hands to steady himself. Still, he said nothing, staring straight at Trisha and her boyfriend. The girl talk with Carissa about someone else, not him. *Looking for the missing piece right in front of you?* Who knows what that meant? David began to hate this man for taking what he wanted. He began to hate Trisha for betraying him.

The boyfriend put his arm around Trisha. She nuzzled into his shoulder and they both began to look up toward David. He jerked his head down to his notes. He wouldn't let her see him like this. He felt stupid, ashamed, angry, and desperately lonely. He wanted to run away, never to return, never to see these people again, to be rid of them, their petty complaints from their ungrateful hearts, their cries of "me, me me! I want! I want! I want!" But David didn't know where he would go. He was trapped, so he did what was expected of him. He performed.

Somehow his eyes read the letters on his script and his mouth formed the words. He began to feel the same numb detachment he'd felt at Wayne's workshop the night of the septic tank disaster, as though he were watching another person preach from his body, through his voice. He couldn't tell how he must have looked to the congregation, but it must have been very strange, for everyone in the auditorium was transfixed by his sermon. Even Sid was paying attention instead of playing on his phone. David avoided looking at Trisha and this man with his arm around her. It was just too painful.

He worked his way through his script, with tales of Old

Testament heroes who remained faithful amid hardship, whom God rescued from their deepest despair. The people sat spellbound. He'd practiced his vocal inflections so much that he produced them effortlessly. Now, he just wanted to get through it.

Mercifully, he reached his final page.

"And so, let us take courage from the examples of Joseph, Esther, and Daniel. For even in their darkest moments they stayed faithful and God rewarded them. God saved them and he will save you, too. Remember that the darkest day in all of history, when Jesus was crucified, dead and buried and all hope seemed lost, even then, victory was just around the corner. If you are in the valley of despair, don't give up. God is in the business of rescuing from the darkest valley and putting our feet on the mountaintop. In Psalm forty the psalmist writes:

> *I waited patiently for the Lord;*
> *he inclined to me and heard my cry.*
> *He drew me up from the pit of destruction,*
> *out of the miry bog,*
> *and set my feet upon a rock,*
> *making my steps secure.*
> *He put a new song in my mouth,*
> *a song of praise to our God."*

The psalm was the cue for the band to come back up on stage. They quietly slipped past him to their instruments. David looked away as Trisha went past him to the piano.

David continued, "Let us stand together and sing a song of praise, a prayer that God would lift us up out of our valley and place us on the mountaintop."

Calvin quietly counted in the band and they began to play the opening chords. David stepped away from the pulpit and strapped on his guitar. He strummed along with the band and began singing. The congregation joined in. They knew it well. David sang with his eyes closed to avoid having to look at Trisha's boyfriend.

As they reached the chorus of the song, David's resistance to his emotions finally crumbled. He could no longer sing, and tears began streaming from his eyes. He loathed himself even more for this weakness, this public humiliation. As he cried, Carissa took up the melody, but seeing David in tears moved her too, and she began to cry. And then people throughout the congregation began to weep as well. Mrs. Garcia was wiping her tears with a lace handkerchief. David opened his eyes and took in the scene in front of him. Dozens of people were crying as they sang "You take me to the mountaintop." Charley took his glasses off to rub his eyes. Chuck was teary-eyed as he quietly mouthed along the words to the song. Even the boyfriend was crying. *Tears of joy, no doubt*, thought David.

By the time they finished the song, David had composed himself enough to pronounce a benediction. "Go in God's grace, Amen." Then he put down his guitar and walked up the aisle to stand at the auditorium doors and shake hands as people left, just like Pastor Rick did every week. He would've preferred to continue through the doors, and leave without ever turning back, but he never even made it to the end of the aisle.

Mrs. Garcia met him halfway up the aisle. Clutching both his hands in hers, she spoke in Spanish between sobs and then kissed him on both cheeks. Charley and his wife were next — Charley's wife telling him what a good job he did, and Charley smiling at him as they shook hands. "Good word, Pastor. Well done!" His eyes were still a little red behind his glasses.

For the next half hour David shook hands, hugged, and spoke with members of the church, all deeply moved by his message.

"The way you spoke," said Carissa. "So... gravely. With such a burden on your heart! It was amazing, David. I had no idea you could preach so well. And then... when you started to cry... oh my."

At this point Carissa began to cry again. "Oh, I just broke down. It was as if the Holy Spirit came and just released the whole church from their bondage! Oh David, this was the best service I've ever been to at this church. Thank you. Thank you for pouring yourself out. For being real, and vulnerable."

"You're welcome," David said, reflexively, as she embraced him again. He was completely spent, hollowed out. He stood there, limp as if a butcher had de-boned him. Then he heard another voice.

"David, that was amazing," said Trisha. "Great job."

He turned to see Trisha, holding hands with the grinning boyfriend.

"There's someone I'd like you to meet. This is Chad. He's

another teacher at my school."

So that's what she meant by finding the missing piece right in front of her.

The boyfriend took David's hand and shook it. "David, it's really nice to meet you. I have to say, that was amazing. And it is so true. You know, I was so down when I first moved here this year. I didn't know anyone and I couldn't figure out what God was doing. And then, I met Trisha, and well — It was so amazing how God turned everything around in my life. Your message was so good. God is really amazing."

David wanted to die.

"Oh. That's great to hear. I'm really happy for you," he said, and tried to think of a way to end this conversation and get away from the two of them.

"Oh, David, you wanted to talk to me after the service, remember?" Trisha said.

David cursed to himself as he remembered his plan. This was to be the moment he revealed his true feelings for her. Another stab of shame pierced through his body.

"Oh. Yeah. I forgot. It's been a long morning. I forgot. It wasn't important." With that, he turned and left them. He went to his office and waited inside until he was certain that they'd left. Then he locked up the church and began his long walk home.

David spent the afternoon walking aimlessly through Lachance, trying to forget.

He arrived at Beans of Production, ordered a coffee and a muffin and sat alone at a table in the corner, staring out at the street. He thought of his mother, the familiar ache of wondering whether she was still alive. He might wonder about her whereabouts, but he knew for sure that she'd rejected him. He sipped his coffee, black and bitter, and caught his reflection through the window. He didn't like the man he saw, so tired and defeated. He took out his phone to distract himself.

He opened up Twitter and saw a tweet from Tom Lindsey.

> @Tomlindsey: "Big news, yo! I'll be appearing on the America's Choice Awards Show!"

Well, good for you, thought David as he scrolled through his Twitter feed. He looked out the window again and tried to think of something to live for, something to care about, something to hope for. He kept staring as his coffee turned cold.

MONEY

The buses started the next morning and David had a vague feeling that he was forgetting something important. As the fog of an uneasy night's sleep cleared he remembered it. He was heartbroken.

He completed his morning ritual under a cloud, making his way to church, settling into his office. Pastor Rick would be back today, his cheerful, menacing presence across the hall. David was feeling too dark and foul to be afraid of Pastor Rick any more, though.

Pastor Rick knocked on his door and came in, sitting down in the chair opposite David's desk. "Well, I didn't know you had it in you. But I guess you learned from the best," he said.

"I'm sorry?"

"The service. Wayne tells me you preached a real stem-winder and then had everyone in tears at the end. I guess I have some competition." Pastor Rick laughed. "No, seriously David, good job. I'm glad I could count on you to fill in. How'd you think it went?"

"Best sermon I ever preached," deadpanned David.

Pastor Rick didn't get the joke. "Well, good. Hard to keep that up, though."

David passed him the keys to the pulpit. "Anything else?"

Pastor Rick was surprised at David's abruptness, but it only showed on his face for a second, and then the mouth-only smile re-appeared. "Yeah. Listen. Easter's coming, and I want an update on the web streaming plan. It will be in place, right? And it has to be in HD."

"Well, about that. I know that guy at Leaderfest said you could do all this for free, but to do it right, it's gonna cost us. Especially if you want it in HD. We'll need a camera, a new computer, and we'll have to subscribe to a service. It'll be about a hundred dollars a month."

Pastor Rick bit his lip and shook his head. David realized he'd never spoken to Pastor Rick like this, bluntly telling him something he didn't want to hear. But today, he just didn't care.

"Listen David, by your own admission, you don't know anything about this. So I'm supposed to believe you over an expert who teaches seminars on using the internet to grow churches? He said you could do all this for free, and now you're telling me we need to buy all this stuff?"

David sighed. "I called that pastor's church and I talked to his technical director. He said he told his pastor to stop telling people they can web stream in Hi Def for free, but he won't listen. He walked me through it. I figure we need about five grand in equipment plus the subscription service." He pushed himself away from his desk, leaned back in his chair, and threw his hands in the air.

"David, you can't be telling me this now. You are going to have to make this happen. Beg, borrow, steal. You go back to the drawing board and you figure this out. You hear me? That tech guy, he's from some big church with lots of money, so what does he know about doing things on a budget? This has to happen, David. This has to happen. We are committed to this. I've been telling people this. And you, David, you are going to make it happen."

Pastor Rick turned on his heel and marched out of David's office, firmly closing David's door behind him.

David spent the rest of the afternoon working out what a 'free' option would be for the web streaming. He found an ad-supported service that offered a free thirty-day trial. He could use that to get started. Ideally, he needed a new computer, but he could re-purpose his own computer if he just got a new video card, that would be about five hundred dollars. He could set up the camera in the auditorium and then run the cable through the false ceiling into his office. But he still needed a camera that would output video in the right format. He found a used one online for about eight hundred dollars. Then he'd need to buy cable, a tripod and a few other odds and ends. He went back to Pastor Rick with his new info.

"I think I can rig up something and make it happen for about fifteen hundred. Is that doable?"

"You can ask Bill. He should be here tomorrow night doing some finance work before your rehearsal."

"What about the money we made from the Tom Lindsey concert?"

"You have to talk to Bill."

"Aren't you in charge here? Why can't you just approve this?" David asked.

"It's more complicated than that. Anything outside the operations budget goes to the treasurer. Unfortunately, that's Bill. He might be able to scrounge up a couple hundred bucks for you."

"Well, that's not gonna do it."

Pastor Rick snapped at David. "Well it's gonna have to!"

"Yes sir." David said, shaking his head.

On Thursday night, an hour before his rehearsal, David found Bill doing bookkeeping in the conference room, just as he did every Thursday night. He had a laptop, calculator and stack of invoices and receipts spread out on the table in front of him.

"Bill?"

"Hi, David"

"You have a minute?"

"Sure. Oh, and I've been meaning to tell you, great job on Sunday. It was a good word. And the closing song was very moving. Thanks for that. I needed that."

"Oh, you're welcome," said David, reminded of his unrequited love for Bill's daughter. He sat in a chair across from Bill, took a deep breath, and began his pitch.

"Anyway, I wanted to ask you about some funding for a project Pastor Rick asked me to work on."

Bill looked startled, then laughed to himself, shaking his head.

"Stop right there. I can save you some time. The answer is no."

"Well, hold on, Bill. I haven't even told you what the project is."

"If there's no money then it doesn't really matter what the project is."

"I don't need much. Just, like fifteen hundred."

"Ok, not because there is actually any money, but I'm just curious. What do you think you need fifteen hundred bucks for?"

"Pastor Rick wants me to broadcast our services on the Internet. I need a camera and some other equipment to do that."

"Rick mentioned he was going to do that, but he said it wouldn't cost anything."

"He was misinformed. Don't we have money from the concert we can use? Pastor Rick told me we could use that money towards the live streaming."

"Oh, the concert? Let me tell you about the concert. We were supposed to get three thousand. But they had to rent a generator since we didn't have the right power or whatever it was. So that cost fifteen hundred, which they deducted from our fee. Then we have about twenty-five hundred worth of water damage from the toilets overflowing and I just got an estimate on the repairs to our septic system which will cost another two thousand. So all in all, that concert cost us three thousand, not to mention your unfortunate mishap."

"Well don't we have insurance for the water and septic damage?"

"We do, and I called them. But it turns out our insurance adjuster is a big Tom Lindsey fan. He was at the concert and saw that the building was well over capacity, so they aren't going to pay any claim. That three thousand dollar bill eats up most of our remaining cash reserve, David. We're broke."

"Well, is that *my* fault? So I can't get approval for my project?"

"I'm not saying it is anyone's fault. It doesn't matter if there's blame to lay at anyone's feet, the bills still need to be paid."

"So how does this work? Pastor Rick's plan to grow this church is for us to branch out into online ministry. It's really for him, not for me. I'm just explaining why we need these things for his plan. Don't you think it's short-sighted to say no?"

Bill took off his glasses and methodically laid them on the table with both hands. He looked up at David from his pile of invoices.

"Short-sighted? Short-sighted? David, I want you to understand something, and I fear I may be asking your forgiveness at the end of this conversation for losing my temper. Nevertheless, I take great exception to the word *short-sighted*. I was practically born at this church. I was baptized here, married here. I was part of this church when my daughter was born, and *she* was baptized here. The last time I saw my wife's face was *here*, just before they closed the casket for her funeral, which was also here.

"I've spent all sixty-three years of my life faithfully attending, serving, and giving here. There isn't a task here I haven't done, from Sunday School teacher to treasurer, to cleaning up the overflowing toilets as recently as last week. You've been here for six months, collecting a pay check and you tell me I'm short-sighted? Where do you get that kind of nerve? Is there a special class for that in Bible College?"

"OK, I shouldn't have said that," David said. "But this is what Pastor Rick wants. We have to grow, and this is his plan."

"Oh yes. I know. There's always a plan. Always the next best, greatest, new thing. Fifteen years ago, it was a digital projector. We had to have Powerpoint. Powerpoint would bring them in! We had to speak the language of the visual generation! So we took special offerings and spent five thousand dollars on a digital projector so we could have Powerpoint! We purchased that projector and a screen and had it all installed, and then you know what happened?"

"What?"

"Nothing! Nothing happened. We didn't grow. We had sermons with pretty pictures and bullet points that flew across the screen, but that was it. Nothing else changed.

"Then, it was 'let's renovate the sanctuary! So we took out a ruinous loan, I still don't know why the bank approved it. And we spent all this money, that we don't have, to renovate the sanctuary, oh, excuse me, the auditorium. We have to call it 'the auditorium' now because auditoriums grow, but sanctuaries don't."

Bill's breathing was becoming labored, his face turning red. David was beginning to worry he'd have another heart attack, but Bill continued his diatribe.

"Then, David, then it was you! We need great worship to grow. We need someone young and cool who can give us great music and then, and only then will we grow. That's what all the church growth gurus tell us, and they're never wrong! So that's what we did, we hired you! Well, in case you haven't noticed, we still aren't growing.

"So now it's video-whatever-streaming that Rick wants. That's the latest hole we're supposed to throw money into as if it can save us. Well, I'm not falling for it, David. Nothing else has worked and even if I thought it would work, there's just no more money. The answer is *no*."

Bill's hands were shaking as he picked up his glasses and put them back on.

"Why are we so broke?" David asked.

"David, you have no idea what this church is up against. Back when I was recovering from my heart attack, Pastor Rick convinced the church council to take out the loan for the renovations. I never would've allowed it, but what's done is done. And then, to make matters worse, Pastor Rick decided to hire a worship pastor, no offence."

David shrugged.

"They had to hire you before September first, when I took over again as treasurer. If the position wasn't filled by then, I could remove the funding for it, but once you were hired, I couldn't. The treasurer isn't allowed to fire people."

"So they just snuck me in under the wire?"

"Yes, you can look at it way. In any case, the loan is structured with a balloon payment of eighty thousand dollars due on May first. If we don't make that payment, we could lose the building."

"Oh. I see," David murmured.

"I have a meeting next week at the bank to figure out what's going on. I need to understand why they made this loan in the first place, and then see if they'd be open to some renegotiation of the terms. It may be our only hope."

"Then what am I supposed to do? Pastor Rick is my boss and he told me to start video streaming. I can't just say no. And he's convinced that it won't cost any money. What am I supposed to do?"

"David, can I ask you something? Do you think video-streaming our services is going to make any difference at all? Do you actually think that's the solution to our problems? Like suddenly people will start watching the services and getting saved, and we'll grow and people will give and serve and everything will be better? If people don't want to come to a live service, what's gonna make them want to watch on their computer?"

"Then what am I supposed to do? Everything I do, it seems to just make Rick more upset with me. He even seemed upset that I preached for him last week. He's making impossible demands."

"That's how the game is played. You make impossible demands and when they aren't met, that's your excuse for your own failure. You're caught up in Rick's game, David. You're a pawn."

"Do you honestly think that's what Pastor Rick is up to?"

"I'm afraid of the alternative, that he's so out of touch that he thinks the Internet will somehow solve all our problems. But he might just be deceiving himself so that he doesn't have to face reality — that he's just an ordinary pastor in a declining church whose best years are behind him."

"I wish he wouldn't take his own frustrations out on me. He blamed me for his wife calling Carissa a slut. Why doesn't the board fire him? Why did he get hired in the first place? I mean, who in their right mind would hire him in the first place?"

Bill took his glasses off again, set them down on the desk and rubbed his eyes. David worried that he'd gone too far with his last comment.

"Me! David, Me. I thought it was a good idea to hire him."

David was shocked.

"What could you have possibly been thinking?"

Bill paused. He picked up his pen, put it down again and then rubbed the back of his neck. "He was different back then. He was young. Fresh out of seminary. Happy and full of energy. He really cared for the church. When my wife was sick, he was so caring, he really helped me and Trisha through that time. He spent hours with us, praying for us and encouraging us. He organized the church to provide meals for us.

"It seems like so long ago. There wasn't a day during that time that he didn't call or drop by. He was with us in the hospital room when she passed. He was there for me afterwards, too. I don't know how I could've got through it without him."

"What changed?"

"It was gradual, but we hit some rough times as a church. Young families were leaving us to go to The Flow. It was new and exciting. And I think he envied Dean's success. It seemed like the better things went at The Flow, the more we suffered here, and the angrier Rick got. He's not a happy man. And I'm afraid for you, David."

"Why's that?"

"Rick was a lot like you when he started here, but after some disappointments he started to resent the church. I'm afraid I see that happening in you."

"There's no way I'll ever be anything like him." David resented the mere suggestion that he had anything in common with Pastor Rick.

"Oh, it can happen, all right. You be careful. When things don't quite turn out how you'd like and you start resenting the church, it's no longer a ministry. It's just a meal ticket. Or maybe the church just turns into a vehicle for your own ambitions instead of real people who matter and live and die and need a place where they can belong and serve God and be served."

David felt suddenly exhausted from this conversation.

"What am I supposed to do? How are we supposed to grow this church?"

"I don't know, David. It doesn't seem like old churches like this one can grow, at least not without changing so much that they're no longer themselves. I don't know what we do, David."

"I have to go rehearse now." David wanted to stay with Bill and keep talking. This was the first honest conversation he'd had in a long time. But duty called with rehearsal starting in five minutes. He planted a smile on his face and left Bill to his bookkeeping.

AMERICA'S CHOICE

When David arrived in the auditorium, the team was already waiting for him to begin rehearsal. Inq, Calvin and Sid were playing Led Zeppelin's *The Immigrant Song* while Carissa and Trisha were off in the corner talking. This was the first time David had seen Trisha since he found out about her boyfriend. He felt a stab of pain as he looked at her.

"All right, everybody. Sorry, I'm late. Let's get started," David yelled over the music. The boys reluctantly stopped playing.

"Let's gather around. I want to talk to you all about something," began David. "As you may have heard, Tom Lindsey is going to be playing at the America's Choice Awards on Sunday night. This is really huge for him, and for God's kingdom. Just imagine what an amazing testimony it is going to be for him to be singing a worship song for a national television audience, and in front of the entire entertainment industry. And to think, we had him here just a couple of weeks ago, right here on this stage! So we're going to sing *Mountaintop* this week, and I really encourage you all to be praying that God uses Tom to really be a witness to our nation. I'll pray and then we'll get underway."

He prayed and they began their rehearsal. After five months with David, the team was working well together. He didn't need to say much to them as they efficiently worked through their songs. He kept his back toward Trisha most of the time to avoid the pain of looking at her.

Right after rehearsal, David asked Inq about how things were going with his band, 'The Aqualung Experience,' knowing Inq would talk well past the time it would take Trisha to leave the building.

"...and that is why we are taking a temporary hiatus from live performance, in order to redouble our efforts toward faithfully reproducing the verve of early Tull. And to be perfectly honest, there's only so much demand for our particular work in a place like Lachance," Inq explained.

David was barely listening, but was sure that he and Inq were the only ones still in the auditorium.

"That's great Inq. I better let you go. It's been a long day. See you Sunday."

"Adieu till then, my boy," said Inq, bowing to David.

At home, David settled into bed and checked his Twitter feed for the latest on Tom Lindsey.

> @TomLindsey: "So Pumped - Gonna be on America's Choice Music Awards! Be sure to Tune in!"
> @TomLindsey: "America's Choice Awards - gonna be epic! Sick new arrangement of Mountaintop - Can't wait to work with Killa-Z!"

David was surprised that Tom Lindsey would be working with Killa-Z, a producer known more for working with gangster rappers and R&B artists. But this was great exposure for Tom Lindsey. Despite the debacle at the concert, David still admired Tom Lindsey and found great comfort and inspiration in his music. David remembered that he had Amy's cell number and decided to text his congratulations to her.

David: "Heard the big news about America's Choice Awards. That's great! Are you going?"

Amy: "Not going. He's got new management. We've all been dumped. Just like that. We were all stranded in Wisconsin. I had to buy my own bus ticket back home."

David: "Man, sorry to hear that."

Amy: "I was gonna quit anyway. Tyler's really taking it hard. U didn't ever buy that Worship-XT thing did U?"

David: "No. Couldn't have afforded it even if I wanted."

Amy: "Good for u. Tyler put every dollar he had into it and now it's worthless."

David: "Too bad."

Amy: "Yup. Gotta go."

David was slightly ashamed at the pleasure he felt in hearing of Tyler's ruin. But Tom Lindsey was much too big a talent to be working with a huckster like Tyler. Tom Lindsey deserved better.

When Sunday arrived, David was still heartbroken about Trisha, but he managed to look at her and say good morning. When they took the stage at the start of the service, he was disappointed to see Chad in the second row. David chose to lead the opening songs with his eyes closed. He didn't open them until it was time to introduce *Mountaintop*.

"This next song we're going to sing is a familiar one. It's one of my favorites and it's by Tom Lindsey. We hosted him for a concert just a couple weeks ago, and I had a chance to spend some time with him after the show." David couldn't resist mentioning this, even though they didn't even shake hands. "I really admire Tom Lindsey and God has honored his faithfulness by giving him the opportunity to sing on national television during the America's Choice Music Awards. I encourage you to watch it, at eight o'clock tonight on channel five. It's a going to be a great testimony and witness to a world that really needs the message of the hope we have in Jesus. Let's sing it together now."

After the song, David prayed, "Father, we thank you for the truth of these words, we thank you also for people like Tom Lindsey who write these songs to bless the church. We ask that you would bless him tonight and use him to shine your light to the world. Amen."

That night, David and Chuck sat together in the living room and watched the America's Choice Music Awards together. They chatted and poked fun at some of the performances and speculated as to which award recipients were inebriated and which ones were naturally incoherent. During some of the more risqué performances, David was worried about his recommendation that people watch the show. He was imagining what Charley would be thinking. However, he wanted them to watch Tom Lindsey, not these other artists.

Then, the time came. The host announced that "a bright new star, an up and coming artist named Tom Lindsey is going to be singing a brand new song for us after the break."

"Chuck, get back in here! This is it!"

Chuck came back from the kitchen where he was getting a soda.

"Wow, David. To think you were hanging out with this guy just a few weeks ago."

"Yeah, God is amazing!"

The show returned from the commercial break. The stage was dark and a hush came over the live crowd. A hip-hop drum beat began, and a back-lit silhouette of a female dancer was now visible centre stage. A very curvy dancer. She began to throb suggestively to the beat.

"They must've messed up. This isn't Tom Lindsey," David said.

And just as he said it, Tom Lindsey appeared upstage from the dancer, illuminated by a single spotlight. He began to sing the familiar opening verse of 'Mountaintop.'

"O, How I long for you, to see your face,
To feel the warmth of your embrace.
Your love lifts me to the sky,
Your love alone can satisfy."

But the words took on an entirely new meaning as more dancers appeared on stage, writhing along with the song. And now Tom Lindsey was writhing with them, hips thrusting back and forth. When he got to the chorus of the song, hundreds of stage lights flashed on and lit the set with dizzying brilliance. Behind Tom and his band, an enormous screen magnified the lead dancer and Tom as they throbbed hip-to-hip.

"You lift me to a highest place,
I see the beauty of your face,
My love for you will never stop,
Because you, You take me to the Mountaintop."

Now the lead dancer was practically wrapped around Tom Lindsey, arching her back suggestively every time Tom sang the word "Mountaintop." David couldn't believe what he was seeing. Tom Lindsey had sold out his song. It turns out Charley was right all along, you *could* sing it to your girlfriend. David thought about all the people from church who were watching the show. His phone started buzzing. He had texts from Trisha, Carissa, and Inq.

Trisha: "U watching this? What the…"

Carissa: "Did that just happen?"

Inq: "Boethius wrote, 'Music is a part of us, and either ennobles or degrades our behavior.' I believe we've seen the latter this evening."

The song ended and the live crowd cheered loudly. David picked up the remote and turned off the TV, still in shock.

"I'm confused," said Chuck.

"Me too."

When David checked Twitter, it was exploding with condemnations of Tom as a sell-out. His thousands of Twitter followers and fans were venting their frustration, but Tom Lindsey was unrepentant.

> @TomLindsey: To all the haterz out there: U don't know me. U can't judge me.
> @TomLindsey: So Proud of tonites performance!!! Off da hook!

Tom Lindsey had attached a picture of himself to the last tweet. He was at a party, holding a bottle of Hennessey cognac in one hand, his other arm wrapped around one of the scantily clad dancers. David recalled the times he boasted that Tom Lindsey had what it takes to make it as a secular artist. He'd been right.

David went to bed with a knot in the pit of his stomach. He continued to watch the growing Twitter war between Tom and his faithful fans on his phone. Then he received an email from Pastor Rick.

> To: David
> From: Pastor Rick
> Subject: Totally Inappropriate
> David,
>
> See me first thing tomorrow morning to discuss consequences. Don't be late.
>
> Pastor Rick

David turned off his phone and stared at the ceiling, wondering if God really loved him.

MOPPING UP

"Man, David. You really stepped in it this time," said Pastor Rick.

"Yes, I suppose I did," said David, wanting to get this meeting over with as quickly as possible.

"Oh, you suppose? You just suppose? Were you on the phone last night with moms and dads who gathered their children around to watch that abomination? Were you?"

"No, I wasn't."

"Well, I was. I got emails, too. Oh David, to think I trusted you. You know, I knew there was something about that guy. I had a sense in my spirit from the very beginning." Pastor Rick slowly shook his head as he looked down at David.

"Why didn't you say anything? You could've told him yourself when you met him," David said.

"You watch your attitude, David. Don't you talk back to me like that. I didn't say anything because I trusted you. And now look where that got us."

"So what do we do? Rather, what do I do?"

"You need to have a statement prepared for Sunday. You're going to apologize to the church. I mean, there were families that watched that filth together. This is not what we need right now. And needless to say, we don't do that song ever again. Or any other Tom Lindsey song for that matter. You understand?"

"Yes, of course I understand that. Did you really think I'd still want to play that song after last night?"

"Well, I just can't be too sure. I mean, I never would've thought my worship pastor would recommend the church watch a burlesque act on live TV!"

David sensed that Pastor Rick relished David's humiliation.

"Yes, I can say something about it on Sunday. I should. You're right."

"Yeah. And one other thing. Charley called me last night after the show. He wants to have lunch with you. Today. He said he'd come by and pick you up."

"With Charley? Oh man. I guess I deserve that. Anything else?"

"Yes, how's the video streaming project going? You better have that ready!"

"Yeah, I'm working on it. I have faith."

"Faith? So I guess that means you didn't get any money from Bill?"

"No."

"Then what's your plan?"

"I don't suppose shoplifting is an option?"

"This isn't funny, David. I give you a project, I want it to get done. Come up with a plan."

"OK, OK. I'll do my best."

Charley arrived just before noon and knocked on David's door. David braced himself and tried to appear cheerful and humble.

"Is Broadway's OK?" Charley asked.

"Oh, yes. Sure."

Charley turned and led David out of the church to his waiting car. They got in together and Charley drove to Broadway's without saying a word. David wondered whether he should try to start small talk, but he was terrible at small talk and was afraid he would provoke Charley. When they arrived at the restaurant, the first words Charley spoke were to tell the hostess "Table for two."

They sat in a booth, Charley looking straight across at David, still silent. David couldn't take it any longer.

"Charley, you were right all along. About the song, about Tom Lindsey... I'm sorry."

"STOP. Right. There," said Charley.

"Yes sir," said David, bracing himself for what Charley would say next.

"You think you know what I'm going to say, David, but you're wrong. You think that cranky old Charley is gonna give you what-for because you said to watch that horrible thing on TV and to say I told you so about that awful song. Well, you're wrong."

"Really?"

"Yes. Really. Hold on. Club sandwich, fries, tomato juice. David? What do you want? My treat. You probably don't eat very well. Get whatever you want."

"Um.. Bacon Cheeseburger, fries and a coke."

"Very original. Now where was I? Oh. You think I'm here to chew you out, but you're wrong."

"So, then why are we here?"

Charley took a sip of water, took off his glasses, rubbed his nose and put them back on again.

"I figured you could use a friend today, because I know exactly how you feel."

"How could you know how I feel?"

"You ever heard of Jimmy Swaggart?"

"No."

"He was a televangelist in the eighties. I used to watch him every week. I talked him up to all my friends. I sent him money. On our vacations we'd drive down to his church to hear him preach. I shook his hand after a service once. Well, one day the news reported that Jimmy Swaggart was arrested in a hotel room with a prostitute. And my friends never let me forget it."

David sighed. "I do feel pretty foolish. And a little angry too. That song. Gee, singing it is probably what got me the job here at Lachance. And since then, Tom Lindsey has caused me nothing but grief."

"Jimmy Swaggart taught me not to put my hope in men. Not even famous Christians. *Especially* not famous Christians. They're probably the worst."

"Yeah. I sure learned that the hard way," David said.

Their food arrived and Charley said grace for both of them.

"Lord, bless this food to our bodies and make us truly grateful. And Lord, help us to keep our eyes on you. Amen."

"Charley, can I ask you a question?"

"Sure."

"What should our church do?"

"What do you mean?"

"I mean, we aren't growing. We're trying to be like all those big churches with big budgets, but we can't compete with them. What should we do?"

"David, the thing that I pray about every day, the thing that keeps me up at night is the fact that my children and their families don't come to church. They don't want to come to our little church. They don't go to a mega-church like The Flow. They just don't see a need. They both accepted Jesus when they were kids, but it just isn't a priority for them. And my grandkids... they don't know Jesus from Santa Claus..."

Charley put down his fork, his hand shaking, took off his glasses and wiped his eyes. "I expect that the next time and the last time they'll come to our church is for my funeral."

"Charley, I'm really sorry."

"David, if someone could figure out what would bring them back to church, that's what we should do."

"What do you think that is?"

"I don't know, and I'm pretty sure Pastor Rick doesn't know either, no matter what he says."

"I don't know either."

The waitress came and cleared their empty plates. They made small talk until the bill came, which Charley paid. They got back into Charley's car and drove back to church.

"Thanks for lunch, and for the talk," David said.

"You're welcome. It was my pleasure. David, you're a good man. Just be faithful with what God puts in front of you."

"Thanks. I'll do that," David said as he got out and closed the door. He stood in front of the church watching Charley drive away. He wondered what it would've been like to grow up with a father like Charley, or any father for that matter. He turned and went into the church. Pastor Rick was standing at the reception desk talking to Rhonda. They both stopped talking and looked at David as he came in.

"So? How'd that go?" asked Pastor Rick, grinning.

David shrugged at him, not wanting to play along.

"So did Charley chew you out? I hope you at least paid for lunch," Rhonda said.

"No, Charley didn't chew me out and he insisted on picking up the bill." David looked Pastor Rick right in the eyes.

"Oh," said Pastor Rick, taken aback. "What did he say?"

"He told me to be faithful."

David walked past the two of them into his office and closed the door behind him.

CHARLEY

David sat at his computer, checking Twitter for the latest news on Tom Lindsey. An all-out war now raged between Lindsey's original fan base and his new fans and Tom Lindsey himself. Millions of others were simply enjoying the spectacle of watching the online Christian community cannibalize itself.

@Tru4Jesus: @TomLindsey betrayed me, my church, my Savior. I guess he never was a Christian.
@TomLindsey: Hey @Tru4Jesus, go forgive yourself, if you catch my drift.
@PstrGuitar: @TomLindsey = Judas Iscariot with leather pants and a personal hair stylist.
@TomLindsey: Just loving all the grace, love and peace I'm getting. I'm living my life and winning. Deal with it, h8erz!!!
@Granka57: Wow. I always thot Christians were annoying but at least they were forgiving. Guess they r just annoying!
@TomLindsey: @Granka57 Tru' Dat!

Someone had posted a cell phone video that looked like Tom Lindsey on his knees vomiting on the sidewalk outside a hotel. The video had millions of views and thousands of comments. The most vicious comments were the arguments between those who thought Tom Lindsey should be condemned and rot it hell and those who thought we should pray for his return.

@ChriWyl: Praying for @TomLindsey #prodigalTom
@AliceT97: Lord, have mercy on @TomLindsey #prodigalTom
@TomLindsey: Losers, get over yourselves #prodigalTom #dorkylosers

Tom Lindsey's new record label was certainly enjoying the publicity. Radio stations across the country had picked up the new version of *Take Me to the Mountaintop*, fanning the flames of controversy. Tom Lindsey's Twitter account gained millions of followers overnight. He became Exhibit A in the case against contemporary Christian music made by ultra conservative pastors and bloggers. The whole affair made David nauseous, yet at the same time he couldn't take his eyes off the unfolding disaster. He spent the rest of the afternoon reading articles and blog posts about Tom Lindsey's fall from grace.

Pastor Rick told him he'd have to apologize for telling people to watch the awards show, and for his endorsement of Tom Lindsey. David planned to do it right at the beginning of the service, to get it over with quickly. David's suspicions grew that Pastor Rick was enjoying watching him struggle. But David no longer cared what Pastor Rick thought. He wasn't sure if this was a good thing or a bad thing, but he had given up trying to please Pastor Rick. Charley had told him to just be faithful. So David tried to just be faithful. He still served Pastor Rick to the best of his ability without worrying about the results. It was liberating.

Sunday arrived. David had his statement prepared. He wasn't worried about having to apologize in front of the congregation. He'd suffered so much humiliation over the last few months that this act of abasement would be mild in comparison. When the service began, he got right to the point.

"Welcome, everyone. Those of you who were here last week will remember that I recommended we all watch Tom Lindsey perform at the America's Choice Awards on TV. Well, it turns out I was very wrong in doing that."

The congregation sat quietly, completely still. All eyes on David. The latecomers at the door just stood at the back, waiting.

"I'm sorry about that. I'm especially sorry for those of you who watched with your children and that it turned out to be completely inappropriate. I've learned a lot from this, and I will be much more careful in the future about what I recommend."

The entire congregation remained still, except for Pastor Rick and his wife. She leaned over and whispered something to her husband, after which they both shook their heads ruefully. David felt contempt begin to rise as he watched them, but maintained his mouth-only smile.

"I'd like to say something!" said Charley, standing bolt upright from his seat. The congregation gasped, the loudest gasp coming from Charley's wife, Agnes.

Charley made his way up to the platform and David stepped back from his microphone stand to allow Charley to speak.

"I'm Charley. I've been going to this church my whole life, just about. If you know me, you know I don't much care for most of this new music we sing, and I never liked that mountain song. But I'm not mad at David. I watched that show last week out of curiosity and when I saw what happened it reminded me of something from my life about thirty years ago. Those of you who've known me for a long time know that I used to be a big fan of Jimmy Swaggart. I bought everything he sold, went down to see him preach on my vacations. I shudder to think about how much money I sent him. We all know how he turned out.

"Sometimes people let us down when we put our faith in them. I've been let down. I bet if all of you are honest, you know you've done the same. David just made a mistake like we've all made. But I think he's a good young man and we're lucky to have him here at our church. So let's forgive and forget this business with that singer character. We probably aren't the easiest church to work for, so for once let's be gracious and support this young man. That's all."

The congregation erupted into applause. David didn't know what to say or do. The applause continued, people began to stand. David felt his eyes moisten. The emotional armor he'd donned in preparation for this morning began to fall off. Even Pastor Rick and his wife joined the standing ovation, somewhat reluctantly, unenthusiastically clapping along with partial smiles pasted on their otherwise blank faces. David motioned for the band to join him on stage and the congregation stopped clapping as David stepped up to his microphone.

"Well, thank you, church. And thank you Charley. I'm afraid I don't know what to say, so I guess we should sing. Let's worship God, together."

David cued the band and Calvin clicked his drumsticks together, counting in the first song. As they launched into it, the church sang along loudly and David fought back tears as he thanked God for his goodness. For the first time in months, he sang from his heart.

After the service, as the last few stragglers made it out the door, David was coiling up some cables on the stage. Pastor Rick came into the auditorium and walked down to the stage.

"Well, well, well, David. Very well played. I must say. You and Charley planned that quite well. Impressive."

David stopped coiling cables. He knew that Pastor Rick had been enjoying David's embarrassment about Tom Lindsey, holding it over his head. And now the fun was ruined.

"Actually, I had no idea Charley was going to do that. It wasn't planned at all."

"Oh, really? Well, you were so tight-lipped about what you talked about with Charley over lunch, it just seemed like a plan was hatched. In any case, it couldn't have been planned any better, could it?"

David was trying to resist the irritation he felt at Pastor Rick right then, but was losing the battle.

"If you don't believe me, ask Charley." David went back to coiling up cable.

"Whoa, whoa, no need to get touchy. Of course I believe you. We all believe you. After all, you have the support of Charley! Of course, he liked Jimmy Swaggart, too, so take it for what its worth!" Pastor Rick chuckled at his own joke, stopping abruptly at David's reproachful look.

"OK, low blow, I admit it, low blow. But you know David, we handled this really well. It was very wise for you to start the service with your apology, get it right out there."

David knew things must have gone well if Pastor Rick was trying to take credit.

"I just knew that our congregation, my congregation really, that my flock would respond with grace and forgiveness. Even for the regrettable counsel they were given from this very stage. Well, all's well that ends well, right David?"

"Sure. It ended well. It meant a lot to me to have someone encourage me in public. I'm very grateful to Charley."

Pastor Rick evidently felt the reproach from David with that remark.

"Well, yes, of course David, you're doing a fine job. You know that. But we aren't in ministry for the praise of men. And we must beware when all men speak well of us, mustn't we?"

"That's never happened to me, but if it does, I'll be careful."

"Oh, come on David. It was a good morning. We're doing good things here, you and I. So how's the video streaming thing coming along? Got it all figured out?"

"Still working on it."

"Well, time's ticking. I don't have to remind you how important it is." Pastor Rick turned and walked back down the aisle.

David finished coiling up the cables and realized how exhausted he felt. He sat down in the front row, bowed his head and prayed.

"O God, thank you for this morning. Thank you for Charley. Thank you for encouraging me when I needed it so much. Help me to be strong. Help me figure out this..." at this point David wanted to pray "stupid fricking video streaming thing" but felt he ought not to use "stupid" or "fricking" in a prayer. "Lord help me to figure out the video streaming. Amen."

David sat for another few moments, a sense of peace and warmth enveloping him. Out of habit, he pulled out his phone and checked Twitter, learning that last night Tom Lindsey had driven his brand-new Porsche into a tree, and had been charged with Driving Under the Influence.

Another week went by and David was listening to Pastor Rick wrap up his sermon. David spent the week trying to come up with a way to do the video streaming but still didn't know exactly how he was going to pull it off. He'd made some progress, however. He borrowed a cheap camcorder from a church member to try out, but the lighting in the auditorium was very low and the resulting images were blurry and out of focus. He still didn't have a way to get the video from the camera to a computer and onto the Internet. David continued to worry as he listened to Pastor Rick.

"Church, listen. We know that we have something really wonderful here at Lachance. And we know that if we had a way to share what we have here with the world, why, there's no telling what God could do. Well, I am very excited to tell you that there is a way. We are going to be taking Lachance Community Church online to the Internet."

Some of the older people let out an audible "Oooo."

"That's right. There was a time when a church would have to spend hundreds of thousands of dollars to build a television ministry to spread the word of God beyond their own four walls, but now, with the power of the Internet, we can do that for a very affordable price. And we are talking about a high definition, first-class viewing experience! David is right now working on our plan."

David winced, then realized people were looking at him so he slowly changed his wince into a smile.

"We've done some amazing things as a church, but I believe our best days are ahead of us. We are launching our online video ministry on Easter Sunday and we believe God is going to do amazing things through this ministry.

"Now church, we know you want to partner in this with us, so we will be holding a special faith offering on Easter Sunday in order to prepare for the growth we will experience. This offering will ensure that Lachance will be well equipped to thrive in this new online Internet era of ministry. Our goal is eighty thousand dollars. I know that sounds like a lot, but I have faith. Do you? Let's pray.

"O Lord, thank you for all you've done for this church. Thank you for what you're going to do. I pray that you would guide each one of us as we consider what we can sacrifice to be a part of your kingdom expansion, both here in our community, around the world, and over the Internet. Amen."

David was still worrying about the live streaming after the service as he was cleaning up the stage. Inq must have noticed.

"Are you troubled, David? You don't seem yourself," Inq said.

"Oh, I'm fine. Yeah. Good service this morning. Any gigs coming up?"

David would routinely parry inquiries into the state of his soul like this, not trusting himself to be discreet if he began to genuinely share his feelings.

"Now, David. Something is obviously amiss. Is there a problem?"

"Oh, nothing that a Sony XDCAM EX3 wouldn't solve. Other than that, no."

"Oh! Well I have the previous model, the EX1. You could use it if you like. Would that help?"

"You have a Sony XDCAM EX1? Really?"

"Yes. I bought it a while back to shoot footage for the annual Lachance Medieval Fair. But the rest of the year, it's just at home in a closet."

"Medieval fair? I had no idea. But, anyway, Yes! That's amazing. Thank you! Inq, you have no idea. You may have just saved my life,

I mean, my job. Thank you!"

"Most happy to oblige, David. I can bring it next week. I'm glad to see it get some more use."

"Oh, Inq, you are an answer to prayer!" David wanted to hug him.

"You just need to ask, David. You just need to ask."

MORE COUNCIL

They all sat quietly around the table in the meeting room, straining to hear the raised voices from the foyer on the other side of the door. David had arrived early for the monthly church council meeting, prepared to review his draft version of the tablecloth policy. Jillian sat beside him. She stopped leafing through her copy of the new policy when they heard the voices in the foyer. Pastor Rick and Wayne were sitting next to each other, also listening to the voices on the other side of the door. Pastor Rick had a concerned look on his face. Spencer, also at the table, was looking at his phone. Gerald, the council chair, and Bill had yet to come into the room. It was their raised voices in the foyer.

The door opened, and Gerald and Bill entered and took their seats. Gerald looked around the table, then looked at his watch. "I'm sorry we're late, everyone. We better get started. Pastor Rick, would you open us in prayer?"

"Of course." Pastor Rick bowed his head. "Dear Lord, give us your wisdom and guidance as we lead your church. May we know your presence here among us tonight and may we further your kingdom. Amen."

David looked around the room. Spencer was still on his phone. Jillian was adjusting her orthopaedic seat cushion. Wayne and Pastor Rick were both leaning back in their chairs, arms folded. Bill was staring grim-faced at Pastor Rick, as he had been since he entered the room.

"OK, everyone," Gerald began. "We're going directly to item four in your agenda. Bill, would you share with everyone what you just told me in the foyer?"

"Excuse me," said Jillian. "Why are we jumping around like

this? Will we be getting to the tablecloths? David has worked very hard on his draft policy."

"I'm sure David won't mind waiting. Bill, please proceed."

Bill cleared his throat. "I've been to the bank and some new information has come to light."

Pastor Rick twisted in his seat and ran his fingers through his hair. He sat up and glared across the table at Bill.

"I met with the bank manager to discuss the details of our renovation loan—"

" — Hold on, Bill," Pastor Rick interrupted. "Not everyone needs to be here for this. If this is what you and Gerald want to discuss tonight, then Jillian, Spencer and David can be excused."

Spencer quickly stood and left the room, as if he wanted to be gone before Pastor Rick changed his mind. David began to get up out of his chair, too.

"This affects David as much as anyone. He should stay," Bill said.

David froze half-way out of his chair and looked over at Pastor Rick.

"He can go. David, you are excused," Pastor Rick said firmly.

David continued to stand.

"He should stay," said Bill.

"He's my employee, and I say he's excused," said Pastor Rick.

"I'm council chair," said Gerald, "and I request his presence in this meeting."

"No, really." David finally straightened to his full height, "I'm happy to be excused, I'll leave—"

"SIT DOWN!" snapped Gerald.

David slowly sat back down and looked apologetically across the table at Pastor Rick.

"Fine." Pastor Rick conceded. "As a staff member, it might be good for David to stay and observe the discussion. Now, as a volunteer, Jillian, you don't need—"

"I'll stay," said Jillian. "As a ministry leader and donor, I'd like to hear what Bill has to say."

Pastor Rick smiled his mouth-only smile, nodded at Jillian and turned to Bill, "Fine. Please proceed."

"Actually, Rick, I'd like to hear from you. Can you tell us all how it came about that we got the money for our renovation?" Bill asked.

"I'm no accountant, like you Bill, but we went with our proposal for a loan to the bank and they weren't willing to give it to us at first. I talked to Dean at The Flow. He put in a good word for us and arranged for the loan to happen. That's all," Pastor Rick shrugged.

"'Put in a good word for us.' Is that all they did?" Bill asked.

"Bill, you're the accountant. Why are you asking me?"

"I'm just trying to figure out if you really know what's going on. Specifically, what's going to happen if we miss our payment."

"We aren't going to miss our payment, Bill. Where's your faith?" said Pastor Rick, practically spitting the word 'faith' at Bill.

"The Flow did a lot more than put in a good word of us. They guaranteed the loan, didn't they? And the arrangement means that if we default, The Flow assumes the mortgage, along with the title on our building. We're finished."

Jillian turned toward Pastor Rick, her face the definition of dismay. "Is that true, Pastor?"

"Jillian, first of all, we are going to make our payments. Secondly, Dean and I go way back. He isn't going to kick us out of our building. He would never do that." Pastor Rick kept smiling

Bill was not amused. "I hear that The Flow is looking to start a satellite location in our part of town. And from what I hear, it was Dean that talked you into doing the renovation, guaranteeing the loan. Why would they do that if they didn't have plans for taking over our building? It's brilliant, actually. For the price of the renovation, they take over our entire property."

"Look, Bill," said Pastor Rick, "All of this went through proper channels. The treasurer, Roger Davis, signed off on all of this. You should be asking him these questions. It's not my fault if you were off recovering from your heart attack when this opportunity came along."

"Rick, you and I both know that Roger Davis is a nice guy who would sign anything that you put in front of him. You rammed this thing through while I was sick because you knew I'd never allow it," said Bill.

"I don't have to put up with this, you know," said Pastor Rick, "This church was stuck. We needed a game changer. We had a tired old building and I went out and found the money to upgrade our facility to give us a chance to grow. Is that wrong? I have given the best years of my life to this church, trying to bring change and growth and this is the thanks I get? Accusations and innuendos. From you, Bill, from you. All those nights we spent, together, when your wife was sick..."

At the mention of his wife, Bill slammed both hands down on table.

"YOU SOLD THIS CHURCH FOR A MESS OF POTTAGE!"

Pastor Rick and Bill glared at each other across the table.

Wayne spoke first. "What does that mean? Mess of what?"

Pastor Rick snapped at Wayne "For God's sake, Wayne, do you ever read the Bible?"

Bill shook his head. "It doesn't matter Wayne. It doesn't matter. It's over."

"Bill, how exactly would this play out?" asked Jillian.

"If we don't make our payment of sixty thousand dollars by May first, then The Flow assumes the mortgage, along with the title to our property. I know they are already assembling their leadership team for a satellite location. It's pretty obvious what their plan is. They'll kick us out of our own building and turn it into a satellite location."

"We'll sue. We'll get a lawyer and we will stop this," Wayne said.

"I don't see how we can afford a long legal battle, either. Besides, I think the Bible says something about lawsuits among believers."

"Then we simply must raise the funds for the eighty thousand payment, regardless of whether or not this business with The Flow is true," said Jillian. "So, Pastor Rick, what is the plan?"

"That's right, Jillian, we should be focusing on our plan for success, not failure. We have a vision to radically expand the reach of this church. We are going online. We are going to launch on Easter Sunday and start video web streaming our services. David, tell them about it."

David blinked three times. "Oh, well, I have good news. Inq actually has a good camera for this kind of thing, and so that's a huge relief because buying one would be really expensive. And, yeah, I will be setting up live web streaming of our services, just like Pastor Rick says. Very exciting." David grimaced at how unconvincing his pitch was, even to himself.

"That's not all," continued Pastor Rick. "We are going to have a special offering on Easter Sunday to help us launch this ministry.

We have a very special service planned, with a surprise that I can't even tell you about. Once that service gets online, people can watch it live and forward it to each other on email and Facebook. It will be a huge evangelistic tool. You know, people drive by this church every day and just ignore it, but they can't ignore it when it shows up in their email!"

"I ignore email all the time," said Gerald.

"Gerald, come on, if a friend of yours sent you a link and told you to check out something, wouldn't you be curious?" Pastor Rick was now warming to his subject.

"We are going to give people a new reason to be excited about Lachance, about what God is doing here. And they'll have an opportunity to partner with us through our special Easter offering. Oh, don't you worry. God is so much bigger than a mortgage payment. God can do this."

"Our offerings are barely covering weekly expenses, said Bill. "It will take a miracle. Our reserve fund was eaten up by the Tom Lindsey fiasco. We don't have any assets to sell, or any other streams of income. It's gonna have to be God doing it, alright, because the cupboard is bare. Completely bare."

They agreed to table the rest of the agenda items. David quietly slipped to his office to get his coat, hoping to leave unnoticed.

"David," he heard Pastor Rick say to him from his office. David steeled himself as he walked toward it. He stood at the door and looked in at Pastor Rick, sitting as his desk, head in his hands, downcast eyes. He spoke, still looking down.

"You will not breathe a word of anything you heard tonight. Not one word."

"Yes sir. Not a word."

Without looking up, Pastor Rick waved David away with one hand. David turned and closed the office door behind him, careful not to make a sound.

DETENTE

David and Pastor Rick spent the rest of the week carefully avoiding each other. David wondered how the contours of their relationship would change after the council meeting. Up until now, Pastor Rick held all the power over David. But now, David knew Pastor Rick's secrets. In Pastor Rick's injunction to remain silent was the admission that if David did talk, it would hurt Pastor Rick. And therein lay David's new-found power. Neither David nor Pastor Rick probed the limits of this new balance in their relationship. David remained wary.

For the first time, David possessed the means to strike back. That realization reopened old wounds — being taken for granted, resented, and manipulated. He remembered being forced to make an apology that Pastor Rick's wife should have offered to Carissa. Pastor Rick fell far short of the expectations David had when he first came to Lachance. David fantasized about revealing the details of how foolish Rick had been, a parting shot at a flailing pastor of a dying church.

But David knew these things would all come to light soon enough, without him breathing a word of it. He need not sully his own reputation by trading in gossip. But along with his fantasies of revenge, David pitied Pastor Rick, an imperfect man who faithfully served many years but had been denied a share of the professional religious success of his peers, like Dean Goodwin. David was haunted by the image of Pastor Rick at his desk with his head in his hands, downcast and defeated, waving him away.

Early one morning as the buses were starting up, David realized he'd been so wrong about Pastor Rick. He knew he'd been expecting too much of the man — to be the father he never had, to meet his needs for guidance, friendship and affirmation. In fact, David had expected Pastor Rick to be God. In that moment, David felt a new liberty. He no longer saw Pastor Rick as the man who fell short of his expectations, but merely a man who was good and bad, strong and weak, able to help and in need of help. In that epiphany, David asked God to forgive him for making Pastor Rick an idol. And in that moment, David purposed in his heart to help Pastor Rick as best as he could, to serve him faithfully to the end, even if that was only weeks away.

Later that morning David decided to talk to Pastor Rick. He left his office, walked across the hall, knocked and opened his door a crack. "Pastor Rick, you have a minute?"

Pastor Rick looked up from his desk, his expression brightening as he saw David. "Oh, David, sure. Come in. What can I do for you?"

"I just wanted to talk about my progress, you said to keep you updated..."

"Oh, sure. Have a seat. Really excited about where we're headed. How are things coming along on the technical side of things? All squared away?"

"Well, yes, I think I have a way to do it. Inq loaned us his camcorder which is really high quality. He also had a video card we can put into my desktop computer to do the... well, the details aren't really important. Um, I just think there's a way it will work. I found a service that has a free trial period, so we can use that to get started."

"Great! Very resourceful! I knew you'd work it all out. I told you we could do it for free!"

David was unnerved by how cheerful Pastor Rick was, but he continued, trying to get to the heart of what he wanted to say.

"What I really wanted you to know, though, is that I really want this to work. I'm going to do everything I can to make this successful."

"Oh, of course, David, I expect no less of you. You've been doing that from day one. I probably should tell you that more often."

"No, what I really wanted to say, is, you know, since the meeting the other night, I—"

But Pastor Rick cut him off.

"Oh, David, don't you worry about that meeting. Things just

got carried away. I've sorted it all out. The bank, Dean, Bill, we're all square and there is nothing to worry about. You understand me now? There is nothing to worry about. God will provide, and we will be just fine. No need to even think about that any more. Anything else?"

That was it. The door was closed, and Pastor Rick wasn't going to let David in. David was about to give up, but made one last attempt.

"Just wanted you know I care about this church and about you."

"Oh, of course you do, I know that. And I care about you, too. I'm glad we had this talk. Easter is gonna be great. I have a great plan for the sermon, might be my best ever! I just love Easter. Don't you? Anyway, I better get my nose back to the grindstone. Glad we could chat."

Pastor Rick stood up from behind his desk and ushered David out the door. David went back to his office. *At least I tried*, he thought.

David spent the rest of the afternoon on Twitter. Following his arrest for DUI, Tom Lindsey was in an all-out war with his combative ex-fans, who, like jilted lovers, were out for revenge. Then there were those from the far-flung fringes of conservative Christianity who disapproved of all the so-called Christian rock music ever since the first drum set defiled a church sanctuary back in the seventies. They crowed proudly that Tom Lindsey's fall vindicated what they'd been saying all along, that allowing Satan's music into church would lead many astray.

Then there were the peacemakers, who looked upon Tom Lindsey as the prodigal son, and believed the church should be praying for him, not condemning him. There were also former Christians who identified with Tom and defended him, applauding him for seeing the light and leaving behind the backward morality and superstition of the church.

These groups all tangled with Tom Lindsey online and he goaded them on. The most vicious exchanges were between the different factions themselves in the comment sections of web sites. Charges of heresy and condemnations to hell were routine. In the midst of this storm, Tom Lindsey became one of the top accounts on Twitter, gaining millions of followers. His new version of *Mountaintop* was a smash hit, DJs often sharing the most outrageous tidbits from the social media firestorm as they introduced the song. A world tour was in the works. Tom Lindsey was on top of the world.

David's Facebook feed was filled with friends from all different factions posting their opinions. He scrolled through headline after headline:

> "What Tom Lindsey teaches us about the corruption of the Worship Industrial Complex"

> "Why I'm Praying for Tom Lindsey and why you should too"

> "Nine Things the church can learn from Tom Lindsey"

> "Worship Leaders: Repent, lest you fall like Tom Lindsey"

> "Tom Lindsey exposes the hypocrisy of the Church"

And David, like millions of others, was continuing to follow Tom Lindsey on Twitter. Each time the superstar tweeted, it would set off a new round of reaction, analysis, condemnation and praise.

> @TomLindsey: Livin' abundantly y'all - making it rain!!!
> <Posted with a picture of a shirtless Tom Lindsey tossing money in the air at a dance club>

While David was very distressed that his hero had fallen so far, he did get some perverse enjoyment out of watching the train wreck unfold, wondering how it would all end up. He set his phone to vibrate every time Tom Lindsey tweeted so that he wouldn't miss one. At every worship team rehearsal, they talked about the latest gossip about Tom Lindsey, reacting and speculating about the state of his soul, his family and his friends.

David kept in touch with Amy via text. She had the inside line on what was really happening with Tom.

> David: Amy, were u surprised by all this?
> Amy: Well, not really. He was always a little shallow.
> David: How's Tyler?
> Amy: He's already managing another band. I think they picked him because he got TL up to the big time.
> David: Figures, people see the TL sell-out as a plus.
> Amy: Yup. Gotta go.

David: K bye.

That night David sat with Chuck to watch a basketball game on TV.

"David, what's this about putting the church on the Internet?" said Chuck.

"It's a way for us to expand our reach, I guess. People can watch it on their computer or their phone."

"How do they find it?"

"It will be on the church website. Why do you ask?"

"Well, my daughter, I told her I was going to church. I think she thinks I'm in some weird cult. Anyway, she invited me to come visit for Easter."

"Wow! That's great Chuck!"

"Yeah, and I thought I could show her our church on the computer. We could watch it on Easter Sunday."

"That's a great idea."

"So just go to the church website?"

"Yeah. That's all."

"Now what's the big offering that Pastor Rick's been talking about?"

"Well, the church is in sort of a tight spot financially. We really need to raise eighty grand."

"What for?"

"That's a good question. Money is fungible. It's for the fungible fund."

"What does that mean?"

"Sorry, it's just to pay some major bills. They took out a mortgage to do renovations and there's a big payment due."

"What if they don't raise the money?"

"We need to have faith, Chuck."

"Yeah, yeah. Faith. But seriously, what if you don't get the money?"

"Well, I'll be out of a job, probably. They'll have to make cuts and there's a lot of changes that would have to happen, probably. But don't worry about it."

"Really? You'd be out of a job?"

"Oh, I don't know. Listen, it's nothing to worry about. I have faith. I'm sure people will give. It will be fine. Anyway, I'm getting tired. I'm gonna go to bed. Good night."

"Good night."

David felt bad that he'd mentioned losing his job. He didn't want Chuck to worry about him. He also wanted to protect Chuck's innocence and faith in Pastor Rick by not divulging how ugly the situation really was. As he settled down into bed he said a short prayer for Chuck. There was a knock on his door.

"David?" Chuck said.

David went to the door and opened it. "Hey, Everything OK?"

"David, I just wanted to say that if you did lose your job that you wouldn't have to worry about rent, you know. Like, until you got back on your feet. That'd be fine. Besides, I cut back my drinking, so I don't need beer money any more. OK?"

"Oh, Chuck. That's really nice. I really appreciate that, but I'm sure things will be fine."

"Well, I'm serious. It's nice to have you around, you know? It's good. I'd hate for you to have to leave."

Chuck rubbed his eyes, clenched his jaw and looked back up at David. "I'm gonna pray for you, David," said Chuck.

"Chuck, thanks. I mean it. We just need to pray that God provides. I'm sure it will all work out."

David winced as he said those last words. The truth was, he didn't think it would all work out. But it was nice to know he wouldn't be thrown out on the street.

PREPARATION

Palm Sunday. Lachance Community Church celebrated Jesus' triumphal entry into Jerusalem like many other churches, parading the children onto the stage, waving their palm fronds while singing "Hosanna." This Palm Sunday was no different. At the appointed time, David and the band began leading the congregation in the singing of the designated "Hosanna" song and the procession of kids made their way from the back doors of the auditorium to the platform. The congregation stopped singing to watch. Some kids waved their palm fronds and smiled, a few cried, but most simply looked confused. Even the babies, in various stages of distress, were not spared from being conveyed down the aisle by nursery workers. As they moved forward, parents and grandparents took pictures and video, children dutifully waving to beaming parents.

The parade bottle-necked at the front as the two-year-olds slowed down to negotiate their ascent of the stage steps. Eventually, they all found a spot on stage, mindlessly waving palm fronds — except for a few unruly boys staging a sword fight with their palm branches, much to the delight of their peers. And so went the annual pre-Easter sacramental exhibition of child-like adorableness.

David dutifully continued the song as the children waited on stage the requisite amount of time. When the song finished, they began their descent from the stage, marching out the auditorium doors and back to their natural habitat in the lower recesses of the church building.

David relished each minute of this ritual, even with all its apparent absurdity, knowing that his time at Lachance may be coming to an end very soon. He tried to fool himself into a sense of peace, believing that the special Easter offering would produce the required money to stave off a hostile takeover by The Flow, but his faith was weak. As they sang the words "Hosanna, You are the God who Saves us," it came out from his heart as more of a question than a proclamation. He looked out on the congregation this Sunday, when attendance was always up (the parade of the palms being very popular with young families) and wondered what would become of them if Lachance ceased to exist? He thought of the seniors, the ones who had paid for the building that was now in grave danger of being taken away from them. How would they feel? Did they have any idea what was really going on? These thoughts swam through his mind as he sang. He chose to give them voice as he closed their time of singing in worship.

"Oh Lord, may we truly experience You as the God who saves us this Easter season. We truly need it. Amen."

Before David could even open his eyes, Pastor Rick was on stage, turning the key to his hard-wired wireless mic, and smiling to the congregation as the loudspeakers hissed warmly.

"Good morning Lachance! Oh, how I love seeing the kids all dressed up and waving their palm branches. I know they're cute..." Pastor Rick's expression changed from cheerfulness to gravity. "But they are our future. Yes. Our future. And I know that each one of you cares about our future just as much as you care about our children. Next week, we'll be receiving a very special offering to go towards the future of our church. Here at Lachance we are launching into the future of ministry. We are taking church online! That's right. We are taking Lachance Community Church onto the Internet."

In the front row, Pastor Rick's wife looked around the auditorium while vigorously nodding her head. Several ladies throughout the church took their cue from her and offered their own gestures of approval.

"David has been working to get us ready for this new era of ministry and we are excited about what it means for us. Did you know that when we are online, anyone anywhere in the entire world with an Internet connection can watch us online? We can only fit about five hundred people in our building, but we can reach over a billion people online! Now, in order for our church to be well positioned for the future, for our children, for our online ministry, we are taking a very special offering. Our goal is eighty thousand dollars and we are asking each one of you to do two things.

"Pray. First, begin by thanking God for all the good things he's done for you. For your family and for your children. And then ask him what role you can play in securing the future of your church for your children. Ask him what he can provide, and then come prepared next Sunday to give. We want Lachance to be well positioned to be around for generations to come, and I don't want to alarm you, but we are a little behind our budget. We need to make that up, so part of the offering will go toward that, and the rest, every penny, will go toward preparing us for future ministry success.

"I believe God will provide. I believe he wants to use each one of you to be his provision. I'm excited to think of the blessing he will pour out on us as a church as we dig deep and sacrifice for the furtherance of his Kingdom. Let us pray.

"Oh God, the maker of heaven and earth and the provider of every good gift, we ask you to speak to each one of us, to inspire us to be generous toward your church, to be a part of the amazing work that you are doing here and to provide the means for us to give sacrificially. As we take up our offering today, I ask that you'll bless these gifts, multiply them and use them to bless the entire world, both here in our community, and on the Internet. Amen."

The congregation muttered *Amen* in response to the prayer.

Pastor Rick continued. "Now church, I have a very special sermon planned for Easter Sunday. I want every one of you to invite your friends and family, anyone you can think of. Let's have them here on Sunday. We want this auditorium filled. I always look forward to preaching on Easter Sunday, but I have something extra special planned. And email, Facebook and Twitter your friends as well, tell them they can watch online. Just link them to our website, lachancecc.com and they'll be able to watch online."

As Pastor Rick launched into his sermon, David's phone buzzed. There was another tweet from Tom Lindsey:

@RealTomLindsey: Sunday mornings like a boss

There was a picture attached to the tweet — a selfie of Tom Lindsey in what appeared to be a hot tub flanked by two women.

After the service, the band was packing up their gear on the stage when David realized he may have only a few more Sundays to work with them. Leading the church in worship with this group, his friends, had been what kept him going in the darkest times over the last six months. Trisha and Carissa were at the corner of the stage, holding hands as Trisha talked, Carissa smiling as she listened. Calvin was watching Sid demonstrate the features of his latest guitar pedal, with Inq interjecting his comments as well. Eric was coiling cable.

"Hey everyone, can we just take a minute and head into the back room? There are some things we need to talk about," David said.

Carissa and Trisha stopped talking, looked at David and then back at each other with slight alarm. David had never done this type of thing before. Calvin, Sid and Eric shrugged at each other and walked toward the back room. Eric quickly finished coiling the cable in his hands, set it down and followed. Once in the back room, they sat in the chairs in a loose circle and waited for David to start.

"I probably should do this more often, but I just wanted to say how much I appreciate being able to work with all of you. We've really come a long way in the time I've been here. I want you know it means a lot to me.

"Sid, you are a great guitar player, and in the past few months you've learned when to hold back and when to go for it. You're not just a guitar player now, you're a musician.

"Calvin, thanks for working so hard with a metronome. You've really improved your sense of time. You love to have fun and you help all of us have fun. This is supposed to be fun.

"Inq, you've been so encouraging to me ever since I came here. You're always on time, prepared, and eager to help however you can. Thanks.

"Eric, you're always the first one here, setting up the sound system and the last to leave. Thanks for serving us — and the Lord — so well, and for putting up with so many complaints. No one ever notices when you do a good job, only when something goes wrong. You've been doing a good job. And I wanted to say that."

Calvin patted Eric on the back as David said this. The room was filled with warmth as David affirmed each of the band members.

"Carissa, you and I both know what you've been through. A lot of people would've given up, but I'm so thankful you didn't. You really shine God's light on us when you sing."

"Trisha," David caught himself as he looked at Trisha. This was the first time he'd looked her in the eye since she began dating Chad. He stuttered, swallowed and continued.

"Trisha, you've served so faithfully, and you've been a good friend. Thanks. Everyone, we've all come so far. I'm really looking forward to next Sunday. I love working with each of you. I guess that's all. Thanks for listening."

David looked around at his team. Most of them looked stunned. Carissa had tears welling up. She was the first to speak. "David, I want to pray for you." She started moving a chair. "Sit here. Let's gather round and lay hands on you."

In spite of being a Christian for as long as he could remember, David never felt comfortable being prayed for, and didn't particular enjoy being pawed over. But for Carissa's sake, he sat in the chair she'd dragged into the middle of the circle. The team gathered around and each laid a hand on him. David closed his eyes. He distinctly felt Trisha's delicate touch on his right shoulder. Inq plopped his meaty paw square on David's head as Carissa began to pray.

"Father, we thank you, Father, for bringing us David, Father. Father, we ask that, Father, you would fill him, Father, with your spirit, Father. That, Father, he would know, Heavenly Father, how precious, Father, he is, Father, in your eyes, Father, and how much, Father, we appreciate, Father, all he's done for us, Father. Bless him Father, Father, Father, fill him with your grace. Father, in Jesus Name, Amen."

It was a particularly heartfelt, fervent prayer. David knew this because of the high number of 'Fathers.' After she prayed, they let go of David. Carissa hugged him. David sat back down in the chair and waited as they all left the room. Trisha, however, stayed back.

"What is going on?" she asked.

"What do you mean?"

"Are you leaving? Are you quitting? Or are you going to get fired?"

"No, what gives you that idea? I just thought I should try to be more encouraging."

"I talked to my dad. I know what's going on."

"Do you? Well…"

"So you did this because you think you might be gone soon. Am I right?"

She saw right through him. He couldn't deny, but he tried anyway.

"I have faith. This is not a problem that's too big for God. There's no such thing as a problem for God. He owns the cattle on a thousand hills. He is faithful."

David knew he was rambling. He still got nervous when he talked to Trisha.

"Well, I don't know what to say either. But… you deserve better. Than all this."

"I don't think of it that way. Whatever happens, I'm glad I came here. I'm thankful I got this chance. There's been a lot of good."

David wondered if this was the last chance he would ever have to speak to Trisha alone. In that moment, he decided to disclose his feelings. He didn't know quite what to say, but he stood up, looked at Trisha, opened his mouth and began to talk.

"Trisha, I'm really glad I got to meet you and for us to become friends. I've enjoyed every minute we've spent together. I think Chad is really blessed to have you. I envy him. I wish I could have that kind of happiness."

David was amazed at himself. For the first time, he felt like he said the right thing to Trisha when the pressure was on. He made his feelings clear to her, acknowledging the fact that she was dating another guy, but letting her know the door was open. It was a master performance. He had no idea he had it in him. He was still admiring himself when he realized Trisha had turned and quickly left the room, without even saying goodbye.

David didn't recall seeing Chad at church that morning. *Huh*, he thought. *Might there still be a chance?*

The door opened and Inq stuck his head in. "We ready to set things up?"

"Oh! Yes. I ordered pizza during the sermon. It should be here soon. Let's eat first and then we'll get things going."

Inq brought his video camera and promised to help David get the web streaming set up for next week. They walked to the front doors where the pizza had just arrived. David paid for it, and he and Inq sat together in his office to eat..

"So, what happens if we fall short of our offering goal?" Inq must have been as curious as Trisha.

"Lots of people have been asking me that. My answer is that I have faith. God will provide. He'll provide the money in the offering. And if not, he'll provide something. He always does."

"Well, I couldn't help but speculate. Your inspirational words reminded me of what a general might say to his troops on the eve of a particularly perilous battle, one in which survival was by no means assured. Am I not far off the mark?"

David tried to parse 'Am I not far off the mark', but quickly gave up and simply said. "Hmmm. Hard to say."

"Well, David, whatever happens will be good. As I'm sure you recall, Boethius said 'All fortune is good fortune; for it either rewards, disciplines, amends, or punishes, and so is either useful or just.'"

"Right. Good old Boethius. He sure knew his stuff, didn't he?"

"Indeed, he did, David. Now, let's get to work. Things may not work out just as we desire them, but it won't be because you and I didn't do our part."

"Where do we start?"

"May I have a piece of paper?"

David found him one.

"Ah, thank you. We'll start with a picture. Here is what we'll do." Inq began drawing boxes, lines and other figures. "Here is the Sony camera, capturing video in the auditorium. The video comes out of the camera into this little box here, a converter which allows us to use an existing CAT5 cable running from the control room to the offices here. We'll have to find it up in the ceiling and run it down to your computer.

"I have another converter here which allows us to plug it into your computer, once we've installed the new video card. Then the video is processed for upload and heads up here to the anyStream servers where it is distributed to the entire Internet, as represented by this cloud. I've modified the church website so that any time we are streaming, the video appears right on our home page, easy as pie. Does all this make sense?"

"Most of it does not."

"Ah... well, nonetheless it was helpful for me to put it all to paper. Shall we begin?"

"You bet. What's first?"

"Well, we're here. Shall we install the video card?"

They installed the video card. As Inq was loading the software, David went to the custodian's room and found a step ladder. He brought it back to the office and began removing ceiling tiles, poking his head through with a flashlight and looking for 'about 30 feet of blue wires coiled up,' as described by Inq. After several tiles and two sneezing fits, he found the cable above Rhonda's desk and tossed it over toward his own office. It was now running down the corner of his office, along the floor and into a converter box connected to the newly installed video card on his computer. Phase one was complete.

In the auditorium, David was playing with Inq's camera while Inq Googled the manufacturer of one of the converter boxes to determine the proper dip switch settings. David pressed *play* on the camera and watched the display. To his delight, he saw recorded footage of Inq in front of a green screen in an ill fitting suit of armor, swinging a sword as if battling an array of imaginary adversaries. He looked utterly ridiculous. David was laughing so hard he didn't hear Inq enter the room.

Inq, looked over David's shoulder. "Oh! I forgot that was in there."

"Inq, I'm really sorry, I don't mean to laugh. I shouldn't have looked at that. It's none of my business."

Inq ignored the apology and kept watching the footage. "Not bad, if I say so myself. Though my technique is more Japanese aikido than anything from King Arthur's court. The plan was to have me doing that at Stonehenge or some such place and use it as a promo video for the medieval fair. Never got around to it. Pity. But... I digress. Let's keep going."

Inq showed David how to set up the camera on the tripod, then fidgeted with several settings to get the best-looking picture. "OK, it's running. Let's get back to your office. Time to test it out."

They returned to David's office where Inq showed David how to use the video control software and test the incoming feed from the camera. It was working. David then logged into the anyStream website in the free account he set up. He followed the instructions and clicked on the big green "Begin Streaming Now" button on the page and began streaming the video of the empty auditorium.

"So far so good?"

"I think so."

Inq had his laptop out and was typing.

"OK, I've switched over the church home page to show the video feed. Now we test for real. I'll go into the auditorium and you look up the church web site on your phone. You should see me in the auditorium."

David waited for his phone to load the church web page. When it did, he saw the church auditorium with Inq on the platform using a mic stand as a sword and rehearsing the same Japanese aikido moves he'd seen in the saved footage on the camera. It was working. David ran into the auditorium.

"Inq! It's working. It's working. You saved my life. Oh man, I can't thank you enough."

"My pleasure. Now you stand up here and move around. I want to check some things out on your computer, make sure our settings are optimal."

"OK, but I'm not doing any imaginary sword fighting."

"You're no fun!" Inq jogged back out to the auditorium towards David's office.

David paced from one end of the auditorium to the other, thanking God for Inq's help in getting the streaming up and running. Things may not work out at Lachance, but it wouldn't be because of him.

A few minutes later, Inq returned.

"All set, my boy. I've shut things down. I'll help you get things up and running next Sunday morning, but it all looks good. We are ready to go."

"Inq, you're the best. Thanks. Thanks so much."

"It is truly my pleasure to serve you, my church, and my God. Allow me to drive you home, or wherever you may be headed."

"Home would be great. Thanks again."

Once home, David spent the afternoon searching the web for worship pastor jobs. He also added "successfully designed, installed, implemented, and tested worship service live web streaming solution" to the achievements section of his resume.

SURRENDER

The band practice on Thursday night went well. The team was eager to do their best, for the church, for David, even for Pastor Rick. They were nervous about being broadcast on the Internet, but David reassured them that very few people would be watching. David only knew of Chuck and his daughter who planned to watch online for sure, but it was something to get people excited about, even if it wasn't going to make any real difference. It seemed like that was enough for Pastor Rick.

Pastor Rick dropped by at the end of rehearsal.

"Hey gang, I just want to let you all know how much I appreciate what you do every Sunday. And this Sunday is so huge in the life of our church. I don't have to remind you of that. I mean, it is Easter, of course. I expect we'll have a huge turnout. And, of course, we are taking our special offering at the end of the service. I have faith that God will move in the hearts of our people. I was wondering, what song do you have planned during the offering at the end of the service?

"I Surrender All!" offered Calvin. Carissa and Trisha rolled their eyes at Calvin's attempt at humor. Inq laughed in spite of himself.

Pastor Rick did not get the joke.

"Excellent choice! We need to remind people that it all belongs to Jesus. That is one of my favorite hymns. It's a favorite for our seniors, too. And they certainly give the lion's share of the money around here, so it makes good sense to appeal to them. David, you have really thought this through. It is going to be wonderful, I can tell. Wonderful."

Pastor Rick turned and walked back out of the auditorium. When he was out of earshot, Calvin was the first to speak. "Sorry, I shouldn't have joked. What do we do now?"

"Surrender," said David. "We'll change the song."

"Really? That's so... manipulative," Trisha said.

"Obviously, it is what Pastor Rick wants. Look, he's under a lot of pressure. Maybe it isn't the best choice, but I don't want to change it, and then we don't get enough in the offering and it's my fault for not doing what he asked."

"Oh please! Just go and explain the joke and let us do the song we practiced instead," Calvin's appeal was met with nods from the others.

David persisted. "No. We're going with 'I Surrender All.' That's that. It's late. Let's go home."

"Oh David," said Carissa, "You're in a tough spot, I know. We'll support you. Maybe we should run through the song."

"Good idea."

Trisha found some old hymnbooks stored in the piano bench. She passed one to David and Carissa and one for Sid and Inq to share.

"These books smell funny. And it's just notes. Where are the chords?" asked Sid.

"It's in the key of D. You'll catch on," David said.

Trisha played an introduction and they began to sing.

All to Jesus I surrender,
All to Him I freely give;
I will ever love and trust Him,
In His presence daily live.
I surrender all,
I surrender all,
All to Thee, my blessed Saviour,
I surrender all.

David could almost hear his grandmother singing along with him. By the third verse, Sid had figured out the chords and was playing along. Calvin was playing the drums softly, using his brushes instead of drumsticks. The effect of this simple hymn was hypnotic, tranquil. David prayed in his heart as they sang the final chorus. *O God, this is all yours. To give, to take away. It is all yours.*

They finished the song and each of them stood in reverent silence, wanting the moment to linger as long as possible.

"Maybe God wants us to sing that song after all, Calvin," Carissa said.

Calvin just smiled and shrugged.

"Well the good Lord spoke to Balaam through an ass, so I suppose it is possible he spoke to us through Calvin," Inq said.

Calvin threw a drumstick at him.

David grinned. "Yeah. Well, who knows what God is going to do. But this is a good sign, I suppose. At least I hope so."

"We all hope so." Trisha didn't sound the least bit hopeful.

HOLY SATURDAY

The buzz of David's phone woke him on Saturday morning. It was Tom Lindsey tweeting again. David's former role model had spent the night of Good Friday at another bacchanalian gathering of celebrities and hangers on. It was a stark contrast to the quiet communion service David and a few dozen members of Lachance Community Church had attended.

Throughout the night, Tom Lindsey had tweeted pictures of himself, each one looking more inebriated than the last. Each image sparked another round of online recriminations. David suspected the tweets were intended to create a spectacle and generate publicity. If that was the case, it was working. Tom Lindsey's Twitter account now had over five million followers, seemingly split evenly between new and former fans. David was beginning to find it all tiring and predictable, but at the same time he couldn't bear to look away.

After breakfast, he went for a walk. He stopped for a coffee at Beans of Production and then found himself headed toward the church. He recognized Bill's car alone in the otherwise empty parking lot. He decided to go in and see what Bill was up to.

"Hey Bill."

Bill looked up from the pile of invoices spread out on the conference room table. He pushed himself back from the table when he saw David, let out a long sigh and put on a weary smile.

"David. What brings you in on this Holy Saturday?"

"I was out for a walk and saw your car. I thought I'd say hi."

"So. Are you all ready for tomorrow?"

"Yeah. The band is rehearsed and ready to go."

"No, I mean, are you prepared for whatever happens tomorrow? You know we've never raised eighty grand on a single Sunday in the history of this church. I just don't know. Do I lack faith? What do you think?"

"I'm at peace. Boethius said that 'All fortune is good fortune; for it either rewards, disciplines, amends, or punishes, and so is either useful or just.' So tomorrow will either be useful or just."

"You've been spending too much time with Inq."

David leaned on the door jamb, his arms folded. "Maybe. But I'm really happy that I had the chance to work here. I've learned a lot. It was nothing like I thought it would be, but it has been good. I'm at peace."

"You've done well, David. I know it hasn't been easy. Even though I didn't think we should hire another staff member, I'm glad I got to know you. And if, you know, things change around here and you find yourself looking for another church, I'll do whatever I can to help you."

"Thanks Bill. I'll let you get back to work."

David walked into the auditorium. He thought of his first time here, how nervous he was. He thought about singing *Mountaintop* during that first meeting, and again the next Sunday morning. He marvelled at how different things had turned out. How he'd been let down by just about everyone he looked up to. He thought about the joy and the agony he'd experienced in that room in just half a year. And how it might all be coming to an end. A wave of sorrow rushed through him, leaving his heart feeling hollow, empty of the hope he held that first day he arrived.

He said goodbye to Bill on his way out and walked the road back toward his house. He felt his jaw tighten as he wondered what the next few days would bring. Where would he go, what would he do if the church went under, or was taken over by The Flow? As he walked, he asked God to give him a sign.

He looked up and saw a hearse driving up the road toward him.

WHY DO YOU SEEK THE LIVING AMONG THE DEAD?

On Easter Sunday, David arrived early at church and was perplexed to see a large object on the auditorium platform, covered in two white table cloths. It was about eight feet long, three feet wide and three feet high, and it took up the space where David and Carissa normally stood. David approached it and reached down to look beneath the tablecloths to see what it was.

"Don't touch that!" A voice called out.

David looked back to see a grinning Pastor Rick hurrying up the aisle toward him.

"Don't touch that," he repeated. "That's the big surprise. Got it? And make sure nobody touches it or moves it. Understand? It's very important. I want to make sure everyone gets to enjoy the surprise. Even you."

"Did you fill out the tablecloth request form for these tablecloths?" David quipped.

"Nope. Senior Pastor's exemption." Pastor Rick winked at David.

David was relieved to see him in good spirits. "Well, can you at least tell me what it's for?"

"It's for my sermon, an illustration. Don't you worry. It's going to be fantastic. I can't wait! But we absolutely must not ruin the surprise."

"It's huge. It's in the way of where I normally stand," David said. "I mean, if I had known, I could've set things up differently."

"I couldn't set it up until yesterday, I didn't want to ruin the surprise. Anyway, there's room on the other side of the pulpit for you and Carissa."

"Right, no problem."

But it was a problem. They would have to move mic stands and monitor speakers. Sight lines for the camera were now all wrong. As David thought about it, he began to feel angry at Pastor Rick, and realized the reaction was coming from his own anxiety about what was riding on this Sunday: his future, and the future of the church.

"I'm looking forward to the surprise. I'm sure it will be great," he said, not believing a word of it.

"It will be!" said Pastor Rick. "And you have the web streaming ready to go?"

"That's what I'm checking right now."

David turned on the camera in the back of the auditorium and then went back to his office to check the live stream on his computer. He loaded the software on his computer, logged into the streaming website and saw the image from the camera. He saw Eric arrive, walk up the aisle and stop dead when he saw the object on the stage. Then he heard Pastor Rick tell him it was a surprise and not to touch it. *Good*, thought David. *The audio is working as well.* All he had to do was click on the "START STREAMING" button and he would be ready to go.

David returned to the auditorium. Eric was moving the microphones over to the other side of the pulpit. David could tell from the way he was manhandling the mic stands that Eric was not pleased. David went up to the platform and put his hand on Eric's shoulder.

"Sorry about this. I just saw it this morning. But it is important to Pastor Rick."

"Yeah, I guess so. Just seems like—"

"What the heck is that!" called out Calvin as he came through the auditorium doors.

David shrugged at Calvin. "It's a surprise. Pastor Rick doesn't want anyone to touch it."

"Oh, man. You can't see the drums behind it. The Internet is going to be deprived of my sick drumming skills!"

"I don't make the rules, Calvin."

"Yeah, yeah, it's fine. Whatever."

The rest of the band arrived, each reacting in turn to the mysterious object on stage. David sensed an energy and an urgency to their music as they ran through their songs. *I'll miss this,* he thought, and then tried to tell himself, unconvincingly, that it wasn't necessarily all ending. They finished their rehearsal with 'I Surrender All' and still had thirty minutes before the start of the service. Some of the seniors who always arrived early were sitting in the auditorium and singing along, perhaps a good sign.

The band finished their sound check and retired to the back room, where they found Pastor Rick and Wayne. Pastor Rick started putting on his hard-wired-wireless microphone and transmitter pack.

"You tested the wireless?" Wayne asked.

"Sure did. Worked like a charm. Elizabeth could hear it even with the lid closed," said Pastor Rick.

"OK, everyone, let's pray," David said.

"I think we should gather round and hold hands," Carissa suggested.

Calvin pretended to spit on both of his hands, as he did every time they held hands to pray.

"The holding of hands embodies a greater spiritual truth: our unity in the risen Christ. And you mock, Calvin. Shame," said Inq.

They held hands and Pastor Rick led in prayer. "Oh God, we are gathered here in anticipation of a great morning. We are celebrating new life in Christ, and a new era for Lachance Community Church. O God, we ask that you provide everything we need, that hearts will be moved by the message of hope, moved to give, to surrender it all. Amen."

At this, David began to sing, with everyone joining in.

All to Jesus I surrender,
All to Him I freely give;
I will ever love and trust Him,
In His presence daily live.
I surrender all,
I surrender all.
All to Thee, my blessed Saviour,
I surrender all.

It's all up to God, now, David thought. "OK team, let's do this like it's the last chance we'll ever get!"

Trisha looked sharply at him as soon as the words left his mouth. David hadn't meant it to be a prophetic utterance, but

Trisha surely took it that way.

"Five minutes everyone, I'll meet you on the platform. I have to go start up the web stream."

David walked out the back room, down the aisle through the auditorium full of people dressed in their Easter best. Every seat was taken, and the ushers were bringing in the ugly grey folding chairs and setting up extra seats in the back, oblivious to the fire code.

David reached his computer and clicked on the "Start Streaming" button.

A dialog box opened up on his screen.

> "You have reached the end of your free trial period.
> Upgrade to Premium for just $299 per month!"

David froze. He clicked 'No Thanks' and prayed for a miracle. A new window popped up.

> "Continue using our Ad-Supported service?"

David clicked "Yes."

The image of the auditorium returned to life. A banner appeared on the screen.

> "Streaming Live NOW."

David breathed a huge sigh of relief, left the office and hustled back to the auditorium with a couple of minutes to spare. He pulled out his phone to check the church web site. He refreshed his browser and saw the live image of the church stage. He could even see the back of his own head. He smiled and said a prayer of thanks to God. He kept watching as the image of a large cockroach scurried across the lower third of the screen and was struck by a bolt of lightning. The ashen remains of the cockroach appeared to be blown away, revealing the words "Zapperz Pest Control" followed by an eight hundred number.

Oh my. What have I done? thought David. But it was too late. Pastor Rick was coming out and the band was taking the stage. The service was about to begin. David went up to the stage, took his guitar and spoke into the microphone.

"He is Risen!"

"He is Risen, indeed!" came the reply from the congregation.

Calvin counted in their opening song. Sid hit the opening power chords and they launched into their set, each song full of joy and celebration of the risen Christ. David drank in every second. He poured his heart into each word of every song. The congregation sang along with gusto.

They finished, and the congregation applauded. David wasn't sure if the applause was for Jesus' victory over death, or for how good the band sounded, because, to David's ears, they sounded really good. David exited out the back as Gerald took the stage to make some announcements and talk about the offering they'd receive at the end of the service.

David circled through the basement to come back upstairs to the foyer where he could get to his office and check the live stream on his computer. Gerald was just finishing and David saw Pastor Rick on his computer screen, coming up to the stage, inserting his key into the hardwired-wireless ignition switch in the pulpit, turn it and then return the key to his inside coat pocket. He turned directly to the camera and smiled. As this was happening, a blue banner ran along the lower third of the screen reading 'Bud Light' while the right edge of the screen showed a girl in a bikini dancing with a bottle in each hand.

"Good morning all, and especially to all those of you who are watching online."

Pastor Rick now waved to the camera. David shook his head in dismay. The viewer count read three people. David figured that one was probably his own computer, the other was his phone and the third was probably Chuck and his daughter. David's mind wandered as Pastor Rick preached, but he sat up and took notice when Pastor Rick walked over to the large object on the stage.

"You are all, I'm sure, wondering what this is."

With a theatrical flourish, Pastor Rick ripped away the tablecloth, revealing a shiny, dark brown mahogany casket.

The congregation gasped.

"Our Saviour willingly went to his death. He was not forced onto that cross. It was not the nails through his hands and his feet that held him there, but it was his love."

Pastor Rick summoned his tears for this crucial point in his sermon.

"His love for you, and His love for even me." His voice cracked.

David's phone buzzed. It was a new tweet from Tom Lindsey.

David ignored it and went back to watching Pastor Rick.

"Most of us, when our time comes, will be placed inside one of these." Pastor Rick ran his fingers along the length of the coffin.

"But Jesus — well, I could tell you, but I think we have to see it to really understand it."

Pastor Rick opened the lid of the coffin. He pulled a short step stool out from behind it and climbed in. The congregation gasped as he did so. David couldn't believe his eyes. The view count was now up to seven hundred eight-three viewers.

His phone buzzed again, a text from Amy.

> Amy: U there? Can u talk? Call me! Urgent!

David called Amy as he watched Pastor Rick close half of the lid over his legs and address the congregation from a sitting position in the coffin.

"Hello, David?"

"Hey Amy, what's up?"

"Have you seen Tom Lindsey's Twitter feed?"

"No, why?"

"He sent out a link to your church web site."

"What?!"

David checked his Twitter account and saw the tweet.

> @RealTomLindsey: Check out what I'm watching right now: www.lachancecc.com

David looked at the view count. It was now at three thousand and rising. The Bud Light girl was still dancing. There were also a hundred and seventy-nine viewer comments.

David was stunned. "How did this happen?"

"Listen," said Amy, "Back when you met with Tom Lindsey, we all heard what happened to you in that septic tank. I felt really bad for you. When your pastor came in asking Tom to tweet out the church website on Easter morning, well, I used to run Tom's twitter account and I wanted to do something nice for you, to help out your church. So I pre-scheduled that tweet to come out this morning. I guess they forgot to erase all those when Tom, you know, changed. I'm not sure what to say. I honestly did it because I wanted to help you. But is this really what you planned? I'm watching it now and there's a cockroach on the screen. And is that your pastor inside a coffin?"

The lightening-stricken cockroach had returned to the lower third of the screen. Pastor Rick continued preaching from his seat inside the casket. David went limp, dumbfounded by what was unfolding before him. He couldn't imagine how this would turn out.

"Hello? You still there?" Amy said.

"I gotta go." David hung up on Amy.

He stared at his computer screen as Pastor Rick continued to preach from the casket.

"And then, in his final act of love, he allowed himself to be sealed in a tomb!"

In another dramatic flourish, Pastor Rick flung his torso down into the coffin, reached up to the open half of the lid and slammed it down, closing it on top of himself. The congregation gasped. David could hear a woman scream.

Pastor Rick continued to speak, the invincible hard-wired wireless continuing to transmit his sonorous voice as if from beyond the grave.

"And so Jesus lay in the grave for three days, but the grave could not hold him! 'O Death, where is thy victory? O Grave where is thy Sting?' For after three days he burst forth!"

There was a pause, for dramatic effect, David thought. The view count was now above a hundred thousand. David watched the stream of new user comments coming in.

> "What kinda wack church sells beer?"
> "That Pastor is crazy. But I'd go to that church if they had the bud light girl!!!"

"He burst forth!" Pastor Rick repeated.

Pastor Rick could be heard laboring inside the coffin.

"Oh, Oh, Oh, it seems. Oh, dear God. Open the coffin. I can't open..."

The casket did not open.

"Well, yes, Jesus, must've felt such, Oh, the drama of that tomb... He was, O GOD PLEASE SOMEONE OPEN THIS THING. O GOD, I CAN'T BREATHE."

The view count was now past two hundred and fifty thousand. David's phone buzzed again, another tweet from Tom Lindsey.

> @RealTomLindsey: OK, dunno who hacked my account, but can u believe this church? www.lachancecc.com

David heard cries and screams from the congregation. Wayne was now up on stage struggling to pull open the casket lid. Pastor Rick could still be heard screaming and struggling inside the casket.

David picked up his mouse and moved the curser over the STOP STREAMING button. He hovered there for a second, listening to Pastor Rick wail from within the coffin, watching the viewer count rise above four hundred thousand. He thought of all the terrible things Pastor Rick had done to him. A small voice from somewhere deep inside of him asked *Why should you protect him now? Why should you step in and end this humiliation?* David's finger quivered above the mouse button. The viewer count was still rising.

David shook his head and silenced the voice. He clicked on "STOP STREAMING" and quickly left his office to go see how he could help in the auditorium. As he came to the foyer some of the people had left the auditorium, many looking quite distressed.

Elizabeth Avery was up on the stage clutching the casket.

"Won't someone get him out of this thing!" she screamed.

David passed Eric at the sound booth. Two men were yelling at him to turn off Pastor Rick's mic. Eric trying to explain that he had no control over it.

"I can't do anything with it! It is only controlled by Pastor Rick's keys and they're locked in the casket with him!"

Wayne went out to his truck and returned with an angle grinder.

"Out of my way!" Wayne screamed as he ran against the flow of people leaving the auditorium. He reached the platform, plugged the grinder into an outlet, and walked toward the pulpit and the steel conduit that carried the wiring for the hardwired-wireless.

"What are you doing?" asked David.

"I'm gonna cut through the wires! It's the only way to turn off the mic. Pastor Rick has the only keys in his pocket. IN THE COFFIN!"

David stepped back as Wayne began cutting the metal pipe. The remaining people in the congregation screamed as sparks flew from the grinder all along the width of the stage. A siren could be heard in the distance, getting closer. Wayne continued grinding through the metal conduit, until there was a loud crack and a bright arc of light from the angle grinder all the way down the pipe The angle grinder had contacted the live power cable, shorting it out. The lights on the left half of the auditorium went out as Wayne dropped the angle grinder and fell backwards into the drum set, knocking it over with a crash. His body went limp and he lay motionless next to an overturned cymbal stand.

At the same time, Elizabeth fainted and fell from the edge of the stage to the floor, landing with a thud. It was suddenly quiet, except for the muffled cry of Pastor Rick from within the casket. Three firefighters had arrived and were coming down the aisle. The first one rushed over to Elizabeth, the next one ran to Wayne.

The third firefighter called out, "Who's in charge? What happened here?"

"Um, I work here," said David, "That man may have been electrocuted. This woman fainted and I think she landed on her head. And our pastor is locked inside that coffin."

"What? Is he still alive? How did that happen? What kinda church is this?" The firefighter was shouting.

"It was a... it's not important. He's locked inside and I don't know if he can breathe. Can you get him out?"

The firefighter turned to the casket, hearing Pastor Rick crying from inside. He ran his finger along the top edge, found a keyhole and took a small tool that looked like a nail file out of his pocket. He inserted it in the keyhole, wiggled it and the lid popped open. Pastor Rick gasped for air. He was trembling and drenched in sweat.

The firefighter looked around at the crowd. "Everyone, listen up. Everything is under control here. Everyone just go home, OK? It's all over. It's all over."

No one left.

Wayne was now sitting up, talking to the firefighter. Elizabeth was lying on her back, her glazed eyes staring straight up at the ceiling. Pastor Rick tried to get out of the coffin, but the firefighter wouldn't let him.

"No, you just stay right there, Pastor. Paramedics are coming. They'll take a look at you when they get here."

The firefighter then turned to the remaining members of the congregation. "All you folks, just go on home now. The excitement is over. We'll take care of these folks. Best thing you can do is give us some space. Please clear the room."

The people began filing out. Paramedics arrived and began attending the wounded. One of the paramedics was shining a flashlight into Elizabeth's eyes as she still lay on the floor. When they opened the entire lid to the casket, David could see that Pastor

Rick had soiled himself in his panic.

David looked around the room. Most people had left, but he saw Bill and Trisha standing in the back. They looked at each other, shaking their heads. It was over. They hadn't even collected an offering.

David walked back toward his office. He stopped in front of Bill and Trisha. "I'm sorry. I'm sorry for everything," he said.

"You tried your best. We all did," said Bill.

Trisha said nothing.

David got back to his office, slumped down in his chair and looked at his computer screen. There was a window on the screen that said. "Are you sure you want to stop streaming? Y/N."

David's heart began to race. The stream was still live. It had captured the entire service. It had broadcast Pastor Rick getting stuck inside the coffin. It had broadcast his panic. It captured the sparks flying as Wayne's angle grinder cut through steel conduit. It captured Wayne's near electrocution and subsequent crashing into the drum set. Hundreds of thousands of people watched Elizabeth faint and fall to the floor. It captured the firefighters and paramedics showing up to restore order. David looked at the view count. It was now over seven hundred thousand . The screen showed two firefighters helping pastor Rick out of the casket, above a dead cockroach and a one-eight hundred number. He clicked on 'Yes', confirming that he wanted to stop streaming.

When David returned to the foyer, Pastor Rick was being wheeled out on a stretcher to an ambulance waiting by the front doors. He had an oxygen mask over his face, the rest of his body wrapped in a blanket. *I wonder if he'll tell them it was a workplace accident*, David thought .

Strapped securely to her stretcher, Elizabeth followed Pastor Rick out of the foyer to the ambulance, similarly shrouded in a blue medical blanket. Wayne followed, walking with the assistance of a firefighter.

David went into the auditorium and surveyed the damage. The empty coffin, with its upholstery now stained by Pastor Rick's panic, remained on stage. Parts of the drum set were toppled over where Wayne had fallen. Bare wires hung out of the steel conduit Wayne had severed.

Someone cleared their throat behind him.

David turned and saw Calvin, Inq and Eric at the back of the auditorium.

"Oh, Hey," David said limply. He looked shrugged and slowly threw up his hands.

Only Inq spoke. "David, would you like a hand cleaning up?"

Chuck was still away visiting his daughter, so that evening, David sat alone on the couch looking over the remains of his canned ham and baked beans. It was a far cry from the honey-glazed ham his grandmother used to make for Easter. He wondered how many of the seven hundred thousand viewers of the live stream would have recognized him. He wondered what it would mean for Pastor Rick and for the church. They certainly wouldn't raise the money they needed now. At least the ordeal of the morning was over. David hoped that Lachance Community Church's brief flirtation with online fame would quickly fade from Internet memory.

His phone buzzed. It was an email from anystream.com

> To: dsinger@lachancecc.com
> From:admin@anystream.com
> Subject: "Your Video Archive Now viewable at anystream.com"
>
> Dear Anystream Content Administrator,
>
> Your live stream video is now available for viewing at anystream.com.
>
> Thanks,
>
> The Anystream Team.

David didn't know this would happen. He opened anystream.com on his laptop. The home page featured "Most watched video today" at the top. It was their video. David felt his heart racing again. He signed into his anystream.com account and tried to delete the video, but he was unable to. He called the technical support number, but got no answer. He checked the online help and discovered that videos streamed with the free ad-supported service became the property of anystream.com. Only premium users could delete their archived videos.

His phone buzzed again. It was tweet from Tom Lindsey.

@RealTomLindsey: for those who missed it...
www.anystream.com/txjeiofsk&FEg.

David clicked on the link and was sent to the video of their service, right at the time when Pastor Rick climbed into the casket. The view count was already past eight hundred thousand from those who watched the video in real time. David watched it rise and rise. He turned off his computer when it passed one million.

His Twitter feed was filled with people retweeting the link, along with their reactions. David wondered what would become of the church, how they would ever recover from this.

From his bed, David stared up at the ceiling. Lying there in the darkness, he tried to pretend all was well, that the Internet didn't exist and that he was just the music pastor at a small church that had one rough Sunday, that none of this was a big deal. Eventually, he drifted into a fitful sleep.

He dreamt that he was at a Tom Lindsey concert with Trisha. Tom was singing *Mountaintop*, surrounded by dancing women in bikinis holding bottles of Bud Light. Suddenly, David took Tom Lindsey's place on stage, surrounded by the Bud Light girls. He looked out at Trisha, who screamed, "Look out!" as she pointed behind him. The Bud Light girls turned, screamed, and ran away. David looked up to see what they were afraid of. A horde of giant cockroaches, each the size of a coffin, stampeded toward the stage. David stood helpless as the roaches trampled him amid a hail of lightning bolts.

RECKONING

It was noon on Monday when David finally got out of bed. The buses had disturbed him as usual, but he'd stayed in bed and drifted in and out of sleep. Chuck was waiting for him when he went upstairs.

"Hey, David. Taking Monday off?"

"I'm probably taking every day off from now on."

"Oh, what happened? How was Sunday?"

"You didn't watch it online with your daughter?"

"No, we decided to go to a real church instead. It was nice, sort of like being a real family, all of us going together. But the music wasn't as good as yours. So, how did it go? You raise the money?"

"You haven't heard?"

"No."

"I can show you how it went. I'll be right back." David went down to his room to retrieve his laptop. When he returned, they sat together on the couch with the laptop on a TV tray in front of them. David opened the anystream.com home page. The video of their service was still the number one rated video. The view count had reached three million. David clicked on the play button.

"Picture looks good. And you guys sound good. What's that big thing in the middle of the stage?"

"I'll show you," David said.

David slid the timeline bar of the video to the point when Pastor Rick removed the tablecloth from the casket.

"Whoa, is that a coffin?" Chuck asked.

"Yes."

"There's nothing in it, is there?"

"Not yet."

They continued watching the rest of the video. Chuck's jaw fell slack when Pastor Rick climbed into the coffin. By the time Wayne was electrocuted, Chuck's mouth hung wide open.

"I guess that wasn't how you planned it?" said Chuck as he raised his eyebrows.

"No, it was not. We didn't even get around to taking the offering."

"Oh, man. So what does that mean for you?"

David sighed. "Only God knows."

After a grilled cheese sandwich, David left the house with the intent of walking to church, but instead found himself at Beans of Production nursing a coffee and staring out the window. He knew he was avoiding Pastor Rick. He told himself he had to face him sooner or later, so he drained his mug and set out for the church.

He arrived just after two o'clock. He expected to see Rhonda's blue hatchback and Pastor Rick's tan Buick, but the parking lot was empty. David used his key to get in. First, he walked into the auditorium. The casket was gone.

As he walked toward his office, he noticed Pastor Rick's office door ajar. He set down his knapsack and walked over to it.

"Hello?" David slowly pushed open the door. The office was completely bare. There were no books on the bookshelves or pictures on the wall. The desktop was empty. A few folded-up moving boxes stood in the corner. Pastor Rick had vacated.

David crossed to his own office and wondered what to do. He decided to call Bill.

The church treasurer answered on the first ring. "Hello?"

"Bill, this is David. I'm at the church. There's nobody here and it looks like Pastor Rick has moved out of his office. Do you know what's going on?"

"David, there have been some developments. Things are still fluid. There's a council meeting tonight and I'll know more after that. Can you and I meet tomorrow morning at the church? First thing?"

"Sure, but what's going on? How are Pastor Rick and Elizabeth, and Wayne?"

"One thing we can be thankful for, maybe the only thing is that no one was seriously hurt. They were all released from the hospital and are doing OK. Rick and Wayne were just shaken up. Elizabeth has a mild concussion, but she oughta be fine."

"That's a relief. So, what's going to happen now?"

"I'll know more by tomorrow. But, David, can I ask you something?"

"Sure."

"Why didn't you stop the web stream when things started going wrong?"

"Bill, I tried. I clicked on the 'Stop Streaming' button and then I came into the auditorium to try to help. When I finally got back to my computer, I found out there was an additional confirmation window to stop the streaming. I'm really sorry, Bill. I really am. And I tried to delete the video from anystream.com, but I'm not allowed to. The video actually belongs to them. I guess you really should read the terms of service before you click 'I AGREE.'

"I'm sorry, Bill. I didn't mean for any of this to happen. And I didn't know Tom Lindsey would Tweet a link to our website. I'm really sorry. I'm so sorry."

"Oh, David, this is all so sad and surreal. There's still a lot to figure out. I'll see you tomorrow morning."

"OK."

"See you then."

David retrieved the empty moving boxes from Pastor Rick's office, assembled them and began packing up his belongings. He would ask Chuck to borrow his truck some time to take his stuff home.

Walking toward the church on Tuesday morning, David saw Bill's car once again alone in the parking lot. He found Bill seated in the conference room with papers spread out on the table in front of him. David went in and sat down next to him.

"Morning Bill," he said.

"Hi David. Thanks for coming in." Bill pushed the papers aside, took a deep breath, and then looked at David.

"David, this isn't easy, but I suspect you knew it was coming. First of all, I want to thank you for your service here. But I'm sad to tell you that we have to let you go. As you know, we are at a crisis point financially, and the most likely outcome is that we'll lose the building and the church will cease to exist. I'm very sorry." Bill took off his glasses and rubbed his eyes and forehead. "I'll be happy to give you a letter of recommendation. We'll pay you out the last two weeks of your contract plus your unused vacation. I wish we could do more, but there it is."

David nodded. "Thanks, Bill. Thanks for the opportunity. I learned a lot, that's for sure. So what's happening with Pastor Rick?"

"Pastor Rick resigned. It's probably for the best. I think he needs a break, and possibly a change. I don't see how he can recover from his new-found fame and stay in ministry." Bill shook his head and sighed. "In any event, I've been appointed as the interim executive leader by the church council, so I'll be looking after things until... until the end, I guess."

"Yeah, I'm really sorry," David said. "But even though you can't pay me, I can still look after the music here, until something else comes along for me. Would that help?"

Bills eyes welled up with tears. "David, that would be helpful, yes. That's very thoughtful. Thank you."

"OK. Thanks." David walked back to his office and turned on his computer. He began composing an email to the worship team, thanking them for their service and letting them know he was no longer on staff. As he was wondering how to begin the message, he received an email from anystream.com

> To: dsinger@lachancecc.com
> From: do-not-reply@anystream.com
> Subject: Account Balance Update
>
> Dear Anystream account administrator:
>
> Please find below your current account balance:
>
> Live Video Banner Ad Revenue: $21,645.78
> Archive Video Banner Ad Revenue: $43,235.24
> Archive Video Sidebar Ad Revenue: $ 5,251.20
>
> Total ad revenue: $70,132.22
>
> To set up direct deposit, click here
>
> Sincerely,
>
> The Anystream Team

David stared at the screen. He read the email over and over again. Their Easter service video was viewed so many times that they'd earned revenue from all the advertising. David ran out of his office to the boardroom.

"Bill, Bill, come and look at this!"

"What is it David? Is everything OK?"

"Yes, just come. Come! I need to show you something!"

Bill pushed back his chair from the table and followed David into his office.

"Bill, you know how ads were running during our video?"

"Yes, you mean the Bud Light dancers? And the cockroaches?" Bill rolled his eyes.

"Yes, well, when a video is viewed enough times, it can earn you money. Look at this email I just got from anystream.com."

Bill sat down in David's chair and peered at the screen over the top of his glasses. His mouth opened when he got to the numbers.

"David, is this real?"

"I think so."

"Seventy thousand dollars? For a video on the Internet?"

"A video with millions of views!" David said.

Bill stared at the email, shaking his head for a moment before he spoke again. "David, this is a miracle. This is a *miracle!*"

Bill took off his glasses to wipe his eyes. He got up from the chair and put his arms around David, hugging and squeezing him tightly.

"I can't believe this, David. This is enough to make that first balloon payment. If giving holds up, and with what we'll save on Pastor Rick's salary, we just might make it. We've got a fighting chance, anyway. And forget what I said about letting you go. If we're going to keep things going here we'll need someone like you around. You'll stay, won't you?"

"You bet I will, Bill. You bet!"

Bill and David set up direct deposit for anystream.com and then just sat together in David's office smiling, basking in the glory of the moment, like prisoners who'd just received a pardon.

"You know, the funeral home called. They're charging us about a thousand bucks to have the casket reupholstered," Bill said.

"Oh yeah. I guess that stain wouldn't come out. So what do you think Pastor Rick is going to do?"

"Last I talked to him, he was putting on a brave face. He told me he planned on becoming a life coach."

Bill stood to leave, then turned. "Say, David, I just thought you should know, Trisha isn't seeing that Chad guy any more. I guess his ex-girlfriend had a change of heart and he went running back to her. Just thought you might want to know. Anyway, I should let council know about these developments. I'll see you later, David."

David took out his phone and dialed Chuck at home.

"Yo," said Chuck.

"Chuck, it's David. Can I borrow your truck tonight?"

"Uh, sure, I'm not going anywhere. Everything OK?"

"Everything is great, Chuck. God gave us a miracle. I still have a job and the church is saved. I'll tell you when I get home."

David dialed Trisha, hoping she would be on her lunch break and able to take his call. His heart leapt when he heard her answer.

"Hi David, how are you?" she asked.

"I'm good,.

"Have you talked to my dad? I'm really sorry."

"Don't be sorry. I have some good news to tell you. Would you like to have dinner with me, tonight? I was thinking that Italian place downtown."

There was a pause on the other end of the line.

"Um, I'd love to. What time should I come and get you?"

"No, no. I'll pick you up. Seven o'clock sound good?"

"Yes, that sounds great, David."

"OK, then. It's a date. See you tonight."

"Yeah, I can't wait to hear the news!"

"I can't wait to tell you. I can't wait to tell you everything." David sat back in his chair, looked out his window and quietly sang to himself:

"Oh, You, You lift me to the highest place
Where I see the beauty of your face
My love for you will never stop
Because You, You take me to the Mountaintop."

ABOUT THE AUTHOR

Geoff Dresser is the Assistant Professor of Worship Arts at Briercrest College in Caronport, Saskatchewan, Canada. He is married to Pearl and they are the proud parents of Pierce, Gideon and Preston.

Made in the USA
Middletown, DE
21 June 2019